ELUSIVE LOVE

A SMALL-TOWN SECOND CHANCE SINGLE DAD ROMANCE

ALPINE RIDGE

MELANIE A. SMITH

WICKED DREAMS PUBLISHING

Published by
WICKED DREAMS PUBLISHING
info@wickeddreamspublishing.com
Boise, ID USA

Cover design, editing, and interior formatting by Wicked Dreams Publishing

eBook ISBN: 978-1-952121-85-2
Paperback ISBN: 978-1-952121-86-9
Discreet Paperback ISBN: 978-1-952121-87-6
Hardcover ISBN: 978-1-952121-88-3

CONTENTS

CONTENT WARNING

Elusive Love is a small-town second chance single dad romance novel that includes elements that might not be suitable for some readers. If you are sensitive to any of the following, please put your mental health first:

Explicit language
Graphic sexual activity
Infertility issues
Religious hypocrisy
Parental abandonment
Mentions of past cheating
Mentions of past bullying
Mentions of depression, anxiety, and ADHD
Mentions of past injuries/deaths from fire
Mentions of past deaths of parents, sibling
Mention of past statutory rape
Mention of past drug use/overdose

PROLOGUE

RAE

The snow-covered fields around the Alpine Ridge community center sparkle under the December sun as I bustle around inside, readying everything for Greg and Joanie's wedding reception. I've always enjoyed decorating for special occasions, a skill I discovered helping my Grams with weddings back in the day. She may have owned the bakery, but she took care of everything for weddings in town — food, flowers, décor, music — and loved every minute.

Weddings bring more complicated emotions for me, so it's a bittersweet nostalgia that tugs at my heart today.

Still, the mood is lighthearted, as it should be. And as I hang fairy lights with Carrie, she teases, "You know, Rae, you might have a future as the town's official wedding planner. First Mia, now Joanie ..." Mia, Carrie's sister, smirks from where she's adding white winter roses to the cake our bakery made for the wedding.

I give a small good-natured laugh, but the sting of memories burns deep at her words. "Oh, honey, I've done way more weddings than that. Back in the day, my Grams used to cater weddings at the Alpine Ridge Chapel. My momma and I would help with the decorations."

Carrie, Mia, and Brandon all stop helping hang decorations and stare at me, jaws dropped.

Then Brandon voices what they're all thinking, "Wait, you're telling me there used to be a church here?" While Brandon recently returned to Alpine Ridge after a dozen years away, he grew up here. So, I expect the knowledge is even more shocking to him. But the church was before his time. If only just.

The smile drops off my face as I recall the day the church burned down, and the fallout that meant losing my dreams of marrying the love of my life. I internalize a sigh and shove all the emotions back down.

"Sure am. But it burned down when I was sixteen. There wasn't money to rebuild," I explain matter-of-factly.

Carrie, using her diplomatic skills hard-earned while running Alpine Ridge's town elections, changes the subject, clearly seeing my desire not to dwell on the past, and they talk about everything that's left to do.

Joanie joins us just as we're finishing up, radiant in her white silk dress, her dark hair tumbling down her back in sleek waves. "Damn, Rae, you're good at this. Remind me why you haven't been snapped up for your own wedding yet?" she quips.

Her words hit me like a punch to the gut. Not because

they remind me of the wedding I wanted, the one I was just reminded of. No, they remind me of the wedding I got. Which was much shabbier and to the wrong man. As evidenced by my subsequent failed marriage.

Still, I know she meant no harm. She's just blunt and forward by nature, which I'm sure doesn't hurt when you're a lawyer.

I force a smile and respond as honestly as I can. "Not everyone's cut out for marriage. But I'm happy for you and Greg."

Joanie, uncharacteristically chagrined, apologizes for her tactlessness. I brush it off, not wanting to dampen the mood on her special day.

Thankfully, there's no time to dwell on it. As the ceremony begins in the frigid, snowy field outside, I watch Greg and Joanie, king and queen of winter in their white formal wear, exchange vows, their love for each other palpable. While Joanie is a more recent addition to the town, Greg has lived here for several years and, having run the community center, he's connected with so many people in town, me included. So, it's good to see him overwhelmed with happiness.

It's infectious, really, and, for a moment, I allow myself to imagine what could have been — a life with my high school sweetheart, a simple but happy home, children of our own. But I quickly push those thoughts aside. That ship sailed long ago. And it was a dream I never could've achieved for so many reasons.

At the reception, as couples sway on the dance floor, I

busy myself with serving drinks and food. Though I can't help but overhear snippets of Carrie's conversation with her movie star boyfriend, who also happens to be Mia's brother-in-law. Their talk of moving in together and promises of forever send a pang of envy through me, followed immediately by guilt. They deserve happiness, and I truly wish them well.

I see Nate and Mia on the other side of the room, their eyes locked as they move in perfect unison. Husband and wife. It's a catching condition in Alpine Ridge these days. I'm happy for them, too.

For all of them. Truly.

As the night winds down, I find myself lost in thought, memories of the past mingling with the joy of the present. Alpine Ridge has seen me through my highest highs and lowest lows. It's a place of love and loss, of painful endings and new beginnings.

But as I watch my friends — my chosen family — celebrate and support each other, I realize that this town, with all its heavy history, is still full of love and light. And there's hope in that thought that carries me through the darkness that's tugging at my heart.

CHAPTER ONE

RAE

TWO MONTHS LATER

The scent of freshly baked pie wafts through the bakery as I wipe down the counter for what feels like the hundredth time this afternoon. It's slow, which isn't unusual at this time of day. With Alpine Ridge getting more traffic these days, most folks come in first thing in the morning to snap up Mia's most popular goodies. But that makes for a boring closing shift and gives me too much time to think about the visit to my momma I have planned later and the pile of laundry waiting for me at home afterward.

The bell above the door chimes, and I look up, ready to paste on my best customer service smile. But as soon as I see who it is, the smile dies on my lips.

Jerry.

The crusty old bastard I worked for most of my life until Mia came along with a better offer. We've got history,

Jerry and I, but it's at best lukewarm. And at worst … well, I try not to think about that.

Either way, I sure don't miss his grimy tavern, and I don't miss Jerry.

His eyes move around the tables, checking to see who's here. In his usual plaid shirt and faded jeans, he looks as out of place in Mia's cheerful bakery as a vulture at a garden party.

Without a word, I turn on my heel and march into the back room, where Mia is pulling the pie I smelled earlier out of the oven.

"Am I allowed to refuse service to people?" I ask, my voice tight.

Mia raises an eyebrow and purses her lips, setting the tray on the cooling rack. "To who? Why?"

"Jerry," I reply without further explanation. She knows why. Partially, at least. Enough, anyway.

Mia's expression softens into a knowing, sympathetic grimace. "No need. I can serve him. Or …" She chews on her lip. Nervous as to what she has in that devious, intelligent mind of hers, I pop my hands on my hips and look at her expectantly. "Or you could just have it out with him. Alpine Ridge is a small town, Rae. You can't avoid him forever."

I blink, surprised. "You're telling me I can give him a piece of my mind? Even though he's a customer?"

Mia shrugs. "Why not? You've been holding onto this anger for a while now. It might do you some good to let it out. If he doesn't like it, he can go buy prepackaged pastries at the grocery store."

A slow smile spreads across my face. And not just because, after striking a deal recently with the owner, said prepackaged pastries are also from Mia's bakery, so she gets his money either way. But because she's got a point. It's about damn time I let him know what I think of his latest bullshit. I'm not sure why I held back so long, now that she's pointed it out. Especially now that I'm being encouraged to do it.

"You know what? You're right. Thanks, sugar."

She sets the pie on a cooling rack and gives me a teasing salute.

I march back out to the front, squaring my shoulders as I approach the counter where Jerry stands, examining the pastry case with feigned interest.

"Well, well, well," I drawl, crossing my arms. "Look what the cat dragged in."

Jerry's head snaps up, his bushy eyebrows rising in surprise.

"You've got some nerve showing up here," I continue, not allowing him to speak. "After lying to me and everyone else in this town, pretending to be on a town council that didn't even exist yet. And then you had the audacity to run for mayor. Now you waltz in here like nothing happened?"

Jerry's weather-beaten face creases into a frown. "Now, Rachel Lynn Donovan—"

"Don't you full name me, Jeremiah James Allen," I cut him off, shaking my head. Honestly, what kind of parent gives their child three first names? "And I wasn't finished. You know what really gets me? That you had the balls to come in here at all. Did you think we'd forgotten? And don't even get me started on the petition signatures that were stolen. I *know* you had something to do with that."

To my surprise, Jerry's shoulders slump. "I didn't come here to cause trouble, Rae. I came to apologize."

I fold my arms over my chest and fix him with a skeptical look. "Apologize? You?"

He nods, his eyes meeting mine. "You were the best bartender and server I ever had — a loyal employee." I scoff. Of course Jerry only thinks of me as an employee. Even after all these years. But he continues, undeterred by my obvious disdain. "I shouldn't have tricked you or anyone else like that. I understand why people didn't want me as mayor." He lets out a breath. "And I swear, I didn't steal the signatures. But … I may know who did." He huffs out a defeated sigh.

My eyebrows fly up, not having expected him to admit anything. "And?" I prompt.

He fidgets, avoiding my gaze. "Look, I'm not here to go throwing anyone else under the bus. Let's just say it was someone who thought it would impress me." His eyes meet mine. "And it most certainly did not. I'm real sorry it came to that, and I'm glad the town is getting what it needs now, even if I'm not in charge."

I stare at him, waiting for the punchline. When it doesn't come, I narrow my eyes. "Are you pulling my leg?"

"No, I'm not," Jerry says, his voice gruff but sincere. "I know we've had some bad blood in the past, but I'm too old for that kind of shit anymore." He looks up at the ceiling. "I'm sorry, Rae."

I blow out a disbelieving breath. "Well … all right then, I forgive you, I guess." I furrow my brow, still skeptical. Jerry has *never* apologized, despite having done far worse.

He nods contritely. "Good." He pauses, as if hesitant to go on before doing exactly that. "I … was also hoping to speak to Mia about selling her pastries at the tavern. People … well, they miss having your huckleberry pie after a meal."

Ah. There it is.

Jerry is eating crow so people can eat my pie, or my Great Grams's pie, as it were. Though as false as his apology now seems, I have to admit I'm glad he's at least willing to cop to his mistakes. Even if he only did it to shut people up about the pie. It's more than I would've thought him capable of, anyway.

I take a deep breath, letting some of the tension ease from my shoulders. "Well, I'll be damned. I never thought I'd see the day Jerry Allen apologized."

A ghost of a smile flickers across Jerry's face. "Yeah, well, don't get used to it."

I snort. "Wouldn't dream of it." I jerk my thumb towards the back. "I'll go get Mia for you."

As I head to the back room once again, I can't help but shake my head. Miracles really happen. If only they could erase more than some stupid political bullshit. Because despite his apology, I was only partially mad because of his latest stunt. All the ones before? Well, I may forgive, but I don't forget.

By the time my shift ends, all I want is to go home and collapse into bed. But it's Sunday, which means my standing date with Momma.

I swing by the grocery store, still not used to how much nicer it is since the renovation last fall, picking up the usual supplies — TV dinners (because Lord knows Momma won't cook for herself), some fresh fruit (which I'll probably end up eating myself next week before it goes bad), dinner fixings, and a box of her favorite tea.

The drive to Momma's little house on the outskirts of town is as familiar as breathing. I pull into the cracked driveway, noting it needs shoveling and salting again. Driving on it is nothing my Bronco can't handle, but if Momma needs to go out, her old Toyota Corolla isn't going to be able to. Add that to the list of things to take care of next week. Thankfully, it's almost March, so winter will be on its way out soon.

"Momma?" I call as I let myself in. "It's me."

"In here, sugar," comes the reply from the living room.

I find her in her usual spot, curled up in her recliner with a romance novel in her lap. Pamela Donovan might be pushing seventy, but she still has a girlish glint in her eye when it comes to her bodice rippers. I cast a quick eye over the shabby furniture, noting that the crocheted blanket covering her chair could use a washing. But not much else has changed. It all still looks the same as it has my whole life, seventies pinks and browns and all.

"How are you feeling today?" I ask, bending to kiss her cheek.

"Oh, same old, same old," she says. "How was work?"

As I bustle around the kitchen, putting away groceries and starting dinner, I fill her in on the day's events, including Jerry's surprise visit.

"Well, I'll be," Momma says, shaking her head. "Wonders never cease."

"Indeed," I agree. "Oh, and they fixed that pothole on Main Street. The new transportation department is getting things done. I hear tell they're working on setting up police and fire departments next."

"Never thought I'd see this place come back to life," Momma remarks, setting aside her book to set the table, as usual.

"Me neither, but I'm proud to be a part of it," I respond. Even though Joanie did most of the work on the incorporation paperwork, and Carrie handled the election process, it was nice to be part of the team, organizing events and having a say in how it all came together. And though the rest of it is out of my hands now, it's still exciting to see our efforts pay off as our tiny town gets the services it has so desperately needed for years.

We eat dinner together — a simple meal of grilled chicken, rice, and vegetables, with enough leftovers to last her until my next visit. As I tidy up the house, Momma settles back into her chair, flipping on the TV to reruns of her favorite game show.

I join her on the couch, handing over a plastic container of her favorite peach crumble, leftover from the bakery. As I dive into my portion, my mind drifts as Alex Trebek's voice fills the room. It has been an almost typical day save Jerry's abrupt change of heart. But I'm pleased with all the positive changes that came with the town's incorporation. And I'm glad Jerry came to his senses so I could bury that particular hatchet with the old bastard. I can't say I respect him after everything we've been through, and especially all those years of pretending to be something he wasn't just for a power trip, but at least we'll be able to be civil to each other from now on. Hell, we've found our way around worse over the years.

Once Momma falls asleep in her chair, I do a final cleanup, gently kiss her forehead, and cover her with a blanket. Then I head back to my house just off the other end of Main Street.

I open the door to darkness. But even with the lights on, the small two-bedroom home feels empty and forlorn. It's cozy enough, I suppose, with its mismatched thrifted furniture and colorful, though cheaply framed art hanging on the walls, but I sure miss having Carrie living here. She wasn't here long, but we became close. But she's happy in one of the new townhouses Greg's cousin built last year, and it's probably best she's got her own place now that she and Evan are together. Lord knows I don't need the constant reminder of what good sex sounds like.

I sigh, setting my things down and collecting all the laundry of the past week, dumping it into the ancient washer, and starting it up. A step I always forget before leaving for work. Now I'll be up late.

Resigned, I settle onto my old saggy couch and grab the fantasy book I'm reading. Momma may like her romance, but I prefer to disappear into another world for a while. Give me epic heroes, impossible quests, and mythical creatures. But then, both take you into their own worlds, I suppose. I just like being as far away from reality as possible. Somewhere I don't have to pretend that watching everyone around me find love and settle down doesn't hurt.

Who knew it was possible to be bursting with happiness for someone else's joy and desperately sad and lonely at the same time? But that's me and my big old soft heart. Too many emotions for my own good sometimes. But we can't all get swept off our feet like Mia, and her handsome doctor with the body of a fitness model. Or like Joanie with her rugged secret millionaire. Or like Carrie, with her famous movie star boyfriend who gave up his glamorous life to be with her.

But I'm forty-six, and I've been through the wringer a time or three, and I know not everyone gets their happy ending. Even if there were any men for me in Alpine Ridge — which, after having lived here most of my life, I can definitely say there are not — I've been through enough to know that not everyone finds their soulmate. My ex-husband sure wasn't mine. And my father left my momma. She's the best woman I know. Loving, beautiful in her day, beautiful *still*, inside and out. If she can't make it work, there truly are no guarantees in this life. Though it's not like mine is bad.

I've got Momma, a group of friends I love, and my own interests that I'm free to pursue. Most of the time, I'm content. But sometimes, despite knowing how wrong things can go, I just want … more. So apparently, I'm also a glutton for punishment.

CHAPTER TWO

LUKE

Being back in Alpine Ridge after thirty years away is a trip, to say the least. As I drive down Main Street, I'm hit with a wave of nostalgia so strong it nearly knocks the wind out of me. The bones of the town I remember are there — the old buildings, the layout — but there's a freshness to it all. Fresh paint, new businesses, new life.

When I left, being in Alpine Ridge was the source of all my family's problems. And now it may be the answer to them. I've been pushing to get the fire chief position in my South Seattle fire station for years. Despite proving myself in the field and being more than qualified, it's eluded me anywhere in the Seattle area, even with station hopping over the years. On top of which, my twelve-year-old daughter, Zoe, has been struggling in school. I've been wanting to pull her out and homeschool her for a while and get her somewhere a little more mellow.

And as much as my exit from Alpine Ridge was a mess,

my childhood here was pretty good. At least, I enjoyed being able to roam and explore as I pleased. And I know Zoe will, too. So, this opportunity to transition out of my stressful role as assistant fire chief and help Alpine Ridge establish its first-ever fire department is a great one. It's a long time coming for both me and the town. I will work, but at a much slower pace for at least a year before the department is established. And even once it is, I doubt it'll be as hectic as my current job. Even if it is, it's an opportunity I couldn't pass up. It means so much more to me than a title, in ways I'm not ready to face just yet. One thing at a time.

I park in front of the newly constructed town hall, a modern building that stands out among the older structures. Inside, I'm directed to a conference room where I find two people waiting for me: an older gentleman with a kind face who I assume is the mayor, and a striking young brunette.

"Mr. McMillan," the older man says, standing to shake my hand. "I'm Arthur Burton, the mayor. And this is Carrie Anderson, our city planner. We conducted your phone interview. It's a pleasure to meet you in person."

I shake both their hands, noting the warmth in Carrie's smile. "Please, call me Luke," I say, though there's something familiar about Arthur that tells me we've probably met before, back when I was a kid. I imagine I'm going to have a lot of that feeling as I settle in here, seeing people who I knew as a child but whose faces have changed over the years.

It makes me think of one particular face I'd like to see soon.

Focusing back to the present, I follow their lead, and we take our seats. Arthur recaps our discussion from my interview the previous week. Carrie chimes in with details about the proposed location for the fire station, showing me land surveys of the selected parcel.

"As we explained," Arthur says, "you'll be overseeing the design and build of the station itself, then take on the active role of fire chief once we're up and running. The county will be involved, letting us know our minimum requirements for building, equipment, and staffing, but otherwise, everything will be at your discretion."

I nod, having already mentioned that I've witnessed this process before, though not in a role of leadership. I'm practically itching to take the reins.

Carrie slides a folder across the table to me. "This outlines the compensation package we can provide during the planning stages, and then once the department is operational."

I flip through the paperwork, nodding as I go. It's all in line with what we'd discussed before, and honestly, it's more than fair given the cost of living here compared to Seattle.

"This all works for me," I say, looking up at them both. "I'm honored to be back in Alpine Ridge and to oversee the creation of such an important part of its infrastructure."

Arthur beams, pulling out a pen and sliding it across the table along with a contract. "Then let's make it official."

I sign on the dotted line, feeling a mix of excitement and trepidation. This is really happening.

After we wrap up the meeting, I head out to check on my old family home. My dad put it in my name during the divorce from my mom all those years ago, and even though we haven't spoken since not long after, I know he'd never come back here. Given all that he took over the years, I have no qualms about keeping it. Though I don't know what shape it's in. I inhale and exhale slowly, reminding myself not to borrow trouble. It will be what it will be.

As I drive down the long, gravel driveway and break through the trees, I'm surprised to see that the old place is still standing proud. Admittedly, it needs repainting, and the yard needs tending, but it's far from the dilapidated wreck I'd envisioned as the worst-case scenario.

I unlock the front door, my key still fitting perfectly after all these years. Just the fact that I kept it makes me realize that on some level I knew I'd find my way back here someday.

The musty smell of disuse hits me as I step inside, but beneath that, there's still the faint scent of home — pine and cinnamon, just like I remember.

Turns out, it isn't too bad; nothing I can't fix, anyway. And in the meantime, all it will need is a few repairs and new appliances to be livable. The rest will be an excellent project while I'm working on establishing the fire department. A good hands-on learning experience for Zo, too.

I wander through the rooms, memories flooding back

with each step. Here's where I scraped my knee learning to roller skate indoors. There's the spot where my mom used to measure my and my sister's heights each year. And in the kitchen, I can almost see my dad at the table, poring over the newspaper like he did every morning.

Taking out a notepad, I jot down measurements and make a list of what needs to be done. New fridge, definitely. The ancient, yet still functional, stove can probably stay for now. The bathroom will need a complete overhaul, but that can wait.

As I work, I envision how Zoe and I will fit into this space. Her room will be my old one, with the big bay window overlooking the backyard. Maybe we can set up a little study nook in one of the spare rooms for her homeschooling.

It's going to be a change, no doubt. Trading the bustle of the city for the quiet of small-town life. Swapping my hectic schedule for a more laid-back pace. But as I stand in the doorway, looking out over the waist-high grass to the mountains beyond, I can't help but feel like I'm exactly where I'm supposed to be.

I head back to my truck, my mind racing with plans for the move to Alpine Ridge. There's so much to do — packing up our Seattle apartment, figuring out Zoe's homeschooling program, coordinating the move itself. But for the first time in a long time, I'm excited about what lies ahead.

As I drive back through town, I catch sight of the

bakery on Main Street. It's clearly still open, the lot half full of vehicles.

My heart races with anticipation, wondering if she's still there, too. Could it be that easy to find her? Am I even ready for this?

I take a deep breath and turn into the parking lot. Because really, why not? She probably won't even be there. With that voice of hers, she's probably got a singing career that takes her around the world. Though I've looked for her over the years and found nothing, that doesn't mean it hasn't happened for her. Maybe she performs under a stage name. I hope so. She damn well deserved to make it, even if I was never there to see it happen like I promised. Something else I blame my father for.

If nothing else, I could use a cup of coffee before I hit the road back to Seattle, right?

CHAPTER THREE

RAE

The bell above the bakery door chimes, and I look up from the register, a smile plastered on my face as usual. But as soon as I see who's walking in, my smile freezes and my heart pounds like a jackhammer.

Luke McMillan.

My high school sweetheart.

I blink hard, trying to decide if I've had so much sugar today that I'm seeing things.

But I'm definitely not.

My next thought? What in the hell is he doing back here?

Still, despite my shock, I can't help noting that he looks the same yet different all at once. His dark blond hair is still thick, but now it's peppered with silver. His brown eyes crinkle at the corners when he smiles — a new addition, along with the laugh lines around his mouth. And the well-trimmed beard is definitely a surprise.

But his stocky build is bulkier now, his muscles more defined under his fitted T-shirt. Thirty years have been kind to him.

Too kind.

"Rae Donovan, as I live and breathe," he says, his deep, rumbling voice familiar yet a different, older version of itself all at the same time.

I swallow hard, trying to find my own voice. "Luke. Wow. What brings you to town?" I aim for polite but professional, but even I can hear the strain in my tone.

I give myself points for not asking him where he found the balls to waltz back into town like he didn't cheat on me and father a child, abandoning us both for the last thirty years.

He leans against the counter, his smile widening. "I guess gossip doesn't travel around town as fast as it once did," he teases. "You're looking at Alpine Ridge's new fire chief."

"Oh. Congratulations?" I manage, my mind reeling. Luke, back in Alpine Ridge? I feel faint as my mind whirs into overdrive, trying to process what that will mean.

"Thanks." He nods, his eyes roaming over my face. "You look great, Rae. Haven't changed a bit."

I resist the urge to roll my eyes. My golden blond hair might be courtesy of L'Oréal these days, but my face certainly bears the signs of age just like his. Though I don't point that out. But I realize … he's clearly not aware that everyone found out about his little indiscretion.

Wait … does he even know about Brandon?

He can't *not* know, can he?

I freeze, wondering whether I should bring it up.

No. There's no way I'm asking him that. Nope. Not going near that with a ten-foot pole.

And yet, if he sticks around too long, I know I won't be able to keep my trap shut.

Time to get him back out of that door.

"Thanks," I mutter, grabbing a to-go coffee cup. "The usual?" The words slip out before I can stop them while I fill the cup with black coffee and cap it. A reflex from a lifetime ago while my mind is fixed on getting rid of him.

Luke's eyebrows rise. "You remember my order?"

I curse myself silently. Of course I remember. Just like I remember every detail of our time together, every first, every whispered promise of forever.

The memories that once warmed me now twist like a knife in my gut. Because what I remember most is his betrayal.

"Lucky guess," I lie, ringing him up and handing over his coffee.

An awkward silence falls between us. Luke looks like he wants to say something more, but I cut him off with a brisk, "Well, thanks for stopping by. I have to go take care of some things in the kitchen, but I'll see you around."

He blinks, clearly taken aback by my abruptness. "Right. Sure. It was good to see you, Rae. See you around."

I nod curtly, slipping through the door behind me and leaning against the wall beside it until the bell chimes again, signaling his departure.

Covering my face with my hands, I wait for my heart to stop racing. Good god, could it have been more obvious that I couldn't get away from him fast enough?

I'd imagined seeing Luke again over the years, but always pictured myself as indifferent, unaffected. I never expected the rush of hurt and anger that is coursing through me now.

How could I not feel this way, though? He came out of nowhere. And I never got to rip him a new one for cheating on me. Probably pointless since he clearly either thinks he got away with it or maybe just doesn't care, thinking it in the past.

The thought sends another bolt of agony ripping through me, and something deep down knows this shouldn't hurt so much. But that's what I get for shoving things down and not dealing with them. They all come bubbling back up, fresh as the day they were born.

"Rae? Everything okay?" Mia's voice snaps me out of my spiral. I drop my hands and look up to find concern etched on her face, dark wisps of hair escaping the bun she's always got her long hair tied in while she works.

I wave her off, forcing a smile. "Yeah, it's fine. Just a long day. Ready for game night, that's all."

She looks unconvinced but doesn't push. "Okay. If you're sure." She heads back to the long table beside the ovens, clearly going back to some experiment of sugar and flour and butter she'd been working on.

I take a deep breath and steady myself. As I go about

my closing tasks, I ignore the implications of Luke's return for my sake, and my thoughts drift to Brandon.

If this blindsided me, it's nothing compared to how Brandon might feel. But then, I assumed since everyone in Alpine Ridge knew about Brandon's parentage, that so did he.

Since Luke himself didn't act like anything had happened at all, like he hadn't cheated on his girlfriend, knocked up someone else, and abandoned her and his son … maybe neither of them knows? I shake my head, not even sure how such a thing could be possible. It's old news from the rumor mill. Part of the town's fabric.

And yet, if I've learned anything today, it's that sometimes the past can jump out and bite you when you least expect it.

As I go home to clean up ahead of traveling up the mountain to Mia and Nate's house, I can't decide what, if anything, I should say to Brandon. Maybe I know more about him than he knows about himself? He sure doesn't know me all that well.

I left Alpine Ridge when he was still a kid, and he was gone when I got back, only returning recently to claim his place in town as one of our new council members. As far as he knows, I'm just the kooky lady that works at Mia's bakery.

I won't say a word, I decide. It's not my place.

Besides, even if Brandon doesn't know, he won't miss how alike he and Luke look. Or the whispers that will surely start up again. He has his grandfather, John, who can explain anything he wants to know.

Still, doubts plague me as I make my way to Mia and Nate's that evening. I could save him the element of surprise. Give him the heads up. I shake my head and push the thoughts aside, deciding to focus on the comfort of being with my friends. But they linger like an unpleasant taste in my mouth.

The entire gang is in the living room by the time I arrive, fashionably late as usual. Though there's nothing fashionable about it, I'm just scattered as hell, and I always feel like I'm ten steps behind where I'm supposed to be. Always have. But now's not the time to worry about that, so I shove that thought down, too.

I shake off the chill of outside as I step into the toasty living room. Since the snow drifts remain outside and the chill of winter has been clinging to the end of February, Nate is stoking a good-sized fire in the massive fireplace.

Joanie and Greg sit on one couch with Bruiser, their chihuahua mix rescue. As usual, they're a little too handsy for polite company, but that's part of their charm. Evan and Carrie sit on the floor in front of the fire, with his arms wrapped around her from behind. Mia is nowhere to be seen, probably working on food in the kitchen.

"Rae, thank god, come be my date," Brandon calls from across the room, patting the loveseat cushion next to him.

Normally I'd take that comment and run with it, but right now I can barely manage a weak smile. Still, I cross the room and settle next to him, patting him on the knee.

Resisting the urge to point out that I'm old enough to be his mother, for so many reasons. Besides, I lack the … ah … equipment that he's really looking for in a date, anyway.

"Are we lavender dating now?" I tease, digging deep to be my usual peppy self.

Brandon raises a dark blond brow in an expression that is so like his father it physically hurts me. The reaction surprises me, though it shouldn't. I thought I'd long gotten over his resemblance to his father. And I shouldn't be after what happened today. I should've expected seeing him to hit that nerve again, really.

"I'm impressed you even know what that is," he admits. "But no. That would imply I want people to think I'm hetero." He smirks, and I can't help letting out a wry laugh.

"Oh good, you're here, and you're happy," Mia says brightly from across the living room, walking in with a tray of sugar cookies. Of course.

Carrie frowns and looks between us. "Why wouldn't Rae be happy?"

And now Joanie perks up. "Rae's not happy? Why?" She turns to me. "Did someone drop a proverbial turd in your hot cocoa at the bakery today? Tell me who and I'll fight them. You know I can roundhouse kick a bitch like nobody's business."

I snort a laugh. These ladies. I love them for their loyalty and sass, truly. "Nothing. I'm fine. Really." I give Mia a pointed yet joking glare.

She sets the tray down and raises her hands as Greg and

Evan both dive for cookies. Joanie gives Greg a look when he emerges with a precariously balanced stack in hand. "What? Ev and I are working out in the morning, it'll be fine," he says defensively. He shrugs and downs half a cookie in a single bite. Since he runs the community and fitness center and is the epitome of in-shape, I don't know why she's worried.

Joanie shakes her head and turns her attention back to me. "I've heard more honesty from opposing council defending a habitual re-offender," she says drily.

Brandon scoffs. "Speak human, Jo Jo."

Joanie tips her head to the side. "Huh. No innuendo, and I still like that nickname."

I roll my eyes. "She means she can tell I'm full of shit," I explain, then sigh. "I'm just ..." I search for a plausible explanation. Anything that will save me from having to open the Luke McMillan can of worms. "I'm still thinking about my conversation with Jerry yesterday."

"Jerry had the balls to speak to you?" Greg asks, incredulous.

I smirk. "That he did. He even gave me a full apology for pretending to be on a town council that didn't exist at the time and said that he's glad the town is doing well even if he's not in charge. *And* he told me he knows who stole the town incorporation petition signatures at that St. Patrick's Day event we held a couple years back."

Everyone gasps. I suppress a smirk at successfully baiting them with a distraction.

Mia tuts. "Which was great until he showed his actual cards. He only wanted discounted pie."

Joanie scoffs. "No offense, Mia, but who the fuck cares about pie? I want to know who stole the signatures." Joanie turns to me expectantly.

I shrug. "He said he didn't want to 'throw anyone else under the bus'," I reply with air quotes. "But that they did it to impress him."

"I know that happened before I got here," Carrie hedges, "but that has Batty Betty McDonald written all over it."

Carrie may not have come to Alpine Ridge until the summer before Nate and Mia's wedding, just after the incorporation petition signature theft, but she was crucial in wooing all the townspeople into being involved in the election process. I saw how hard she worked to get to know people and listen to them. Betty McDonald included. So, if anyone had a good sense of her during that time, it's Carrie.

Though I've also known Betty my whole life. Both she and Jerry lost their spouses five to ten years back. Even if she's a good twenty years older than me, I know her well enough to know she'd pull some shady moves to woo someone.

"I agree," I reply succinctly. "But we re-collected the signatures, and the incorporation went through. So, I'm going to try to just let it go."

Everyone's silent for a moment, presumably processing that.

"She comes into the wellness center for massages once

a week," Evan pipes up. "I could have Dana, you know, go a little rough on her next time." He wiggles his eyebrows in a way that lets us know he's joking.

Probably.

Everyone laughs, anyway.

"You just hired Dana," Nate objects. "Let's not ask her to do anything sketchy for at least six months."

Mia settles next to him on the couch and smacks his arm. "Nate!"

He grins at her. "I'm just kidding, babe." But he winks at Evan when Mia turns away, and I snort.

"I'm a big believer in karma," I say. "So, nobody needs to do a damn thing. Betty has a pile of karma coming her way, don't you worry."

"But it's so much more fun when you get to watch it happen," Joanie says.

Greg laughs. "This is normally where I'd try to balance your vicious tendencies, city girl, but Betty is … special. And in this case, I agree completely."

"We are not manufacturing a way to make Betty get hers," Carrie interjects firmly. "Even if I agree, we're trying to build a community here, not piss off its long-time residents, no matter how irksome they may be." She perks up. "Oh! And speaking of building the community, we officially hired the new fire chief today."

My heart drops into my stomach.

No. No, no, no, no, no. I worked so hard to avoid exactly this conversation.

"His name is Luke McMillan," she continues. "He grew

up in Alpine Ridge." She turns to Brandon. "And I swear, he looks just like you, B. Is there any chance you could be related?"

I can't imagine I'm hiding the horror on my face. Every word out of Carrie's mouth … it was like a series of horrible accidents I was powerless to stop. And now … the wreckage.

I turn to find Brandon's face strangely blank.

And everyone else is looking between me, Carrie, and Brandon, clearly confused about the vibe in the room.

It's at that point I realize … I'm the only one here who knows. The only Alpine Ridge resident that was around when it happened. When the gossip was flying around town. When Luke's indiscretions came to light. When what was left of my world fell spectacularly and completely apart.

Brandon sighs, running a hand through his hair. "He's my biological father."

His words break through the paralyzing fog I've been wrapped in.

"I wanted to warn you, but I didn't know whether you knew," I say.

Brandon's brown eyes meet mine, and all I see there is warmth. The tightness I hadn't realized was seizing my chest loosens.

"What?" Carrie asks, eyes widening. "Wait. Rae, you —"

"Knew Luke. Know Luke," I correct. "Yes. He stopped by the bakery today."

Brandon nods resignedly, at what I'm not sure. Acknowledgment of his father's presence, I suppose.

"Well, this is going to be awkward as ass," Joanie mumbles.

Mia leans over, placing her hand on Brandon's knee. "Are you going to be okay having him back in town?"

Brandon drags in a deep breath and shrugs. "Yeah, sure. I mean, I couldn't care less that he's here," he says flatly. "My grandfather told me about him years ago. But Luke's never been involved in my life. That says all I need to know about my sperm donor."

I blanch at the frankness that I can't argue with.

"You seem … mad," Carrie points out tentatively.

Brandon shrugs. "That would require caring. Which … okay, I can't honestly say I don't care but I also don't want to care, you know?" He gives another agitated shrug. "But I'll deal with it, and I'm sure if I ever have to interact with him, we'll both be polite. Clearly, we're not going to be best buds or anything."

Greg sets down his crumpled napkin. "Speaking as someone who has a piece of human garbage for a father," he opens, "sometimes you just need to tell someone exactly what you think of them so you can mentally move on. Even if you don't expect or want a response, all those feelings you have … you've got to let them out, man, or they'll fester."

Brandon shifts uncomfortably. Greg is usually on the quiet side, so we're all a little taken aback by his frankness. I mean, most of us know what a blow-hard his dad is, but to hear him summarize it like that … well, I can see his point. It makes me want to give Luke a piece of my mind. I'm not sure if that's on my behalf or Brandon's. Both wouldn't go amiss.

But Brandon still looks unsure.

Carrie, ever the diplomat, seamlessly reassures Brandon with a hug and moves everyone into our first game of the evening. It's somber at first, but eventually everyone loosens up and things return mostly to normal.

Despite putting on my own "normal" face, I still can't shake my unease. Knowing that Brandon is aware of his connection to Luke doesn't make me less anxious. If anything, it makes it worse.

Because I know the gossip mill in Alpine Ridge. Luke's return and his link to Brandon will be all anyone can talk about for months. And while Brandon might be able to shrug it off, for now at least, the idea of reliving the pain of Luke's betrayal, of having to hide it from my friends ... it's already wearing me down.

I thought I'd put that part of my life behind me. But with Luke back, the past is threatening to swallow me whole. And I'm not sure I'm strong enough to keep my head above water this time around.

CHAPTER FOUR

LUKE

The two-hour drive back to Seattle gives me plenty of time to replay my interaction with Rae in my mind. The way her smile froze when she saw me, her chilly reception ... it's clear she's not thrilled about my return to Alpine Ridge.

I got caught up in the idea of catching up with my first love, wondering if she still thought about me like I do about her. But I didn't consider that she may, just not in a good way.

I can't say I blame her.

Thirty years is a long time. And despite our promises to keep in touch, to keep our connection alive until we could reunite in the two short years we had until adulthood ... well, I didn't. In fact, even though I think of her often, I haven't spoken to her since the night before I left all those years ago.

In my defense, my father went to great lengths to keep

me isolated from everyone in Alpine Ridge after the fire. Moving meant a new phone number, which he didn't want given out, and he also intercepted my mail and even threatened to pull me out of school and move across the country if I tried to reach out. And since my mother had left us by that point, I didn't have her normal intervention to save me from his strictly enforced rules.

And he was stricter — and angrier — than ever, so I feared crossing him. He said the town had ruined us, and to have anything to do with it was an insult to our family. While I didn't buy into that, I also had enough on my plate not to fight him on it.

Once I hit eighteen, I wanted a quick and easy way out of what had become a hellish situation. So, I joined the military. I'll admit, I didn't even think about contacting Rae at that point. I'd made my decision, and I assumed she'd moved on.

Or maybe it was easier than facing the truth — that I'd let her down. That I'd broken the promises we'd made to each other.

Well, I'm facing it now. Because she's still in Alpine Ridge, and now I will be, too, permanently it seems. I'll have to tell her what happened and beg her forgiveness.

Hopefully she'll give me the chance.

I push the thoughts aside as I pull up to Danny's house. As I head up the steps, Danny pops out of the front door, running a hand over his jet-black hair absently. I note he's gotten a fresh high and tight fade on our day off. He'd look sharp but for the exhaustion written all over his face. I'd say it's from the twenty-four hour shift we just finished but I can tell it's more than that.

I raise my brows. "Hey, man," I greet him.

"Hey, Luke," he replies somberly.

I stop beside him, putting my hands on my hips. "I'm guessing you're not out here to talk me into rattling the pans next shift."

"Well, I am a shit cook, but no," he replies, then sighs. "The girls had a big fight at school. Thought you should know what you were walking back into."

"Ah," I say, heaving a sigh. "About what?"

Danny's head swings side to side, even though I know he, like me, probably knows what it was about. "Don't know for sure. Neither will talk. To us or each other."

I rock back on my heels. "Okay. Are we talking fistfight here or …"

Danny smirks. "Just cattiness, I think. No blood or bruises that I can see, anyway. Still … Zo's been crying when she thinks we aren't listening. Nia tried talking to her a few times with no luck."

I shake my head and slap him on the shoulder. "Thanks for the heads up. And for having her. I hope it didn't disrupt things too much for you guys. I can look for someone else to stay at the apartment with her while I get things set up in our new place."

"You know I love her, but honestly I think she'd be happier that way." He pauses, assessing me. "So, new place, huh? That mean you're out of here?"

I nod. "As soon as I can work it out with the chief."

"What's the town called again?"

"Alpine Ridge."

Danny smirks. "You must really want that chief title to leave Seattle for some Podunk town in the Cascades, man." His grin says he's teasing, but the comment lands a little too hard.

"Come on, you know I wouldn't do it just for the position," I respond defensively. "I'm *from* that Podunk town, you know."

"Oh shit, sorry, I guess I missed that part," he murmurs. He pops the door and leans in, shouting up the stairs, "Zo, your dad's here." He leaves the door ajar and turns back to me. "So full circle opportunity, huh?"

I heave out a sigh. "More than you know. My family left there because of a fire."

I chew on my lip to keep the rest of the story from spilling out. That it was a fire that burned down so much more than my father's church. It burned down our family, metaphorically. And, unfortunately for my sister, literally.

"Damn. Well, I'm happy for you," Danny offers as I hear Zoe come crashing down the stairs.

She pops out, her sparkly purple backpack slung over one shoulder, a well-worn book in the other hand. Her dark brown curls are in disarray and her right alabaster cheek is ruddy, the puckered scars covering her left cheek paler and starker than usual; by itself, not concerning. But the real tell is her red-rimmed brown eyes. I deflate a little at the evidence of

Danny's warning, and how often this seems to happen lately.

Zoe coming home from school upset.

Zoe fighting. *Zoe.* My little pacifist who used to tell me not to yell at people who cut me off in traffic because, *"Maybe they're just having a bad day, Daddy."*

Zoe crying and inconsolable. My little Zen warrior. It kills me.

"Hey, kiddo," I say softly. "Ready to go?"

I can tell she's trying not to look directly at me, so I don't see the evidence full on, but her eyes betray her, darting my way as if she's thinking about folding herself around me like she did when she was little.

"Yeah."

One quiet syllable is all I get. I sigh and give Danny a curt nod.

"Thanks again. See you day after tomorrow."

"Sure thing, Luke."

Zoe dashes on ahead of me to the truck, climbing in the passenger seat. I head around and get in.

As I start the engine, she ever so nonchalantly asks, "Did you get the job?"

I nod solemnly. "I got the job. We're moving to Alpine Ridge."

Zoe closes her eyes and lets out a sigh of relief. She reopens them and turns her big, beautiful brown eyes on me. "When can we go? Tomorrow? Please say tomorrow."

I try not to let my concern for her show on my face. "I'm sorry, Zo, but no. It might take a few weeks, maybe even a couple of months. I need to get the old family house fixed up first and give notice at my job."

Her expression falls. "So ... I'll have to stay with Danny, Nia, and Piper again?"

"No," I assure her. "You don't. We'll figure something out." I pause, unsure of how far I want to push my luck. "Do you want to tell me what happened today?"

And while Zoe's mother and I were only a couple for about five minutes, we did work together, so I knew her enough that the resolute expression that settles over Zoe's features makes her a mirror of her mother in every way. It's moments like these that make me hurt for her loss the most. Not for myself but for Zoe, and for Virginia too, who would've loved every minute of this pre-teen phase. Certainly, her sass would've been a much better match for the stubbornness I know is coming right now.

"Are you asking me to relive my trauma?" she says haughtily.

"I would never," I assure her in as serious a tone as I can manage.

"Good. Because my answer is *no*," she says firmly, lifting her chin and looking away.

A ghost of a smile pulls at my lips at her theatrics. But this isn't my first time trying to get information out of her. I pull into traffic and let the silence do its work.

When we're almost home, it pays off. Zoe lets out an epic, world-weary sigh.

"They were making fun of me again. For being weird. For my scars ... and for not having a mom," she adds quietly, looking down into her lap. Out of the corner of my eye, I catch a fat tear drop hit her thumb.

"Piper, too?"

She looks up, sniffing deeply and shaking her head. "No, but she didn't say *anything*."

"Maybe she was afraid they'd make fun of her, too," I offer, playing devil's advocate.

This time I feel Zoe's sharp gaze before I turn to see it. "Then she's a coward," she says acidly. Then she deflates just a little. "I would've stood up for *her*."

A sad smile crosses my lips, and I reach over to pat her knee. "I know you would've, Zo. But unfortunately, most people are too afraid or nervous to stand up for what's right."

"Guess I am weird because I don't understand that at all," she grumbles as I pull into an open spot on the street in front of our apartment building.

"You say that like being weird is a bad thing," I reply lightly. "You march to the beat of your own drum. Someday you'll be glad for that."

"Not today," she says, folding her long arms over her chest.

I huff a dry laugh. "Fair enough."

She turns abruptly. "Can't I just come with you while you fix up the house?"

I hesitate. The house isn't in top shape, but it's not unsafe either.

And having Zoe with me would make the process a lot more bearable.

And clearly, she's even more miserable here than I thought …

"Tell you what," I say, tugging at one of her curls. "I'll talk to the chief, see what I can do. But we haven't even started packing, so it still might be a couple of weeks, okay?"

Zoe sighs dramatically. "I guess it'll have to do."

I blow out a breath as she jumps out of the truck. Oh boy.

And she's not even a teenager yet.

Turns out the department was about to furlough someone because of budget cuts so, while they would've rather gone with someone less senior, given the circumstances it only made sense that it be me.

So, to Zoe's great relief, here we are, not quite two weeks later, standing in the driveway of our new home, surrounded by boxes, furniture, and a scant dusting of snow that has fallen.

Well, the house is new to Zoe, anyway. The place is full of memories for me, which is going to make this process extra challenging, because some of them aren't great. The two-story Victorian needs a lot of work. Not least of all a fresh coat of paint. Even if it weren't peeling, the sickly yellow color was never my favorite, but mostly it reminds me of how my parents argued over it.

A sigh escapes me as I try not to get overwhelmed

thinking about all the work that needs to be done to the inside.

Bright side, come Monday morning, I'll officially start as Alpine Ridge's fire chief. And maybe I can finally right some wrongs of my past.

"Well, that's the last of it," I say, unhitching the moving trailer from my truck. "What do you say we head to the tavern for dinner? I'm starving."

Zoe's eyes light up. "Yes, please! I want to see more of the town."

I grin as she jumps into the truck with glee. She's been like a different kid since I pulled her out of school.

Or, more accurately, like her old, carefree self. She's reading less and drawing more. Before we left, she didn't hide in her room at all like she had been, choosing the apartment's furnished balcony to sketch trees, squirrels, and passers-by. I was relieved to see her happy again. I can only hope she continues to be happy living here.

As we drive the few minutes to the tavern, I can't wait to see what she thinks of the house's yard. Well, after we clean it up a bit, anyway. I want to share it with her because at least the outside of my childhood home holds plenty of wonderful memories for me, thankfully.

As does the tavern, which looks practically the same as I remember when we pull in. Funny, since I'd have expected it to look shabbier with the years but clearly, it's been maintained. Recently, by the looks of it, I notice as we step out onto a walkway freshly swept of snow while Zoe rapidly fires questions at me about the town that she doesn't wait for answers to.

"And why is it snowing?" she asks, swinging the door open. "It's March!"

I chuckle and follow her in.

"Welcome to Alpine Ridge," I murmur. Snow in early March really isn't all that unusual here. But thankfully Zoe will be spared the full winter snow experience for a while. As a born Seattleite, she's not exactly used to tons of the white stuff.

Instantly, my focus shifts as the weight of curious stares from the other patrons in the tavern lands on us. It's to be expected — Alpine Ridge is a small town, and my return is bound to be big news. And Zoe definitely stands out.

In any case, she seems oblivious to the stares and whispers as we find a table in the semi-crowded dining area. It's Friday night, but it's still early, so we're lucky to snag a two-seater in the corner. Zoe continues prattling on about her plans to explore the local hiking trails and start "unschooling" — a concept we stumbled on that seems tailor-made for her curious, self-directed nature.

It's pretty much what it sounds like; exactly the opposite of traditional schooling with no set structure, expectations, or limits, directed only by the student's interests. Zoe is thrilled to direct her own learning and escape public schools with their cliques and mean girls.

For my part, I know she'll learn loads. Besides, she's only twelve. There's time to worry about test scores and college applications, but I think both of us need this unstructured approach as we figure out our new life here.

After perusing the menus left between the ketchup bottle and saltshaker on the table, I head up to the bar to order since it seems there aren't any wait staff.

The old guy behind the bar looks terribly familiar. I know the Allen family owned this bar once upon a time, and he has their look about them. He has their average height and build, but he also has their look ... it's something about the shape of their faces that I can't quite put my finger on. The two sons were a good ten to fifteen years older than me though, so I don't remember their names or which one this might be.

"What can I get for you?" he asks curtly.

"Hi," I say pointedly, "I'm Luke. My daughter and I would like a couple of cheeseburgers, fries, and cokes, please."

The old guy tips his head to the side. "You're Luke McMillan, Pastor McMillan's boy."

I hesitate only for a fraction of a second. Shit, he put that together fast.

"Sure am."

He narrows his eyes, assessing me. "Well ... welcome back, I guess." He leans into the cracked door behind him and shouts down our order before turning back to me. "So just visiting?"

My eyebrows bunch together. How has the gossip not traveled around by now? Am I even in the right town? But then ... it was really only Arthur, Carrie, and Rae that I've seen, so clearly all three can keep things to themselves. Good to know.

"Nope. I'm here to get the Alpine Ridge Fire Department up and running." I smile winningly. "And you are?"

There he goes narrowing his eyes again. But after a moment he sticks out a hand. "Jerry Allen."

Jerry. That's right. And his younger brother was Perry.

I hold back a snort as I reach out and shake his hand.

"Pleasure. Be seeing you around, Jerry."

He dips his chin, and I head back to the table. Zoe is swiping around on her phone, probably learning things about the town even I don't know yet.

"Did you know there's no library in Alpine Ridge?" Zoe asks. She turns her phone to show me a map. "The closest one is in a city called Ellensburg."

I smirk. "Honey, this is a *very* small town. I warned you. When I lived here, there was this tavern, a gas station, a history museum, a bakery, a church, and a general store."

Zoe's jaw drops. "Wow. Well, I'm glad it's got more than that now at least."

I nod. "Arthur told me there are plenty more businesses coming soon. You'll see. We'll get to watch this town take on a new life."

"Okay, but first can we go to the library in Ellensburg? I need to make my reading list."

I can't help but smile at her enthusiasm. Zoe has always been a voracious reader, devouring books well above her grade level. It's one of the many things that makes her unique. Special.

"Sure thing. We need to go into Ellensburg tomorrow anyway to order new appliances and pick up some building materials."

Zoe bounces in her seat excitedly. Which at first I think is because of what I said, but I'm quickly proven wrong by Jerry arriving with our food.

"Thank you, thank you, thank you," she says gleefully in his direction as she dives on her fries.

Jerry gives her a bewildered but amused look. "Well, you're welcome, young lady."

I smile and pop a fry in my mouth, giving him a thumbs up.

As he heads back behind the bar, I'm also pleased that everyone else in the room seems to ignore us. Like we're just part of the town.

I laugh a little. Could it really be that easy?

"What's so funny, Dad?" Zoe asks around a mouthful of burger.

"I think we're going to do just fine here, that's all." I say, then I point a fry at her. "And don't talk with your mouth full."

I should've known it was all too easy. On the way home, Zoe spots the bakery.

"Ooh, there's the bakery you mentioned! Can we get dessert? Please?"

Anxiety churns in my gut at her innocent request.

"Not tonight, kiddo, it's already closed," I reply. Since checking the hours was the first thing I did after I walked out last time so I knew when I could come back and try again with Rae. "But I'll bring you another day, I promise." Suddenly my burger and fries aren't sitting so well.

Zoe looks a little crestfallen, which isn't a surprise given that she's visited every bakery in Western Washington, but she immediately starts asking questions about what other businesses might come in next.

I'm glad she quickly moved on from talking about the bakery because I'm not sure I'm ready for Rae to meet Zoe. Not yet. It feels ... complicated.

It takes me a while to figure out why. It's not until I watch Zoe skipping up the front steps into the house that it clicks. Something about watching her come back to my childhood home.

Introducing Zoe to Rae would flaunt a life I've built without her. A life that was supposed to be ours, here in this town.

It was supposed to be our daughter skipping up the steps, racing to see her momma after a night out with her pops.

A sadness I haven't felt in a long time tugs at my heart.

But then I remember the tavern, the curious looks from the other diners. In a town this small, Rae is bound to hear about Zoe soon enough. Whether I'm ready or not.

That night, as I tuck Zoe into bed, she asks for a story, *"Like when I was little."* The request catches me off guard — it's been years since our bedtime story ritual. But something about the new house, the big changes in our lives, seems to have brought out a neediness in her I haven't seen in a while. It pulls harder at that feeling in my chest.

And as I sit on the edge of her bed, spinning a tale about a brave princess on a quest, my mind drifts to Rae. To the life we'd dreamed of together all those years ago. A life filled with love and laughter. A house echoing with the sound of little feet.

It further occurs to me that's why I don't want to let Rae see this part of my life. Because in a way, it's more than what could have been. It feels like … a betrayal. Like I'm living the future we'd planned, just ... without her.

The thought sits heavy in my chest as I kiss Zoe goodnight and slip out of her room, settling into my own freshly made bed. I know it's ridiculous — it's been thirty years, after all. For all I know, Rae has built a beautiful life of her own, with a husband and children and a home filled with happiness.

I shift uncomfortably, even though it's my same old mattress.

But I know it's not the bed that's bothering me.

It's the idea that Rae has a whole life that I wasn't a part of either.

It's hypocritical.

It shouldn't bother me.

But it does.

I shake my head, as if I can physically dislodge the thoughts. I can't go down that road. Not now. Not when I have so much on my plate already.

Get settled. Fix up the house. Make sure Zoe has everything she needs. That's what I need to focus on. The rest ... well, I'll just have to figure it out as I go.

One thing at a time.

CHAPTER FIVE

RAE

Another day, another round of pretending (badly) that I'm not worried Luke will pop out from behind every corner. I'm fooling no one at this point, myself least of all. So, I'm not surprised at all when I'm at the sink in the customer-facing area of the bakery, washing up with a little more force than necessary, when Mia corners me. A mix of concern and determination fills her big blue eyes, and I know she won't let me avoid this conversation.

"So," she begins, dusting flour off her hands, "I've been giving you some space, but it's clear you're not coming out of this funk on your own. I think it's high time we talk about Luke and whatever happened between you two that has you so upset."

I sigh, my shoulders sagging. "Mia, I've been quiet about it for a reason. It's in the past; I'd really prefer that it stayed there."

Mia raises an eyebrow. "Really? Because from where

I'm standing, Luke is very much in the present. He's the new fire chief, and whatever it is with him is obviously affecting you. So, spill."

I close my eyes briefly, knowing she's right. "Fine. Luke and I ... we were high school sweethearts. But then he left town, and that was that." I bite into my lip as I dry my hands. Because that *so* was not that.

Mia scrutinizes me for a moment, and I can practically hear the wheels turning in her head. And I definitely see it on her face when it clicks. Her eyes widen as understanding dawns on her features. "Oh my god! He cheated on you, didn't he? And Brandon ... he's the result of that?"

I nod, my throat tight. "Bingo." It was only a matter of time before she figured it out, even without my help, but it still hurts to hear the words spoken out loud. To remember the raw feelings of losing the love of your life ... only to find out that he'd been going behind your back with your best friend.

Mia's expression softens, and she reaches out to squeeze my arm. "Oh, Rae, I'm so sorry. I can't imagine how difficult it must be, having that reminder constantly in your face, what with Brandon's return and now Luke's."

I take a shaky breath in. "It's been a challenge," I admit. "But I adjusted to Brandon being back. It helped that it wasn't his fault. I'll adjust to Luke being back, too. Might just take a bit longer."

"I can't imagine what that must've done to your ability to trust people," Mia says, studying me. Then, softly, she asks, "Is that why you never got married or had kids? Because of what happened with Luke?"

I side-eye her, debating how much to reveal.

Well, in for a penny, in for a pound.

With a sigh, I mutter, "I *was* married, actually. Once upon a time."

Mia's eyes go wide again, and she opens her mouth to ask more questions that I'm not prepared to answer, but before she can, the bell above the bakery door chimes. We both turn to see Betty McDonald walking in.

I glance over at Mia with an arched brow. She gives me a small nod, having already convinced me to help karma along when the chance arose.

Now it's a double win for me: getting out of a conversation I don't want to have and taking this old bat down a peg or two.

"Hi, Betty. The usual?" I greet her, keeping my voice as casual as possible.

"Yes, and it best be *fresh* this time," she replies imperiously, looking down her nose at me. I fight back an eye roll and give her a sugary sweet smile.

"Of course," I murmur. But as I pack up her order, I lean in, smiling invitingly while lowering my voice. "By the way, a little birdie recently told us who stole those town incorporation petition signatures St. Patrick's Day before last."

And I've never seen someone pale so fast in their life. She turns her head, pretending to look at, well, anything but me.

"Why would I care about old gossip?" she sniffs.

I chuckle. "Oh, I think you know why." I pause for effect. "I didn't take you for a thief, Betty," I say mock-sadly, shaking my head.

She sputters, her face reddening as her wide, enraged eyes return to meet mine. "How dare you accuse me? As if I would ever do such a thing!"

Setting her bag down between us, I give her a razor-sharp smile. "Oh, I think we both know you would. And did," I reply firmly. "But like you said, it's old news, and it didn't stop the incorporation from happening. So, I'd be willing to forgive and forget … *if* you were to apologize."

"I have nothing to apologize for!" she insists indignantly. "And … and even if I did — which I *don't* — there isn't a world where I'd ever owe an apology to an uppity piece of trash like you."

Despite knowing that's exactly how she's always thought of me, the words still sting, and I blanch as she snatches the bag from the counter.

Mia steps forward. "No charge for that today, Mrs. McDonald."

A smug smile crosses Betty's face, and she turns her nose up at me. "As well there shouldn't be! I can't believe you let the help speak to customers like this. She'd better be fired!"

Mia tips her head to the side. "Oh, I'm sorry. I didn't mean to imply that Rae did a damn thing wrong. In fact, I think she's being gracious even giving you the chance to redeem yourself. I sure wouldn't. But it's her call, since she had to do all the work to replace the signatures you stole." Mia shakes her head. "No, I was saying I don't want your money *or* your business until you do as she asks." Betty sputters, but Mia holds up a hand to show that she's not done. "But now I think that since you've been so insulting, we're going to need a *public* apology before you're permitted back here ... or in any of the businesses that our family runs in this town. And make no mistake, Mrs. McDonald, Rae is my family." Mia turns to me. "So, that's also Nate's new medical practice, Evan's wellness center, Greg's community center, Joanie's new law practice, Brandon's new art gallery ... hmmm ... I'm missing someone ..."

"Sera's new realty office," I offer, lips twitching, presuming she didn't mention Carrie because, while she's the town planner, she doesn't actually own a business.

"Ah, yes, Greg's cousin. She's definitely part of the family. Oh! And she owns the grocery store, too. Goodness me, well, that's pretty much everything but the tavern and the gas station!" Mia says with feigned alarm.

"And the mail place, since Jerry owns that now, too," I correct, stifling a laugh.

"Ah. Yes, and the mail place," Mia agrees with a serious nod.

"You ... she ..." Betty's eyes flick between us as she sputters incoherently. "Your pastries are barely tolerable, anyway!" With a frustrated noise, she throws the bag with her maple bar on the floor, *stomps on it*, and storms out.

For a moment, we silently stare at the crushed pastry bag and bits of donut that have scattered out of the top.

"Well. I'd best let everyone know what went down as soon as possible," Mia murmurs. She looks over and gives me a small, self-assured smile. "Hope she has fun driving into Ellensburg every time she needs something."

I can't help but laugh. "Thank you for talking me into doing that. It was the most satisfying thing I've done all year." I pop around the counter with a broom and quickly sweep the mess into a dustpan.

"That *was* more cathartic than I expected," Mia agrees. "And it was a good message to send. The new Alpine Ridge won't put up with any bullshit."

With a chuckle of agreement, I dump the mess into the garbage can and put back the broom.

Then I turn to Mia, untying my apron. "That seems like a perfect note to end the day on. And anyway, Arthur asked me to stop by town hall this afternoon."

Mia nods, her expression a mix of concern and curiosity. "Okay. But don't for one minute think I'm going to forget you told me you've been married before. We're definitely finishing that conversation later."

I give her a sweet smile, grab my purse, and walk toward the door. "Not if I can help it," I call over my shoulder as I head out the door.

I hop in my Bronco and drive the short distance to the new town hall, windows down, so the slightly less frigid March air can blow away my worries. Dodging yet another conversation about my past with Mia. Betty's stinging words. Thoughts of Luke.

It kind of works, as I'm a bit perkier when I step out onto the newly paved walkway to the building, breathing in the crisp, clean mountain air. One of my favorite parts of living here.

I enter the building to the smell of new. Like the subtle aromas of paint, brass, and paper mixed, and I find I like it. It's the smell of progress.

I wave at Meredith, the newly hired office manager.

"Here to see Mayor Burton?" she asks with a bright smile.

"Sure am," I confirm. "Is he in his office?"

She shakes her head, her beautiful curly ginger locks swaying. "He's in the conference room. He should be just wrapping up a meeting. If the door is open, you can go on in."

I nod my thanks and slip a pastry bag to her on my way by. "For you."

She opens the bag and inhales deeply. "Oooh, one of Mia's chocolate croissants," she breathes. "Thanks, Rae."

"Anytime, sugar," I reply with a wink.

I head down the hall, appreciating the classical architecture. Simple, understated columns line the main hall, each topped with domed lighting, ending at the sizeable meeting room. The decoratively paneled double doors give the relatively small space a sense of importance and grandeur.

It all just feels so … official. A swell of pride moves

through me at getting to be a part of making this town grow into something even better.

Since one door is propped half-open, I peek inside. I find Arthur, Carrie, and Greg at the opposite end of the long, black walnut conference table. They all look up at my arrival.

"Were you ready for me?" I ask Arthur tentatively.

A warm smile spreads over his friendly, wrinkled face, and he gestures for me to enter. "Nearly. Please, come in. We're just about done here."

I step inside tentatively. "Is it okay to ask how everything is going with setting up the town?" I ask. "Fire chief aside, of course. I think we all know about that." I give my best impression of a smile, but it feels more like a grimace.

Carrie's smile, however, is radiant, as she brushes her long dark waves behind her shoulders and smooths her cream pantsuit. Clearly, she's quite pleased with herself, but understandably so. "I'm working on the police department next," she offers. "We're making good progress."

Greg nods in agreement, his blue eyes lit up. "And I've just agreed to run the parks and rec department."

"Well, I'll be. Congratulations!" I say, genuinely happy for him. I slink up and squeeze his shoulder before taking a seat. "So, what does that entail?"

"Well, first, cleaning up and maintaining the hiking trails. But also establishing parks, running events, that sort of thing," he explains.

"How does the community center fit into that?" I ask with a frown. "I know how hard you worked to get it set up. Surely, it'll be part of the plan?"

Greg smiles indulgently. "I'll split off and continue to run the gym portion. We just agreed to hire someone to run the other side for workshops, special programs, and events."

Arthur chimes in, "That's actually why we asked you here, Rae. The young lady who will take on the role is based in Leavenworth and will only come on an as needed basis until she's able to move permanently in a couple months. We'll need someone to show her the ropes and help run things until then. And since you've been the driving force behind many of our events, we were hoping you could help. The St. Patrick's Day event this year should be a good way to get Layla up to speed and kick things off. We'd like to pay you as a consultant."

"Oh, gosh, I wouldn't say I've been the driving force," I demur. "Greg has really been at the forefront —"

Greg snorts. "I own the space, show up, and do what I'm told, Rae. You absolutely make those events shine. You're who *everyone* looks to when planning an event around here. Give yourself some credit."

I wrinkle my nose. "Okay, fine, I *might* have already come up with ideas for that event ..."

Carrie chuckles and Arthur smiles knowingly.

I sigh. "All right, all right. I'm in."

"Excellent," Arthur says, clapping his hands together. "Now, if that's all —"

"Did I miss the party?" a deep voice asks from behind me.

We all turn toward the door to see Luke standing there, looking uncertain. My eyes involuntarily trail down his body, taking in the fitted polo and slacks he's wearing that show off his toned physique spectacularly.

I swallow hard as my stomach does an uncomfortable flip.

"Ah, Luke," Arthur says. "You're early."

"Before you move on, Arthur, I have one more thing I'd like to talk to you about," Greg says.

Carrie rises, and I follow suit, all too happy to get out of any room Luke is in. "Of course, we'll give you all the room," I say with a smile in Arthur and Greg's direction.

Arthur dips his chin. "We'll reach out soon."

I nod and follow Carrie out. She's already headed back to her office, and I'm making to leave when I hear someone call, "Rae, a minute, please." I turn to see Luke has also stepped out of the room and closed the door behind him, presumably to give Arthur and Greg privacy. But that also leaves me alone in the hall with Luke.

Shit.

I take a subtle deep breath and plaster on my best impression of a smile. Even though my palms are already sweating.

"What can I do for you, Fire Chief McMillan?"

Luke gives me a look. "Well, if I didn't suspect you were upset with me before, that would've done it," he responds drily.

"I don't know what you're talking about," I reply airily, lifting my chin.

He cocks an eyebrow and my insides curl tightly. "It's been a long time, Rae, but I can still tell when you're lying."

I clench my jaw. The audacity of him to pretend like he still knows me. But I presume Meredith is listening, so I do my best not to lose my cool.

"Don't be silly," I reply with a forced laugh.

"Rae, we should talk about —"

"So, you're a firefighter," I blurt out, hoping to head off wherever he was taking this conversation, as I'm certain it's somewhere I don't want to go. Not here. Not now. Probably never.

His deep brown eyes examine my face for a moment before he replies. "Just registered that, did you?" he murmurs, a hint of teasing in his tone.

I lift a shoulder. "I was too busy being shocked that you were back for it to fully sink in."

He raises a brow. "It was long overdue. Me coming back, I mean."

I snort derisively. "That's sure one way to put it." My first instinct is to be horrified at showing my irritation and anger, but I realize I'm not the one here who has something to be ashamed of.

"And how would you put it?" he asks, curiosity lacing his tone.

I frown, unsure of how to frame this, given that I don't know if he knows about Brandon. But Mia's encouragement seems to have freed my inner thoughts lately.

"It is what it is, and I have no interest in gossip. Never did. So, I wouldn't put it any way. But the townsfolk … well, as you can imagine, they've got their own opinions."

His brows pull together. "What? Why?" he demands.

My own brows pop up. It seems like he doesn't know … yet I find that hard to believe. So, I can't resist putting out one more piece of bait.

"You didn't think they'd find out?"

An unnatural silence settles over the hall. Now I *know* Meredith is listening. It's so quiet I'm afraid Luke might hear the rapid pounding of my heart as I wait breathlessly for his response.

His brow furrows deeper. "Why would they care that we broke up? That my father made damn sure I could never speak to you or anyone here after we left? At least until it didn't matter anymore, anyway," he replies gruffly.

I let out my breath, and my chest constricts as his words sink in. Pastor McMillan stopped him from speaking to anyone in town? Well, that would sure as hell explain a lot. But … why?

"I'm sorry. I'm not sure I understand. He did what?" I pull back, distracted by this new information. "Why would …" I shake my head "… but even if he did, that's not … I'm not talking about us, Luke." My hands ball into my fists at my sides, and I can't help the frustration in my voice.

But now it's Luke's turn to shake his head. He's clearly

bewildered. "Then I have no idea what you *are* talking about, so you're going to have to clue me in."

I couldn't imagine how he wouldn't know. But … he *doesn't*. Holy shit.

My stomach drops as certainty settles over me.

"You really don't know," I whisper, more to myself than him.

"I don't know what, Rae?" he asks tightly.

The blood drains from my face. I put a hand over my mouth, shaking my head. I can't do it. I can't be the one to tell him. That he has a son. That he's missed out on Brandon's whole life. That he created a reputation for himself he's going to have to contend with. That I know of his betrayal.

It's so much. Too much. I never should've gone down this road. Never should've had this conversation. It's none of my business. Hasn't been since he stepped out on me. This is between him and Brandon.

Thankfully, Greg comes out of the meeting room, and I seize the opportunity to leave the conversation.

"Greg!" I cry in relief. "I need to talk to you alone for a minute." I give Luke a tight, fake apologetic smile and drag Greg away.

I can practically hear Luke's teeth grinding, but he doesn't stop me from leaving. He just watches as I loop my arm through Greg's and practically drag him down the hall.

Greg looks at me questioningly, clearly missing the tension. "What's up, Rae?"

I take a deep breath as we exit the building, pausing just

under the awning and turning toward him. I realize all at once that I have to stop letting my past control me. That the only way I can stop caring about Luke and what he knows is to just let go.

"I've been mulling over something for a while," I tell him. "And it just came together for me. You said you'll only have half the community center for the parks and rec department?"

"Yes?" he says uncertainly.

I take a deep breath. "Surely you could use more space?" I offer.

He tilts his head back and forth. "I mean, yes, but I figured we'd just build it. Lots of that happening right now, anyway." He shrugs.

I huff out a breathy, on-edge laugh, preparing to get rid of the only part of my past I have control over. "Sure. Or you could use the museum." I lick my lips nervously. "I've decided it's time to let go of it."

Greg's eyebrows shoot up. "Really? I mean, that'd be great, but are you sure?"

Am I sure that I want to get rid of the museum my daddy ran once upon a time — the unexpected inheritance I received when the man who'd abandoned us died, hopefully alone and miserable? Even before he caused the fire that broke our family apart, he did awful things, and I've never mourned him. The better question is, why have I held onto it this long?

I'd laugh, but I'm already teetering on insanity with

everything that's happened. And it's time to do something to stop it.

That museum doesn't just hold Alpine Ridge's gold rush history, it also represents everything that went wrong during that time of my life when both of the men I loved left me. I can think of no better symbolic gesture than getting rid of it. And maybe it'll give me the courage to let go of all of this hurt and anger, too.

I meet his gaze, my voice steady. "I'm sure. It's time I let go of the past."

CHAPTER SIX

LUKE

I stare after Rae's retreating form, her sudden departure leaving me reeling. What the hell is she talking about? What don't I know? I rack my brain, trying to unearth some long-buried memory, but come up empty. Unease settles in my gut like a lead weight.

Shaking my head, I turn my focus to the task at hand. I have a fire department to establish, and that will require all my attention. Pushing thoughts of Rae aside, I step into Arthur's office to discuss the next steps.

Arthur is all business as we go over the preliminary research that I've done on the county regulations. We discuss how to work with them to grease the wheels for getting everything approved smoothly. He recommends I talk to Carrie first, as she's established contacts there, but cautions that it can't be tomorrow, as he's asked the rest of the town council to meet us in the morning so he can introduce me to them. Then he plans to take me on a full tour of the town so I can familiarize myself with what building sites and projects will be upcoming as I prepare to take responsibility for fire department coordination and inspections of new builds.

By the end of our meeting, I'm a little overwhelmed, but not in a bad way. Aside from being the perfect distraction from whatever this unknown drama is, it's exciting to sink my teeth into this huge new responsibility. Having always been on the periphery of it, I underestimated how involved the process is. And this is just the tip of the iceberg. I'm equally thrilled by and terrified of that fact.

That evening, my mind is so busy working on the events of the day that once I dry the last dish after cleaning up from dinner, I'm staring out the kitchen window, gazing blankly at the near-dark sky when Zoe pokes me in the side.

"Earth to Dad," she teases, waving a hand in front of my face.

I turn to her with a smirk. "What's up, kiddo?"

She raises a sassy eyebrow. "You were going to teach me how to use the escape ladder?" she reminds me.

Shit. That's right. We replaced the old smoke detectors and installed new carbon monoxide alarms over the weekend but hadn't gotten around to a full emergency drill. Since we lived in an apartment building with external fire escape stairs, she's never had to mount and navigate a hanging ladder, so that's definitely job number one this evening.

"Sure am," I respond. "Follow me." I toss the towel I'd been holding on the counter and take her upstairs.

I talk her through hanging the ladder herself and have her go down it several times until she's comfortable with the less-sturdy feel from what she's used to. She doesn't complain once, but she never does with these things. She and I, of all people, know how important fire safety is.

Not that it saved her mom, who, being a firefighter herself, knew it all. Knew it and pushed too far to save others, dying herself in the process.

My thoughts are so distracting I don't even notice Zoe packing up the ladder until she stops and approaches, wrapping her arms around my middle.

"I miss her when we do this, too," she murmurs into my chest, clearly understanding where my head is at.

I wrap my arms around her and rest my chin on her head. "Gosh, you're getting tall," I respond evasively. And then, so she doesn't think I'm ignoring her, I add, "She would've been so proud of you."

"Thanks, Dad."

Zoe's deep sniff tells me she's crying. It's been a while since she did, about her mother, anyway. At least that I know of. She was so little when the fire that leveled their apartment building took Virginia and left Zoe with third-degree burns on the left side of her face, neck, and shoulder. As if the burns themselves weren't bad enough, they also got her teased and bullied mercilessly from the moment she started school. Bullying that didn't relent, even when we transferred her to a top-shelf private school. And yet, here she is, as sweet as ever.

"I'm proud of you, too," I add. "I know things at school were rough before, but this is a whole new era. One in which I hope you can learn to love and appreciate the gentle person you are. Because it's your superpower, Zo."

She snorts and pulls away, wiping at her cheek. "As if," she scoffs.

I tap her under her chin. "I'm serious. What you've gone through would send most people spiraling to a terrible place. Yet you stay so positive. And empathetic. In this world, that's definitely a superpower."

Zoe rolls her eyes so hard I have to work not to laugh. "Puhleeease," she groans. "You're being embarrassing, Dad."

But I see the little smile on her lips. "Fine," I concede. "Let's practice our escape routes and then we can have dessert, okay?"

Zoe bounces on the balls of her feet, waiting for my direction. I call a series of emergencies, from a fire in different places in the house to an earthquake to power outages. By the time we're done, we've thoroughly earned the banana splits we make ourselves. I use mostly banana, but Zoe piles hers high with everything, naturally.

"So ... am I allowed to ask why there's so much stuff left in this house from when you were a kid?" Zoe asks tentatively. "Like ... why didn't you guys take it all with you?"

I take in a deep breath and set my empty dish down on the new coffee table we bought this weekend. But the sofa we're sitting on is vintage eighties, as is much of the furniture in the house.

I haven't told Zoe much about my family, save that I'm not in contact with any of them. But I knew the questions would come someday. I'm not exactly surprised she's asking now, given our surroundings.

"It's … complicated," I say, not sure how to answer her without dumping more on her shoulders than she wants, or needs, to know.

"I hate when grown-ups say that," she groans. "Try me."

I smirk. "Okay, Miss Mature," I tease her. "You know my father was a pastor. One night, there was a fire at the church."

Zoe's eyes go wide. "Was everyone okay?"

My heart clenches. As a burn victim, of course that would be her first question. God, I should have thought this conversation through better.

"No," I say sadly. "A fallen storage cabinet trapped my little sister. They got her out, but by then, she'd inhaled so much smoke."

Zoe sets down her half-finished dish, clearly having lost her appetite. "What happened to her?"

"Well, Alpine Ridge is pretty far out. So, there weren't any medical services for miles and miles. They called my mom, who came and took her to get help while my dad and another man tried to save the place. They did what they could, but she couldn't breathe like she used to. And while they had things that could help, they didn't have as many options as they do now. Though even if they did, she was pretty bad off. She died within the year." I let out a shaky breath as I note Zoe's frown.

"I'm sorry, I didn't know. We don't have to talk about it anymore," she says.

"Hey, it's okay," I assure her. "I probably should have told you a long time ago." I shake my head. "Anyway, back to your question. With the accident, and my sister being in the hospital, my mom moved out first, only taking what she needed to stay with my sister. And then my dad and I left not long after, since the town didn't have the money to rebuild the church. We didn't have the means or need to take much."

I shrug, trying to feign nonchalance when in reality my skin is crawling with terrible memories of that time. Of all I lost. Of all I left behind. Because to hell with furniture. I left the community I'd known my whole life. Friends. And the girl I'd planned to marry.

"So, the house just … sat here?" she asks, drawing her legs against her chest and wrapping her arms around them.

I nod slowly. "And it's ours now. If you want, we can get rid of everything and make it all new. All us."

Zoe considers that. "I think we can do some of that. It'd be nice to have a dishwasher, at least," she replies. I laugh, resisting teasing her. It's not like she's had to do the dishes, anyway. "But … I think it's good to keep the memories that make you stronger. So, I guess it's up to you."

My brows jump. Well, damn. Maybe she *is* Miss Mature. God, she's growing up so fast.

"You're wise beyond your years, Zo," I commend her. "That's a good plan. I'll keep it in mind. And speaking of good plans, I set up an appointment for Thursday to get satellite internet installed."

Zoe jumps to her feet and does a happy dance. "Yes, I can't wait!" she cries with a fist pump. "I haven't watched YouTube or played *Dress to Impress* in like a week!"

Chuckling, I rise, taking both of our dishes toward the kitchen. But Zo stops me with a hand on my arm. "I think I'll finish mine after all," she says, taking her bowl back.

I ruffle her hair, partially out of affection and partially because I know she likes it even though she pretends it exasperates her.

At the end of the evening, Zoe trots off to bed all on her own. She doesn't ask for a story like she has been the last few nights. She barely even hugs me goodnight. Clearly, despite the slightly somber tone of earlier this evening, she's feeling good about life. More secure.

I'm glad but, unfortunately, I can't say the same. As I lie in bed, sleep eludes me and my mind fitfully refuses to settle, wondering what I'm missing about my exit from town. I try to dismiss it as perhaps Rae's own hurt at my departure seeming like a bigger deal in her mind … but even as a teenager, she wasn't that prone to those sorts of theatrics. But maybe she is now?

I know there's no point in worrying about it, so it's only after reminding myself that whatever it is … well, it's nothing compared to what I've already lived through. It'll be fine. One way or another.

The next morning, I arrive at town hall, ready to meet the council. But instead of the meeting room, I find myself ushered into Arthur's office. It has plain ivory walls and crown-molding detailed to match the rest of the building, but is otherwise simple with a black walnut desk, a few padded chairs, and a couple of filing cabinets. No other décor graces the walls, though there is a framed family photo on Arthur's desk.

Arthur looks up at me without expression as I enter.

"Have a seat, son."

I raise a brow at the terseness and lack of greeting but sit across the desk from him.

"I hope you're not offended, but I overheard your conversation with Rae yesterday," Arthur continues. "And I did some thinking after our meeting. While I'd heard some rumors when your family left town, I despise gossip and did my best to — forgive the language — stay the hell out of it." I smirk despite the churning anxiety I have for where this is going. "After some deliberation, I decided that a bit of well-intended intervention was worth a shot."

"I'm not offended, but I also have to admit I have absolutely no idea what this is all about," I admit, wiping my sweating palms on my dark jeans.

Arthur nods and sighs. "I surmised as much. And there's no easy way to do this." He leans forward and presses a button on his phone. "Meredith, can you bring Brandon to my office, please?"

My brows pull together. "I've heard his name mentioned. He's on the town council, right?"

"Yes, he is. I'm trying to convince him to take on Public Works. He was an aid worker, and he's shown a very good understanding of the basic infrastructure needs of a developing area. But —"

A knock on the door interrupts him and a blond head pokes in. Attached to a familiar face with familiar brown eyes. And as the younger man walks fully into the room, my breath catches in my throat. The resemblance is uncanny, like looking in a mirror that shows the past. I'd peg him at about thirty. Some quick mental math makes my pulse race, and I rise on unsteady legs.

"Luke, this is Brandon," Arthur says, gesturing toward the man. "Brandon, Luke."

Neither of us makes a move toward the other. Me because I'm so stunned. But as the shock wears off, I wonder why he hasn't.

"I'll just give you gentlemen some time," Arthur says after a few painfully silent moments. He rises and leaves, closing the door behind him.

And I still don't know what to say.

Brandon breaks the silence first. "So, what do I call you? Dad seems a little too familiar, don't you think?" His tone is acerbic, clearly communicating a lifetime of feeling rejected. Thirty years of it.

I feel queasy and breathless, like someone punched me in the stomach.

I have a son?

I have a son.

What else could he be? We even *sound* similar. It's almost eerie.

"We're going to need to back up here, because I don't understand what the hell is going on," I manage at last. "I had no clue … I swear I …" I shake my head, my thoughts jumbled and confused. I take a deep breath, willing my mind to settle. "Why didn't your mother tell me I have a son?"

Brandon shrugs and takes a seat in the chair closest to the door. "She was sixteen and pregnant by a guy who'd just left town. What was she supposed to do? It's not like social media existed back then. She had no way of finding you."

I scrub my hands down my face. "Fuck," I swear. But things are clicking into place. "Well, that explains why she's so pissed off."

Brandon's brow furrows. "Excuse me?"

"Your mother. She's clearly furious with me and I had no idea why until you —"

Brandon holds up a hand. "Whoa there. My mother is dead. Who in the hell are you talking about?"

I blanch at his words. "Your mother isn't Rachel Donovan?"

"Who?"

"Rachel Donovan … Rae Donovan," I repeat.

"Oh," he says. "Rae? God. No. My mother was Bethanny Thompson."

And now I'm back to shock. *Bethanny Thompson? Rae's best friend?*

I shake my head vehemently. "That's impossible. I never had sex with Beth Thompson."

Brandon's eyes narrow. "Then why do you look like me with an aging filter?"

I shake my head, baffled as I try to answer that myself.

I've heard of women getting themselves pregnant from used condoms, but Rae and I didn't use them. I'd blame it on the small-town potential for our parents finding out, but honestly, we were just dumb kids. And short of Beth climbing in my bedroom window and looking for used tissue … no, that train of thought leads to wild speculations. That's way too far out there. So … how? How could Brandon look *so* much like me?

When I ask it like that, the truth quickly crashes over me like a tidal wave. I sink into the chair I'd been sitting in, my legs no longer able to support me. Brandon's face, his voice, hell, even his *mannerisms* are so like my own. It all slots into place with sickening clarity.

I feel like puking, and it must show, because a look of concern crosses Brandon's face. "What?" he prompts.

"My dad," I choke out. "It must have been my dad." My eyes flick up to meet his. "I look just like him. And so do you." Though now that I'm looking, there are some differences. Brandon's nose is narrower, his jaw a little rounder. He's a little stockier, too, though with the same fit build as my father and me.

"Wasn't your dad a pastor?" Brandon asks hesitantly.

I blink. "How'd you know that?"

Brandon looks away and shrugs. "I might've done some research after you came back to town."

I huff out a dry laugh. "Yes, he was a pastor," I agree. "And a hypocritical piece of shit." And apparently a philandering predator who then convinced his victim to tell everyone I'd knocked her up and left her to deal with it. But I don't need to say that part out loud. "We can get a blood test done to make sure."

"Well, since apparently everything I knew is wrong … that's probably a good idea," he agrees.

I nod absently, my mind still processing everything. Anger churns in my gut while the betrayal burns like acid in my veins. My dad, the man who preached about morality and sin, fathered a child with a teenage girl and pinned it on me. I knew he was a hypocrite. Preaching about God's plan and the kindness of Christ while unleashing his anger verbally and physically on his family. Forcing us to do what he said, when he said it. Ruling by fear. His actions had an enormous impact on me in my formative years. I thought that part of my life was over, but apparently, I was wrong.

My thoughts continue to whirl with the staggering implications of this revelation.

But now I get what Rae meant about the town's opinions. If that's the person they've thought of me as all these years, that's sure not going to make stepping in as the Fire Chief any easier.

More importantly? That means Rae thinks I cheated on her. That I abandoned my child.

Now I also get why she can't stand the sight of me.

I pull myself out of my thoughts to find Brandon looking at me with an equally contemplative stare. He must be reeling as hard as I am right now. And it finally sinks in that he mentioned Beth died.

"What happened to your mom?" I ask softly.

Brandon's gaze drops to the floor. "She passed when I was five. Overdose. My grandpa raised me."

I search my memories for anything on her father. John, I think? He was a single father, his wife having died in childbirth, if I recall correctly. Not having a mom messed Beth up pretty badly. John seemed like a great father, but I've seen firsthand the emotional toll it takes on a girl to lose her mother.

My brain wants to take that commonality and run with it, but Beth was quiet and kept to herself. The kids in town constantly teased her for her antisocial behavior. Now, as an adult, I understand she was probably depressed. Zoe, however, is compassionate, connected, and expressive. Though many burn victims struggle with depression and anxiety, Zoe has shown no signs of either given her natural positivity and an excellent personal and professional support system that wasn't available to Beth given where she was. So, I don't think for one minute Zoe will meet the same fate as Beth.

But right now, all of my other concerns aside, my heart goes out to the man in front of me, for the mother he lost, for the family he never knew. Including me.

Assuming my guess is correct, and I'm reasonably certain it is, Brandon is my brother.

A fierce protectiveness surges through me. I've lost one sibling. I will not lose another.

For his part, Brandon is silent, so I know this must be hitting him hard.

"I'm sorry for your loss, Brandon," I say sincerely. "If there's anything I can help you figure out about our family, I'm here, okay?"

He nods solemnly. "Thank you," he murmurs. He breathes in deeply and looks up at the ceiling. "Where is our father?"

I frown.

"Honestly? I don't know. I haven't spoken to him in years. But I'm sure as hell going to track him down now."

Brandon nods, a glimmer of hope in his eyes. "Good. Let me know what you find out."

"Of course. I'll figure out how we can do that blood test, too."

"Why don't you let me take that one? I have a friend who might help," Brandon offers.

As we've clearly both had enough for one day, we exchange numbers, a tentative bridge spanning the chasm of years, before calling Arthur back in.

Arthur re-enters his office, his expression guarded. "I'm sorry to have sprung this on you two, but I'd hoped that cutting to the chase right away would be best for you both. And if it wasn't, please know that if you'd prefer not to work together, we can accommodate that," Arthur says.

I smirk at the slightly pompous speech that I know is well-intentioned. "We're good," I reply. "But thank you."

Arthur looks surprised but pleased. "Brandon?" he asks, turning toward him.

Brandon nods. "I'm still a little shocked, honestly. I came in expecting to meet my father, and I'm leaving with a brother." He shakes his head as if he can't quite believe it.

"I'm sorry. Did you say Luke is your *brother?*" Arthur asks, his weathered brow scrunching.

"We think so, yes," I reply. "To be confirmed soon. And I know you don't like gossip, so I'll let you know as soon as it's proven."

"Oh, that won't be necessary. I don't intend to spread your business around," Arthur protests.

I rise and pat Arthur on the back. "Given the false version that's been circulating all these years, look at it as helping me set the record straight."

"Us," Brandon pipes up. "Helping *us* set the record straight."

I meet Brandon's eyes, and a warmth passes between us.

Brothers.

I don't have a son ... I have a brother.

I have so many emotions about that I can't even begin to unpack right now.

"Are we still meeting with the rest of the council?" I ask Arthur.

He shakes his head. "I've requested with the rest of the council to reschedule for Friday. I figured this took priority, as well as whatever came of it."

"You're a good man, Mayor Burton. Thank you," I tell him. I reach out and shake his hand. "If we're done here, I have something important to take care of as soon as possible."

"By all means," Arthur responds.

Brandon eyes me speculatively. "Since you're my brother, you should know I'm terribly nosey," he says with a mischievous twinkle in his eye.

I laugh loudly and honestly. "You got something to ask, kid, just say it," I reply.

Brandon grins. "Where are you going?"

"To set things right with someone who has every reason to be angry with me."

Brandon nods. "You know, I came in thinking *you* were a hypocritical piece of shit, but now I'm thinking you might be a good man, Fire Chief McMillan," he says.

"Glad to hear it," I say sincerely. "I look forward to getting to know you, Brandon. I'll see both of you later this week." A thought halts me as I head for the door, and I turn back to Brandon. "Oh. I have a twelve-year-old daughter named Zoe. You're an uncle."

Brandon grins, but I don't wait for a response. Instead, I stride out of the office, determination quickening my steps. I have a record to set straight with Rae. She thinks I cheated on her. That I fathered a child with her best friend. The betrayal she must have felt ... I can't even imagine. Well, actually, given my father's betrayal, I have some idea. But that's different. She's had to live with it all these years, whereas I'm just finding out.

I practically run to my truck, jumping in and hurrying out of the parking lot. I need to see her, to explain. To tell her it wasn't me. That I never betrayed her. That I never stopped loving her.

CHAPTER SEVEN

RAE

I'm just putting a fresh batch of chocolate chip cookies into the display case when Evan pops into the bakery, a mischievous grin on his handsome face, his light brown hair artfully disheveled, oozing movie star charm. And his wellness center uniform fits against his swimmer's body in a way that should be illegal. I try not to ogle too hard. It'd be a shame to drop a cookie.

"Hello, ladies, what's good today?" he asks, knocking his knuckles on the counter.

I wave a cookie at him. "Just out of the oven. Want a booze pairing or just the cookies?" I ask.

He laughs. "Just the cookie. Two, actually. I have a break between appointments, so no alcohol for me. Though I am curious what booze Mia pairs with chocolate chip cookies," he replies.

Mia pops out of the kitchen as I bag his cookies. "A

Frangelico cocktail," she offers, answering his question. "What's got you in such a good mood?"

Evan grins. "Oh, you know, one of my famous friends may or may not be building a house in Alpine Ridge soon," he announces, leaning against the counter.

Mia's eyes widen. "What?! Who? Tell me, tell me!" she pleads, practically bouncing on her toes.

Evan shakes his head, his grin widening. "Nope, not saying a word. It's all very hush-hush."

Mia narrows her eyes as I hand him the bag. "Does Carrie know?"

"Of course she does. She's the town planner, after all," Evan replies with a wink.

Mia huffs. "Fine. I'll just get it out of my sister later, then."

Evan laughs and waves as he heads out the door with his treats. "Good luck with that!"

"It's a shame Penny left to go to school in Seattle. She'd love to see more celebrities around here," I say as I head back into the kitchen to put the baking tray away.

Mia nods, a thoughtful look on her face, following me through the door. "True, but who knows? Maybe she'll come back at some point."

The bell above the door chimes again, and Mia perks up. "I bet that's Evan, coming back to spill the beans," she says, hurrying back out to the front.

But a moment later, she pops her head back into the kitchen, her expression unreadable. "Luke's here. He wants to talk to you."

My stomach does an uncomfortable flip. I'm not ready for this conversation, not by a long shot.

"Tell him I'm at work," I protest weakly.

Mia levels me with a look. "I can handle things here for a bit. There, now you have no excuse to deal with it. Which you definitely should do, because this is a small town, and you can't avoid him forever."

"Fine, have a point," I grumble. Reluctantly, I untie my apron and hang it on the hook by the door. I take a deep breath, steeling myself, and step out into the front of the bakery.

Luke is waiting at a table, his hands clasped in front of him. He looks up as I approach, his brown eyes filled with a mix of apprehension and determination.

"What can I do for you, Fire Chief McMillan?" I ask brusquely.

He winces. "Can we talk?" he asks, his voice low.

I contemplate him for a moment. I could say no, but Mia's right — nothing keeps in a town this small. Plus, I'd always wonder what he was going to say. Though, while I may begrudgingly agree, I also don't want anyone who walks in to hear whatever he's got to get off his chest, either.

"Guess we'd better. But not here." I glance out the window, remembering the chill in the air as I walked in today. It's gotten cold again, winter not quite ready to release its grip.

"We can sit in my truck. It's probably still warm," he offers, rising.

I glance out the window at what I presume is his vehicle. It's nice, if not well-loved. Mostly, I'm thankful it's not the same truck he drove back in the day. Though being in any truck with him is bound to bring back memories. Still, it's probably our best option.

"Fine," I agree tersely, grabbing my coat off the hook by the door and slipping it on.

Luke leads the way out. As I climb inside the truck, he starts the engine, presumably to have the heat running to keep us warm.

But as soon as I slide in, a subtle but acrid smell hits me. "It smells like smoke in here," I comment.

Luke shrugs. "Comes with the firefighter gig."

"Didn't you shower at the fire station or at least change clothes or something?"

He looks at me for a long moment. "It sinks into everything. Even your skin."

I shudder at the tone that implies he's talking about so much more than the smell. I hadn't thought too hard on how difficult a job it must be.

An uncomfortable silence settles between us as he seems to gather his thoughts. Finally, he takes a deep breath and meets my gaze head-on.

"I talked to Brandon," he begins.

My brows pop up. "Well … okay. That was unexpected," I admit.

"Arthur thought it best that we confront the issue head on. The issue you apparently couldn't tell me about? The one where everybody talked about me having a son and abandoning his mother?" He casts me a look that holds no anger, just hurt.

"I wanted to," I admit. "But I didn't think it was my place." My insides churn.

"Beth was your best friend. In what world wasn't it your place to call me out for that?" he asks candidly.

I'm a bit taken aback. "What good would it do now? He's grown. She's gone. Everyone has moved on." I shrug, uncomfortable with skating so close to the well of anger inside me.

"In the spirit of confronting the issue head on …" he says warily. I feel myself shrink away from whatever else he's about to lay on me. But he looks me straight in the eyes anyway. "I'm not his father, Rae. I didn't sleep with Beth."

I can't help it. I let out a sarcastic laugh. "Really? That's the story you're going with? I mean, you saw Brandon, right?" I shake my head. Unbelievable. It took me a long time to come to terms with how little I really knew Luke, and I think part of me still didn't believe it. But the gall of him denying it is astounding.

A muscle in his jaw flexes as his gaze turns hard. "Did you ever consider that there's someone else who could've had a child that looked just like me?"

I stare at him, baffled. Is he serious? And who the hell could that even be? The only other man in his family … my chest constricts at his implication.

No. He cannot possibly mean who I think he means. I speak before I can even fully process what I'm saying.

"You've got to be joking. Your dad? Are you really that desperate to avoid taking responsibility? Is the idea of being a parent so bad?" I ask accusatorily.

Luke's nostrils flare. "Not at all. I *am* a parent, Rae. I have a daughter. And if Brandon was my son, you bet your ass I'd claim him in a heartbeat. But he's not. And in case it's not crystal clear, I also didn't have sex with your best friend." He shakes his head angrily.

My heart pounds in my chest and my palms go clammy. Luke has a *daughter?* How have I not heard this yet? Maybe she's grown, too, and didn't move here with him, so nobody knew? God, that would have to mean he knocked Beth up, then not long after knocked someone else up. My stomach churns at the thought.

"You're … serious?" I stare at him, struggling to accept what he's telling me. But by far the hardest story to swallow is him pinning this on his dad. "You're saying your father — a married man, pastor, and pillar of this community — slept with a sixteen-year-old girl?" I ask, my voice laced with disbelief.

Luke sighs heavily, staring down at his clenched fists. I can't tell if he's exasperated or exhausted. "That's exactly what I'm saying. And honestly? I was horrified when I figured it out, but not at all surprised. He's not a good man, Rae. I've always known that, even if I never told anyone. But that was part of his brainwashing: best face forward, always. Be the perfect family. And after we moved away … our family fell apart. Then things got even worse."

He looks at me with tears in his eyes and despite my

anger, my heart twists. "But that … that's another story. What I'm worried about right now is making things right with you. I guess I hoped you'd listen. That you'd believe I'd never do that to you. I loved you, Rae. I was devastated when I had to leave you." His eyes roam my face, his lips pulled down in a frown. "And now I'm devastated to know you still believe the worst."

I close my eyes, trying to process everything he's thrown at me. It's too much, too fast.

"When you left, my world shifted," I admit. "And then when Beth herself told me …" I turn away, staring out the window. I can't relive that day out loud. My best friend claiming that the love of my life had only ever wanted her. That I was just easy sex. I shake my head, refusing to dwell on the part of me that died that day, or the rage that took its place. "It took me a long time to come to grips with yet another new reality. And now … I'm being told it was all a lie." I look back at Luke. His anguish is written in the lines around his down-turned mouth. Defeat in the slump of his shoulders. "This is a lot to take in. I'm going to need some time."

We stare longingly at each other for a few moments that do no justice to the years of heartache I can tell we've both suffered. Not for the first time, I wish I'd been stronger than my pain all those years ago.

Maybe I can be now. But not right away. Not right this moment.

"I understand," Luke finally says softly. "For what it's

worth, Brandon and I are getting a blood test done. That should give you some reassurance that I'm telling the truth, at least. I guess I kind of hoped you wouldn't need it, though."

My throat tightens under his disappointment. Not because his opinion matters, though I can't deny it does. But because I feel like my entire life has been one disappointment after another since he left.

But right now? There are too many words to say. Most of them wouldn't mean anything to him, anyway. So, I make a noncommittal noise and crack the door open. "I'll see you around, Luke."

He huffs a sharp breath and nods. "See you around."

I hop out of the truck and swing the door shut behind me. The metallic snap feels like an echo of another heartbreak. I practically stumble back into the bakery, torn between deciding to hate him and his desperate lies for the rest of eternity … and accepting his version so I can go back thirty years and do my life over with hope in my heart.

But there's no going back. So, I push through the bakery door. The bell tinkling heralds a choice made. The choice to walk away from Luke. For now, at least. I have to in order to protect myself.

I look up to meet Mia's concerned gaze. She takes one full look at my face and ushers me into the back room, sitting me down on a stool.

"What happened?" she asks quietly.

I relay the conversation to her, my voice shaking.

She says nothing at first, and I don't ask whether she believes him.

"How are you feeling?" she eventually prompts.

I shake my head. "I want to believe him, but the betrayal I thought had happened ... it changed how I viewed things. That's hard to undo."

Mia is quiet for a moment. "Is there something more going on here?"

I throw her a sharp look. "What does that mean?"

One slender brow raises on her forehead. It says she knows I'm full of shit. "I think you know exactly what that means. And while I know you're hurting right now, I wouldn't be a good friend if I didn't point out that your trust issues seem to go deeper than this thing with Luke." She pauses. Not like she doesn't want to say whatever is on her mind, but like she's trying to figure out how to word whatever truth she's going to hit me with next. "Does this have anything to do with why your marriage ended?"

I flinch as if she's slapped me, even though I should've seen it coming. "That was different," I snap.

But Mia's gaze is unwavering, and I feel my defenses crumbling. Because I'd never thought about it before. But now she asks ... well, she may not be wrong.

"I couldn't have children," I admit, my voice barely above a whisper. "So, my husband cheated on me with my best friend, who we were trying to use as a surrogate. That's why we split." I tip my head back, blinking back tears, realizing I was wrong; it's not different. And that she's right.

"Oh, Rae. I'm so sorry." Mia's eyes widen in horror as she makes the connection. Because I make it, too.

I don't know how I could've missed it before. Two men I loved cheating on me with and impregnating my best friend. It just shows how deep I'd buried both hurts, that they didn't even sit in my mind long enough for me to make the connection. To realize I might disbelieve Luke because, while I didn't catch him in the act, I sure as hell caught Sam. I didn't consciously make the association but apparently my brain did.

And I suddenly get that that's exactly what happened. Seeing Sam fucking Tanya on the couch my mom gave us as a wedding present was irrefutable proof that they were both awful, lying assholes. So, my mind filed Luke and Beth in the same category. Damn.

"Thanks, sugar," I say with a sniff. "But now I think on it, it really isn't different at all. Now that I think about it, catching my ex-husband in the act is very different from believing someone you knew to be a liar." I look over at her and see the confusion on her face. "Beth was … unstable. She lied for attention loads of times. I should've known to question her about it before believing her."

Mia's eyes soften with pity. "Well, I'd say everyone wants to believe their best friend, but …"

I wipe an errant tear off my cheek. "But?" Mia chews on her lip. I huff a dry breath out and gesture at her. "Out with it."

"But maybe, deep down, you wanted to believe the worst? That somehow you deserved to be cheated on? Or that you didn't deserve Luke?" My brows bunch together angrily, and she holds her hands up. "I'm just saying, it's easier to believe things that reinforce our own fears, Rae. It would explain why you didn't question it."

I open my mouth to give her a what-for … but close it when I realize she may be right. Luke always loved me in a way I didn't think I deserved.

"Shit. You might have something there."

Mia smiles sadly and squeezes my hand. "I have a great therapist I do teletherapy with. Would you like her number?" she offers.

I sniff deeply and chuckle. "That might be a good idea," I agree. "I've got a lot to unpack." I shake my head. "Forty-six years of baggage, really. Because lord knows there was plenty of it even before Luke and Beth." I take in a deep breath. "We should get back to it. Someone's liable to come in." I'm deflecting, but I've had enough.

Thankfully, Mia seems to get it, as she nods. "Just … one more thing before that?" she asks tentatively.

"Mia, sweetheart, I love you to death, but I don't want to talk about Luke anymore," I reply wearily.

The corner of her mouth tips up ever so slightly and she shakes her head. "No, it's not … I just wondered … why couldn't you have children?" Mia asks softly.

I look at her, my brow furrowing. That's a whole other can of worms, but I sense she's got a purpose behind the question, and I'd rather not get into my fertility struggles and the surrounding mess. Best to cut to the chase of whatever she's really after.

"Why do you want to know?"

Mia bites her lip, looking away. "Nate and I ... we've been struggling to get pregnant. I'm ... afraid of seeking answers in case they tell me I'll never have children."

My heart clenches. I know that pain. I've lived that pain. I reach out, taking her hand in mine. "Mia. Look at me." She meets my eyes reluctantly. "You need to go get that information. Living in doubt of your own body, the fear every month as the clock ticks down, the devastation of starting to bleed .... even in my day, there was so much they told me they could do depending on how things turned up." I sigh, opting not to add that in my situation, that meant surgery that ended my dream of having a baby. But even in that knowledge, there was comfort. However, it's Mia's journey that's important right now. "Trust me, taking the chance is better than living in the hell of not knowing what could have been."

Mia meets my gaze with a sad smile. "You're right. I know you're right. Thank you." She bumps her shoulder against mine. "You know, that applies to you and Luke, too."

I sit back with a resigned sigh. She's right, of course. Again. As much as I want to cling to the hurt and anger of the past, I know I need to ask all the questions this time. To get all the information I can. To give Luke a chance to prove himself. To give myself a chance to heal and accept the truth, whatever that may be.

Though this whole situation has felt like yet another round of pain and doubt and fear, maybe it's the fire I've got to walk through to find peace and happiness again. I'm suddenly reminded of a quote. One I think we could both use right about now.

"We must accept finite disappointment but never lose infinite hope."

Mia smiles. "Martin Luther King Jr. … Does that mean you're going to give Luke a chance?"

I smile back. "Yeah. I think I am. What have I got to lose?" My stomach flips. Because I've got a lot to lose. It makes me wonder … is it worth the chance?

But Mia cuts off my train of thought with a shake of her head. "I think the question is: what do you have to gain?"

I close my eyes as her words pierce through me.

I open them again and consider her for a moment.

I grab my apron and whack her with it before slipping it back over my head. "I think I've had enough of you being right for one day. Let's go eat some of those damn cookies."

Mia laughs and gestures for me to lead the way. "I think we both could use a few," she agrees. "But Rae?" I turn back and give her a questioning look. "I'm queen of using humor to deflect. But you should know I'm always here for you, no matter what, okay?"

Touched, I pull her into a hug. "I know. Me, too, sugar."

She pats me on the back. "And I promise not to sleep with your next boyfriend."

I bust up laughing. Then we go eat a good chunk of the fresh cookies. And I realize, Mia is just one of my "no matter what" people. I've got a whole family of friends now. So, no matter what truth comes out of this thing with Luke, I know I'll be okay.

CHAPTER EIGHT

LUKE

Yesterday was a heavy day. I wake up still reeling from everything I learned and obsessing over everything I wish I'd said or done differently, particularly with Rae. But I won't change her mind by chasing her, so I get my ass out of bed hoping to distract myself as much as possible.

Unfortunately, I'm almost immediately hit with another letdown. Before Zoe has even come downstairs, I'm having my morning coffee when Arthur calls to let me know he has to postpone our Friday meeting to introduce me to the town council due to scheduling conflicts. I'm disappointed as I was eager to meet everyone and share what I've put together so far, but I understand. Life happens.

Instead of wallowing, I spend the morning setting Zoe up on a website she discovered called Outschool where she can take classes on almost any topic. Naturally, she's selected a drawing class. I'm thrilled, as there are a bunch of other kids her age in it and, listening while I do some minor repairs in the kitchen, it sounds like the teacher really knows their stuff and is great at keeping the kids involved.

Once the repairs are done, I'm still fidgety. I make lunch for Zoe and me before she heads outside to take advantage of the warming weather. Apparently, her instructor wants them to practice drawing trees. Good thing we're surrounded by them.

Alone in the house for a rare moment, I decide to use the time to track down my father. I really don't want to talk to the bastard, but I might as well get it over with. Even though in my mind he's Brandon's father, I want to hear it from him. It's not even about the facts. The blood test will give us those. I want the fucker to know he didn't get away with throwing me under the bus. That I know the truth. Brandon knows the truth. And soon the whole town will know the truth, too.

It takes some digging, and several calls to old friends in Marysville, but I eventually wind up with a phone number. My hand shakes as I dial, my heart pounding in my chest.

He answers on the third ring. "Hello?"

My gut clenches at his familiar voice. The awful memories it brings.

I'm silent a beat too long and he says, "Hello, who is this?"

I swallow hard, my throat suddenly dry. "It's Luke."

Silence. Then, "What do you want?"

No *"Son, so good to hear from you,"* or *"I'm so glad*

you called." Then again, deep down, I didn't really expect that.

I take a long breath. "I know about Beth Thompson."

He scoffs. "And what do you think you know?"

I roll my eyes to the ceiling. "That you cheated on Mom with her. Or I guess I'm hoping it was consensual, anyway." A shiver trails down my spine. I hadn't even thought of the alternative, and I'm not prepared to go there. I've got to stick to what I called for. "And I also know you blamed it on me."

After another beat of silence and some rustling, he finally says, "I don't know what you're talking about. The girl's father called me and said you knocked her up. I did what I had to do to protect our family."

Suddenly, all my anger rushes to the surface. "She had a boy. Did you even know that? And he looks just like us. I know I didn't have sex with her. So, I think you *do* know what I'm talking about, and you did what you had to do to protect *yourself*," I snap. "Never mind what you did to that poor girl. Or your other son." I resist the urge to tell him what a great guy Brandon seems to be. How much he missed out on. He doesn't deserve to know. He does, however, deserve to know how pissed I am. "Or me. Did you think I'd never go back? That I'd never find out the whole town thinks I'm a piece of shit? It wasn't enough to ruin my childhood — all of your children's childhoods — you had to make sure we inherited your legacy of lies and ruin?"

"We're all sinners, Luke. Repent and be saved."

I almost laugh at his false piousness. "That's rich. Because if anyone needs to repent, it's you. But repentance requires regret and change. Two things you're obviously incapable of. Also, if you think that's what it takes to be saved, you clearly never really got the heart of Christianity. Ironic, given your line of work. All you need to be saved is Jesus. I'd introduce you, but I'm pretty sure you've been shitting all over His word while you were cheating on your wife and, at best, committing statutory rape, all while stealing from the churches you were supposed to be shepherding. I'm not the least bit surprised you can't even admit to any wrongdoing. I'm just glad I get to tell you I now know exactly how much of a fucking asshole you are, and I hope you get exactly what you deserve. My only regret is that I won't be there to see it happen, because if I wasn't done with you before, I most definitely am now."

He starts to sputter a protest, but I've had it. This conversation is obviously going nowhere, and I'm only getting madder by the moment. So, I hang up. It makes me miss the days of analog phones. My cathartic rant could've only been improved by the ability to slam the handset down when I hung up on his pathetic ass.

I'm so upset, I stand at the counter, chest heaving, tightness bunching my shoulders inward. Breathing deeply, I close my eyes and meditate until I relax.

I'm tempted to chastise myself for not keeping my cool better. Because it made an already high-stakes conversation even more difficult. But while I may not have gotten what I wanted out of it, I ended up getting what I needed.

Still, the more I think about it, the little he said all but confirms his guilt. I blow out a final, slow breath before calling Brandon.

He answers immediately. "Hey, Luke. What's up?"

I fill him in on my conversation with our father. He's quiet for a moment.

"So, he didn't admit it?" Brandon asks.

"Not directly, no. But I know him. 'We're all sinners' was code for 'so what if I did?'" I explain.

"Okay. I can buy that. But what does 'I did what I had to do' mean?" he presses. "Obviously he said or did something that made my grandfather and my mother let you just walk away from any responsibility," he muses.

"Damn. That's a good point. I hadn't picked up on that," I admit. "I guess my anger blinded me."

"I don't blame you at all," he responds. "Do you think he'd talk to me about it?"

My brows jump. "Do you even *want* to talk to him?"

Brandon chuckles. "Good point. Not really, honestly. But I do want to know how it all played out. Guess I'm too curious for my own good."

"Have you ever asked your grandfather?"

"Huh. Not in a very long time. Since I was still a kid, basically."

"Seems like a good place to start," I respond.

"It's Wednesday, so he's home. Are you busy right now?"

"You want me to come?" I ask incredulously.

"You deserve answers as much as I do," he points out.

I think about that for a moment and decide he's right. And it wouldn't hurt to have a conversation with John, man to man, to clear the air.

"All right. I'm in. I'll let Zoe know I'll be gone for a bit and then I'll head on over."

"I mean, you can bring her if you need to. Can she even, like … be left on her own?" he asks tentatively.

I laugh. "She's twelve going on twenty-five. She'll be fine. Plus, I think this may not be an appropriate conversation for her to be privy to," I point out.

"Ah. Gotcha. You're probably right. Okay, well, I'll see you soon, then?"

"Yep. Bye."

"Oh, hey, one more thing," he adds. "My friend Nate runs the medical clinic. He said we can stop by anytime for a blood test. So, we can do that after if you have time."

"Sounds perfect. Thanks, Brandon."

It takes me almost an hour to meet Brandon, given that I had to look in fifteen trees before I found Zoe. I can't be mad, though. She's curious and intelligent, and I'm thrilled that she's so happy here.

But finally, I pull up to John Thompson's house, a tidy little bungalow on the outskirts of town. I knock, and Brandon answers.

"Sorry it took me so long. Took a while to find Zoe. She was up a tree twenty feet from the house."

Brandon frowns. "No worries, but she should be careful. We get bears and wolves up here."

"Hm, good point. I forgot about that, thanks. I'll head back and have a conversation with her about it when we're done here."

Brandon nods. "As long as she's not still out at dusk, I'm sure she'll be fine. It's just something to keep in mind."

"Guess I've lived in the city too long," I admit with a sheepish grin.

"And I've been in remote locations that make the Cascades look like a petting zoo. Guess it's made me extra cautious," he admits. "Anyway, come on in. I just got here a few minutes ago. I was helping Grandpa use the bathroom." He gives me a loaded look.

"Is he okay?" I ask quietly as I follow him inside.

Brandon nods. "He fell and hurt his hip yesterday, apparently. It doesn't seem too bad, but he's embarrassed as hell. He says only old farts fall and break a hip."

"I can hear you," a voice calls from the room at the end of the hall.

Brandon and I share a conspiratorial chuckle as we enter a cozy living room crowded by a deep red overstuffed couch and recliner set surrounding a long, low knotty pine coffee table. A news program is paused on the wall-mounted flat-screen TV.

"Luke McMillan," John says, struggling to stand.

"Hey now," I say, approaching and holding out a hand. "Don't get up on my account."

John fixes me with an indecipherable look but reaches out and shakes my hand. "Appreciate that, son. Good to see you."

"Good to see you, sir," I reply in kind, taken aback by the warmth of his greeting. Given he apparently thinks I knocked up his daughter and never looked back.

John shoots a look at Brandon. "So, what can I do for you boys?" he asks, settling back into his recliner.

Brandon and I exchange another glance, this one more nervous. I clear my throat. "We wanted to ask you about Beth. Well, more specifically about what happened when you spoke with my father after you found out she was pregnant."

John's weathered face grows somber. He sighs heavily. "Beth insisted you were the father, so I felt like I had to try, even though I knew your family had troubles of its own. But when I contacted your dad ... well, instead of making you take responsibility, he paid Beth off to go away."

I feel like I've been sucker-punched. "He what?"

John nods. "It was a sizeable sum. Too much money to hand a sixteen-year-old. Hell, I'm not sure how she could even legally sign the agreement his lawyer sent over, but I couldn't stop her. She was strong-willed and had dollar signs in her eyes. But I held onto the money until she was legally an adult. And I was right to. Wish I could've held on to it longer. As soon as she turned eighteen, she took off with the cash and her new boyfriend. Used it to buy drugs.

It took her a full three years to snort through enough cocaine to kill her." His voice is heavy with old pain.

I swallow hard. "I hate to ask this, but ... did you ever suspect that maybe I wasn't the father?"

John meets my gaze, understanding in his eyes. "I had my suspicions. I knew you enough to have a sense of you, and you seemed like a good kid. And once Brandon started growing up, it was obvious he looked like you and your pa. But Beth ... even before the drugs, she lied as much as she told the truth, and I don't think even she could tell the difference sometimes." He pauses. "Are you trying to tell me you're not Brandon's father?"

"I am," I agree. "I never ... Beth and I were just friends, and mostly just because of Rae. There was no ... physical component to our relationship." I could not feel more awkward than I do in this moment.

We sit in heavy silence until finally, John speaks again.

"I didn't think so. So, that leaves Pastor McMillan. And honestly, just by the way he handled the whole thing, I'd suspected as much. But once Beth was gone, I didn't see the point in pushing the issue. I was more than capable of raising Brandon. I didn't think dragging it all up would change anything."

Brandon nods slowly. "It may not change anything for you, but I guess I needed to know what really happened. So, thank you."

"The truth will set you free. John 8:32," he says to Brandon. Then to me, "Just wish your father practiced what he preached."

"Me, too," I murmur.

"But would I be here if he did?" Brandon muses.

We both look over at him in surprise. John chuckles. "Guess not, kid. Guess not."

Despite both John and Brandon's seeming acceptance, I can't help but feel awful that my father did this. I turn to John. "I'm sorry for what my father did to your daughter. If I'd known I —"

"It's not your burden to bear, son. Put it down." John looks me square in the eye.

And his words remove a weight from my heart I hadn't known was there. "Thank you," I say, my voice thick with emotion.

Brandon pats me on the shoulder. "Next stop, blood test?"

I nod. "Let's do it."

Brandon points at John. "I'm calling the home nurse service to get someone to hang out with you until your hip is better. Don't do anything stupid until they get here, okay?"

John glowers for a moment before growling, "Fine." And then he resumes his news program.

With the clear signal that he's done with the conversation, we head toward the front door. As I leave, I feel a mix of anger and relief. Anger at my father, at the lies and betrayal. But relief, too. Relief that truth will prevail.

A short time later, we meet up at Nate's clinic and the nurse calls us each back in turn for the blood draw. I go in first, and before she takes the sample, she lets me know the results could take a week, and that we might get them faster if we went to the hospital in Ellensburg. Brandon and I already discussed that option and agreed there was no hurry. That getting the ball rolling was enough for now. So, she goes ahead.

After, I feel lighter.

As we leave the clinic, I turn to Brandon.

"I need to head back and make sure Zoe wasn't eaten by bears. But given the time, I'll probably just be bringing her back down here for dinner at the tavern. Want to join us?" I offer.

"I'd love to," he agrees. "But — and this might sound weird, so feel free to say no — is it okay if I ride back with you? I have a couple more questions I don't think you'd want to answer in front of Zoe, and I think I'd rather meet her for the first time not in public."

I nod slowly, having not even thought about that aspect.

"I think that's a good idea, because there's something you should know before you meet her."

Brandon's eyebrow quirks. I gesture toward my truck and we both get in. Before I start the engine, I turn to him. "Zoe and her mother were trapped by an apartment fire when Zoe was little. Her mother got her out but ... she didn't make it. And Zoe was burned badly. She has facial scars that ... well, I think she's mostly okay with them now. It's other people that have been a problem."

Brandon covers his mouth in horror. "Oh god. I can't even imagine what they've said. Kids can be awful," he says with a bitterness that implies he's suffered being bullied, too. "Thanks for the heads up, though. I'm sorry you lost your wife."

I shake my head and start the truck. "Ginny and I were never married, and by then we'd long since gone back to being just friends. We were barely ever more than that, really," I admit. "That's not to say it didn't hurt. I cared about her a lot. Zoe was devastated, of course. It was a hard time for us both, but mostly for Zo." I take in a slow, deep breath.

"So, not to pile on …" Brandon says nervously.

I huff a wry laugh. "Dude, we're already rolling around in the mud. I'm obviously not afraid of getting dirty."

Brandon chuckles. "That's … apt." He takes a deep breath of his own. "So, our dad … is he really that bad?"

I glance at him warily. Because obviously my gut answer would be "no, he's worse." But I try to put myself in his shoes. I'd be concerned just learning that my biological father is … well, my biological father. So, I guess I'm the best person to answer his questions. Unfortunately, I'm not great at sugar coating things.

"I'd love to tell you that there were good parts of him. But honestly? I can't remember any. He's not a good man, Brandon. Everything was always about him. We all walked on eggshells because he'd explode at us for the slightest inconveniences. Behind closed doors, anyway. At church and in public, he was the doting husband and father.

Righteous and patient and kind. As a kid, even I bought the act, so I always felt like I deserved his punishments. Because clearly, I must've been doing something wrong. Everyone thought he was an amazing man." I shake my head at the memories.

"What made you realize he wasn't?" Brandon asks solemnly.

I snort. "The fire started it. I was sixteen when the church burned down, and we left Alpine Ridge. I should've taken divorce filing from my mom as a clue that something was very wrong. He only got meaner after that. Especially because it took him a long time to get a new job. And things were … rough. Financially and otherwise." I let out a heavy sigh. "Then he got a new job at a church up north of Seattle. Not long after, he started coming home with piles of cash. It didn't take much to figure out he was stealing from the Sunday tithe collection. I remembered times like it when I was younger, when he'd take us all out to a fancy dinner on Sunday nights, and I realized he'd probably been doing that all along."

"Shit."

"Yeah. I should've known his deceit went further than that." I pause as we pull into the long driveway. "I'm sorry for what happened to your mom. For the role he played in it."

Brandon is quiet for a moment. "I'm not sorry I was raised by my grandpa. He's a good man. And my mom … what I remember of her … she was too young. Too selfish. Too unstable. She wasn't ready to be a parent."

I reach over, squeezing his shoulder. "Well, you've got a brother now. And a niece. We're here for you."

He gives me a grateful smile as we pull up to my house. Zoe bounces out the front door, demonstrably not consumed by a wild animal. I let out a nervous laugh as Brandon and I get out.

She looks warily between Brandon and me as we approach.

"Hey, Zo, I've got someone for you to meet," I say, giving her a reassuring smile.

"Okay," she replies, clearly unsure.

I have the urge to crouch slightly to her level, like I did when she was younger. I shake it off. She's far too mature for that. I think it's just my urge to protect her from the nastier aspects of this revelation.

"This is Brandon Thompson. I just learned yesterday that we're related."

Brandon gives me a fleeting, confused look. I shake my head subtly. "Well, duh," Zoe says. "I mean, he looks almost exactly like you."

Brandon and I both laugh. "I guess it doesn't take a genius to see that," Brandon admits. "Nice to meet you, Zoe."

She looks him up and down. "Nice to meet you, too," she says, still with a note of skepticism. Then to me, "So, is he my cousin or something?"

"Well, that's a good question," I reply carefully. "We think he might be your uncle. But we're working on figuring that out."

"Hm," she hums. "How old are you, Brandon?"

Brandon's brows flatten. "I'm thirty."

She scrunches her nose — her thinking face — before declaring, "Okay, I guess you're old enough to be an uncle."

Brandon smirks. "Glad that's settled."

"So does that mean you'd be okay if Brandon came to dinner with us?" I ask her.

Zoe thinks about that for a moment. "Yeah, I guess that'd be cool."

I press my lips together to hold back a laugh. "All right then. Shall we?"

We climb into the truck and Brandon turns around as Zoe's buckling in. "So, Zoe. I hear you're twelve and that you're an artist."

She looks up, her eyes alight.

"Oh boy. Now you've done it," I murmur teasingly.

Zoe spends the drive talking Brandon's ear off about her favorite drawing media, her new class, and the sketch of a bough of fresh pine needles she did this afternoon. As we walk into the tavern, she's describing the softness of the newer needles compared to the older ones lower to the ground.

We get seated and Brandon takes the opportunity to talk to her about the woods around the house and how to keep an eye out for animals — bears and wolves especially — and that she should never go out around dawn or dusk for her safety.

Zoe listens to him in a way she doesn't even listen to

me, and while we wait for our food, I'm happy to watch their surprisingly already strong bond solidify.

It's not until Zoe is chowing down on her chicken tenders, a new favorite, that I'm able to get a word in edgewise.

"So, I hear you were an aid worker?" I prompt.

Brandon nods. "It actually started with photography. I wanted to be a photojournalist for natural disasters. But once you see the destruction they cause and the desperate need of the people affected, it's impossible not to want to help."

"I know a little something about that," I murmur.

"So, the church fire made you want to be a firefighter?" he asks gently.

I glance at Zoe, who is listening raptly. I've told her about Hannah now, but she doesn't know details about my life before her.

"Sort of," I admit. "I had a little sister. She got caught in the fire and sustained extensive lung damage from the smoke. She died not long after. It devastated our family. My mom …" I breathe deeply, slowly. "I think it broke her. She left, and it was just Dad and me."

"I'm so sorry," Brandon says.

I push my partially eaten plate away and lean back. "Thanks. It was a long time ago. Anyway, I guess I thought it could have been prevented. That even if I couldn't go back and undo it, I could save someone else's sister. Someone else's family. So, when I graduated high school, I joined the army and trained for fire-fighting missions. Then once I was out, I went through the Seattle Fire Department's recruit school and bing-bang-boom. Firefighter."

Zoe leans over and wraps her arms around me. "I'm sorry about your sister, Dad."

"I know, sweetheart. And I'm sorry about what happened to you and your mom. Just goes to show that even when there are firefighters in the equation, it doesn't always work out like we want. Though you know if I could've saved you both, I would've."

"I know," she says quietly.

Brandon shakes his head. "I'm so sorry for you both."

I shrug. "If I've learned anything, it's that you can't save everyone. No matter how much you want to. And as devastating as the losses have been, I've found solace in that. So, I do my best, and the rest isn't up to me."

"Alpine Ridge is lucky to have you as its new fire chief," Brandon replies.

"And its lucky to have you as a town council member. It sounds like you've got experience this town is going to need," I reply.

Brandon blushes. "I don't know about all that. But I'm excited to be part of establishing the new Alpine Ridge. I can't wait to see what this town becomes."

I nod. "Me, too."

"I just hope we get a library soon," Zoe pipes in.

Brandon laughs. "I will pass that on to the mayor and city planner," he assures her.

Zoe claps her hands. "So, until that happens, what is there to do for fun around here?"

"Well. There's the bakery. And my friends have regular game nights and a weekly dinner party. But honestly, I spend most of my weekends away," Brandon admits.

"Oh? Where?" I ask, with an arched eyebrow, sensing there might be a reason involving a special someone. I may have been lucky, but I know it's probably hard to date in such a small town.

"At first, I visited Seattle a lot. But these days I'm spending most of my time in Ellensburg. I'm … seeing someone there," he replies.

Zoe grins and makes that "oooooh" noise kids do when they're teasing each other about their crushes. I hide my smile behind my glass as I take a sip.

"What's her name?" I ask as nonchalantly as possible.

"*His* name is Alex," Brandon corrects gently, blushing even harder than before. "He owns an antique shop. We met when I was setting up my art gallery and looking for pieces with local history to include."

I feel like a complete ass. "I'm sorry," I say. "I shouldn't have assumed."

Brandon waves off my apology. "No worries. It's an understandable mistake."

I'm about to ask how long they've been dating when Zoe bursts in, clearly unable to contain herself. "You have an art gallery? Can we see it?"

Brandon smiles at her enthusiasm. "Sure, we can go when we're done here."

And so, after Zoe finishes eating at record speed, we head over to the gallery. It's a small space, but Brandon has filled it with an impressive array of local artwork. Photography, wood carvings, fiber arts, paintings ... it's a celebration of Alpine Ridge's unique beauty and creative spirit.

"This is amazing, Brandon," I say, marveling at a stunning photograph of a line of pine trees just visible under the snowy Cascade peaks at sunset with deep oranges, pinks, and purples highlighting the rugged landscape.

He ducks his head, looking pleased. "Thanks. It's a work in progress, but I'm happy with how it's coming together."

I gesture at the photo. "Is this yours?"

"It is," he admits.

"It's gorgeous. There are so many pieces here I'd love to get for the house. Once Zoe and I finish fixing it up, anyway."

Zoe nods her agreement. "I like the paintings," she says, gesturing to the far wall filled with watercolor renderings of native wildflowers.

"Good eye," Brandon says encouragingly. "They're painted by a Chinook tribe descendant who lives in town. She's one of our oldest town residents."

Zoe's eyes go wider than I've ever seen them. "There's a woman here who *paints?*"

I chuckle. "I don't think you realize what you just started," I tease Brandon.

"I'm glad she's excited. That's why I started this place. To showcase the beauty and talent of the townsfolk, not just the landscape itself."

He finishes showing us through the displays, and when we leave the gallery, I can't help but feel a swell of pride. My brother, building something beautiful in the town we both call home.

Friday morning, I'm just finishing up breakfast when my phone rings. It's Nate.

"Hey, Luke, hope you don't mind my calling," he opens.

"Not at all," I respond. "What's up?"

"I've got your test results," he says. "You and Brandon are definitely half-siblings. Same father."

I blow out a breath. I'm … relieved. That my assumption was correct. That my assessment of my father was dead on. That rumors can now be replaced by facts.

"Wow. Okay. Thanks. That was … fast."

"I went ahead and expedited it. If it were me, I'd want to know."

"Thanks, Nate. I appreciate that." We only met briefly at the clinic, but my sense that he's a standup guy was dead on.

"No problem. I'll make sure you get a copy of the results. Also, we're having a dinner party tomorrow night. Brandon's coming. Why don't you join us?"

"Really? Are you sure? I'd have to bring my twelve-year-old daughter. I wouldn't want to intrude."

"Absolutely. We'd love to have you both. Mia lives to feed people. She'll be thrilled."

I hesitate for a moment. Because if Mia, who I'm pretty sure is the bakery owner, will be there, then Rae probably will, too. And I'm not sure if she'd want me there. Last I checked in, she still needed time. But the thought of spending more time with Brandon, of getting to know Nate and their friends better ... it's appealing. And we can always leave if it makes Rae uncomfortable.

"Yeah, okay," I agree. "We'll be there."

"Great. I'll text you the address."

"Thanks, Nate."

"Sure thing, Luke."

After I hang up, I sit at the kitchen table, thinking. I figured I'd be worried about seeing Rae tomorrow, but my brain keeps sticking on the blood test, and the fact — *fact*, mind you, no longer just speculation and rumor — that Brandon is my brother.

It throws everything into a new light. My parents' marriage. My parents' divorce. My mother's subsequent distance. I always assumed it was because of my sister's death, but now ...

I find myself searching for my mother's address. It takes some digging, courtesy of the internet and what little I remember of the names of family members on her side, but I eventually track her down in Spokane. It's a shot in the dark, but given everything I've been through lately, I find I'm valuing family more than ever.

So, before I can talk myself out of it, I sit down to write her a letter. It pours out quickly as if I'd been writing it in my head for the past thirty years.

Dear Mom,

I know it's been a long time. Too long. But I've learned some things recently that I think you should know. I know about Dad and Beth Thompson. About their child, and how he told everyone it was mine. I know his unfaithfulness was probably part of why you left. I'm so sorry you had to go through that and losing Hannah alone.

I have a daughter now. Her name is Zoe, and she's twelve. She reminds me so much of Hannah. She has the same smile, the same laugh. I think about Hannah, and you, every day.

Believe it or not, I'm back in Alpine Ridge, as their new fire chief. I went into firefighting to save people, families, like ours. I'm building a fire station here. Trying to make something good out of all the pain.

I hope you're doing well. I miss you.

Love,

Luke

I add my phone number at the bottom of the letter and fold it carefully, sliding it into an envelope. I don't know if she'll write back. If she'll even want to hear from me after all these years. But I have to try.

For her. For Zoe. For the family I'm piecing back together, one truth at a time.

CHAPTER NINE

RAE

Saturday morning arrives in a flurry of activity. It's go time for preparing the St. Patrick's Day event, which we decided to hold on Sunday to ensure as much of the town can attend as possible, even though the actual holiday is on Monday. One less day to make the shamrock adorned festivities a reality. On an already short schedule, that has me feeling the pressure. Thankfully, that's when I do my best.

I arrive at the community center early, expecting to get some time to work on my own. But to my surprise, I find Greg, Joanie, Brandon, Carrie, and Layla already hard at work.

While I've spoken to Layla on the phone a few times this past week, this is my first time meeting her in person. It's easy to pick her out, as hers is the only fresh face. And it's an intimidating one; she's beautiful, with big, jewel-green eyes, flawless deep sienna skin, and thick, curly black hair.

"You must be Rae," she says warmly, approaching and wrapping me in a hug.

"Oh!" I exclaim in surprise. She's nice, too. Goodness. "And you must be Layla," I reply, giving her a squeeze before taking a step back. "You're here early. You're *all* here early."

Carrie grins. "You always do so much work for town events, so we wanted to surprise you by taking care of as much as we could. We cleaned the whole place, and we're moving the tables out now."

I put a hand to my chest, moved by their thoughtfulness. "You guys are the best, thank you," I gush, setting down my overstuffed tote bag. "I brought the lightest bits in first, but I wouldn't object to help bringing in the bigger boxes from the Bronco."

"On it, boss," Greg says. I toss him the keys as he and Brandon head outside.

I rub my hands together, eager to dive in. "All right, Layla. Are you ready for your first Alpine Ridge extravaganza?" I joke, considering Leavenworth's event traffic is probably light years beyond ours.

Layla laughs, her dark curls bouncing. "As ready as I'll ever be. I'm just glad we're having it inside, given how unpredictable the weather's been."

I nod in agreement. "True. But we've got plenty of space here, and you've all done a great job of getting started setting up."

"So, what's the plan?" Joanie asks, planting her hands on her hips like she's about to run a race.

I chuckle. "You'll see once the guys bring the boxes in. First, I want to go through what we have to make sure I accounted for things correctly."

First, I give Layla a high-level overview of the events we run. She listens and asks good questions.

"So, your permanent population is how many people?" she asks, tapping a long, slender finger to her chin.

"A few thousand, but we're pretty spread out," I respond.

She nods. "That's about how many permanent residents Leavenworth has, but our events are more geared toward the larger tourist population."

"Ours will be eventually, too, I hope," I say. "But until now, it's mostly been locals. We usually get a few hundred people, give or take. The key is to be flexible and roll with the punches. Weather, turnout, last-minute changes ... I treat it as part of the fun."

Layla mumbles to herself while jotting down notes. "Sounds a lot like the festivals we have in Leavenworth, too. It's always an adventure!"

I take Layla with me to the supply closet and go over what we have. It doesn't take long, and after we're done, I get ready to distribute the boxes I brought. I call everyone back together in the main room.

"Okay. Are you all ready for your assignments?" I ask. Everyone grins and hoots in response, and I can't help but chuckle at their excitement. "Excellent! Greg, I need you to set up a dance floor in the corner with a CD player." I dig through my tote.

"A CD player? Huh. Okay. We might still have one somewhere," he replies skeptically.

I fish out the CD I was looking for and hand it to him. "Mr. O'Reilly will teach traditional Irish Céilí Dancing, and he gave me this for the music."

He takes the CD. "Well, now I *have* to find a CD player. This sounds too good to miss out on."

I wink at him and grab another box. "Carrie, you're on Shamrock Bingo duty," I inform her. "Oh, and you're still bringing the mini shepherd's pies, right?"

She grabs the box. "Absolutely. Evan and I will make them tonight after the dinner party, so they're as fresh as possible."

"Sounds like my kind of after party," I respond. "Brandon, since I already asked you to do a photo booth, the cat's out of the bag on that one." I gesture to the largest box, sitting by the door. "There's a green photo backdrop and a whole pile of St. Patty's Day themed props in there. Let me know if there's anything else you'd like me to scrounge up for you."

Brandon nods. "A few stools wouldn't go amiss, but I think I saw some in the closet."

"Sounds good," I agree. "Mia will provide everything for the Pot of Gold cookie decorating table, along with Guinness cupcakes with Bailey's icing. But for the food table itself —" I nudge a large box toward Joanie with my foot "—Joanie, if you could arrange these platters and serving ware, I'd be much obliged. There are some beverage containers and cups that will go on the drinks table Jerry will be running."

"Can do," Joanie agrees. I give her a look, waiting for her to say more. When she doesn't, everyone else's heads, save Layla's, swivel in our direction. Joanie throws up her hands. "What? I don't *always* have to be sassy. I can be cooperative sometimes."

Everyone laughs except Greg, who looks like he's trying not to. It's sweet that he doesn't want to seem like he's making fun of her, even though I know she wouldn't care if he did.

"What's Jerry bringing?" Brandon asks curiously.

"A non-alcoholic Irish cream liqueur drink and elderflower cordials," I reply.

"Damn. I was hoping for some Guinness," he laments.

I shrug. "Guinness isn't cheap, and Jerry's nothing if not frugal," I point out. "I have no doubt he came up with drinks that would use ingredients that don't move at the tavern. But I'm sure you can go there after and get one."

"Hm. I might do that for lunch because now that I've said it, I kind of want one right now."

"I'm down," Greg offers.

"Babe. Really? Before noon?" Joanie says, poking him in the stomach.

"Well, not right this exact moment, obviously," Greg responds. "Maybe we can all grab lunch when we're done."

"Oh, that sounds good," Carrie agrees. "I'll text Evan to see if he'll have time to come after his morning appointments." Nobody brings up inviting Mia and Nate, as both will be swamped on a Saturday, and we'll see them at tonight's dinner party, anyway.

"I'm not saying no, and I can't believe that I'm the one who has to say this, but can we please focus here?" I tease.

Layla's brows bunch together. "Are you not usually on task?" she asks me quietly.

I lift a shoulder. "I'm easily distracted." Then to everyone else, "So, I get it. But if you want lunch and beer, we're going to have to get this done." I glance at my watch. Considering it's almost eleven, it'll be a late lunch at best. "Anyway. I'll be running the raffle and setting up the prize table, and Layla and I will handle general decorating and coordinate anything you need or the attendees need. Sound good?" Noises of agreement bounce around the room, and I nod, satisfied. "All right, let's do it!"

"I love your ideas, Rae," Layla says as everyone splits off to start their tasks. "This is going to be a lot of fun."

"It is. I really hope as the town grows, we can keep the small-town community feel to these events. It's what makes them so rewarding, knowing my friends and neighbors are enjoying themselves," I admit.

"I know what you mean. You just have to learn to think of the visitors to town as new friends. That's how I do it."

I smile. "That's a lovely way to frame it."

As morning passes into midday, the community center transforms into a sea of green and gold. Shamrocks, leprechauns, and pots of fake gold decorate every surface, and laughter and excited chatter fill the air.

Once Brandon finishes setting up the photo booth area, he meanders over while I'm arranging the raffle prizes.

"You're doing an amazing job, Rae," he says, rubbing my back. "As always."

I smile up at him. I keep the smile fixed on, even though lately I get that gut punch when I look at him. It happened a lot when he first came back, but I thought I'd gotten used to it. Or, I suppose I had, until Luke returned, anyway.

"Thanks, Brandon. I really appreciate your help. Especially given everything that's been going on lately. How are you doing with all the Luke stuff?" I ask as nonchalantly as I can. With the event preparation, I have had little time to dissect my discussion with Luke or check in to see how Brandon was doing. But if he's feeling anything like I am, "overwhelmed" probably doesn't even begin to cover it.

"Honestly? I feel fantastic," Brandon says, to my surprise. "I spent my whole life thinking Luke was the father who rejected me. So, when I heard he was moving back here, I was terrified of whatever would come next. Now I don't have to worry about that, and I also have a brother and a niece who both seem pretty awesome. It's great. I'm great. But thank you for being concerned."

I smile, my heart faltering at his description of Luke. Because his description reminds me that I also found Luke pretty awesome once. More than awesome. Once, Luke was the most important person in the world to me. Which is why what I thought he did hurt me so much. And why, even now, I still have feelings for him. Convoluted ones, but still, feelings.

"I'm happy for you, Brandon." I pause, unsure of whether I should ask, but too curious not to. "So, it's confirmed then? You're brothers?"

Brandon's chin dips. "It is. Nate was kind enough to get us the blood tests results quickly. Brothers with the same father."

I try to smile again, to share his clear relief and joy, but it's a weak attempt.

I can tell Brandon sees right through me. Proven when he says gently, "Look, I know Luke told you all of this, and I know it was probably shocking. Just in case you're not ready to deal with it yet, you should know they'll both be at the dinner party tonight. Luke and his daughter, Zoe."

My stomach does a little flip. Nerves, anticipation, a lingering hint of the anger I pushed down for years ... it's a complicated mix. One I'd like to let go of but am afraid of what that might mean. The unknown is ... scary. Though I know at some point, I'm going to have to deal with it.

"Thanks for the heads up," I manage. "I'll be fine. And I'm sure they'll fit right into the group."

"Hey, Brandon, will you please come help me mount this speaker?" Greg calls from the opposite corner of the room.

Brandon kisses me on the top of my head and goes to help Greg, leaving me distracted and unsettled. I look down at the beautiful baskets I'd put together this week, trying to focus on the joy of bringing joy to others. For the first time in a long time, it doesn't feel like quite enough.

I think about not going. Then I think about going and pretending everything's fine. *Then* I think about going and having the heart-to-heart I know Luke and I need. And that's when I go back to thinking about not going.

Yet here I am, standing on Mia and Nate's doorstep, late, as usual, a bottle of wine in hand. Going won, obviously, but I'm still not sure if I'm going to act like it's not happening or face it head on. Guess there's only one way to find out.

I step inside to the sounds of dishes clattering in the kitchen and multiple conversations going on in the living room across from it. All I have to do is step forward and round the corner into the living room.

I have to force my feet to cooperate. Setting my coat on the rack, I hang my purse over it and force myself down the hall.

As I stop at the entrance to the living room, I take a deep breath. But nobody looks up. Brandon and Carrie are talking to each other by the fireplace. Greg and Joanie are watching a dark-haired girl who, I assume, is Zoe playing with Bruiser on the floor. And Nate and Luke appear to be deep in conversation, leaned against the back wall.

Since nobody's paying attention, I take a moment to really look at Luke. I've avoided it so far, maybe because I feared getting caught, or maybe because I didn't want to remember how attractive he is. Because the reality is that he looks good. Really good. The same yet different, but the gray in his hair, the laugh lines around his eyes ... they suit him.

He's somehow even more handsome than when we were kids. I shake myself, trying to tear my gaze away. And in doing so, I realize Mia and Evan are both notably absent. Since I have a pretty good idea where Mia is, and my nerves are getting the better of me, I turn and head into the kitchen.

As I expected, Mia is busy at work pulling dishes out of the oven.

"Need any help?" I offer.

Mia looks up, little pieces of her dark hair sticking to her neck. "Rae! Hey! Didn't hear you come in." Surprise laces her tone. She blows a piece of hair out of her eyes. "Yes, please." She jerks her chin toward a stack of plates and cutlery. "Mind setting the table?"

"Not at all," I agree, heading to the sink to wash my hands first.

As in the bakery, we work seamlessly in tandem to get everything set up. It smells heavenly; pork roast, buttered fingerling potatoes, garlic rolls, and roasted asparagus sprinkled with lemon and parmesan.

"Cheese?" I ask curiously as she finishes sprinkling the asparagus. "Since when does Nate eat cheese?"

Mia smirks. "A while now. I think I've tempted him into eating most of his food no-nos at this point. But he's on his feet all day at the clinic, so he says he's not worried about the calories." She shrugs, then turns to me and hands me a bowl of steaming rolls. "Go by the living room on your way to the dining room. That ought to get their attention."

I chuckle and do as she says. This time, the second I appear at the wide arch entrance of the living room, everyone's heads perk up, Bruiser's included.

"Dinner's ready," I trill, continuing on to the dining room. I don't miss hearing the excited cries and shuffle of feet as everyone follows. I chuckle to myself as I set the bowl in the center of the long table.

They've all poured into the dining room and are taking seats when Evan finally shows his face.

"Damn, it smells amazing down here," he says, looping an arm around Carrie's waist and giving her a kiss.

I briefly wonder what he was doing upstairs but am distracted by Zoe, who was about to take a seat next to her dad and stops cold, her jaw dropping and her eyes getting hugely round.

Oh shit. Someone forgot to mention the movie star to the newbies.

Mia comes in with the pork platter, the last dish, and sets it down with an, "All right, everyone, let's eat!" just before Zoe screeches, "Omigod, Evan Edwards!"

The room erupts into laughter, and to my surprise, Evan blushes bright red, rubbing at the back of his neck. "Wasn't expecting that," he mutters as I slide into the chair next to him.

Mia props her hands on her hips. "Nate, did you forget

to tell Luke and Zoe about your brother?" she asks accusingly.

Nate scrunches his face. "Sorry, babe." He turns to Luke. "Hey Luke, Zoe. My brother is Evan Edwards. You know, the movie star. Try not to make a big thing of it?"

Mia rolls her eyes and swats him on the arm.

Luke's jaw had dropped, too, but he promptly shuts it and nods. "Sure, of course, no problem. It's nice to meet you, Evan." He sits and pulls Zoe into the chair beside him. "Right, Zo?"

Zoe thunks down onto the chair, her big brown eyes still wide and excited. "I love your movies! You're so cool! Why are you here? Is she your girlfriend? Do you, like, live here now? Oh my god, I live in the same town as Evan Edwards!" She makes a little squealing noise and wiggles in her chair.

Okay, so clearly Zoe's not ready to chill. I chuckle. It's pretty cute to see her honest, awed response. I know I had that reaction internally when we found out Evan was Nate's brother and that we'd be meeting him at Mia and Nate's wedding. Thankfully, he's such a down-to-earth guy, that it didn't take long to just see him as one of the gang. I'm sure Zoe will get there with time.

Nate sighs and puts a slice of pork roast onto his plate, triggering the rest of us to dive in as well.

"Wow, well, thanks," Evan replies. "And, to answer your question, yes, I live here. Welcome to Alpine Ridge." He smiles warmly at her.

"So, Luke, Zoe, what do you think of the town so far?"

Carrie asks, drawing their attention away from Evan, who I notice rubs her leg under the table gratefully as he starts eating. Guess he's still over all the attention that came with his former gig.

"It's already leaps and bounds better than when I left," Luke admits. "I can't wait to see how things continue to develop."

Carrie nods. "We have so much more planned. I think Arthur intends to take you through it all at some point."

"Is there going to be a library?" Zoe pipes up.

Carrie raises a brow. "You know what? I don't think we've talked about that yet, but I love that idea. I'll put it on the agenda for our next meeting," Carrie says to Zoe. "What do you like to read?"

"I like dystopian. My favorite books ever are the *Hunger Games*, but I like *Red Queen* and *Divergent*, though that series ended kind of bad. But I also like fairytale retellings like *A Curse So Dark and Lonely* and *Cinder*."

"I love all of those," I offer. "I'm Rae, by the way."

"Nice to meet you Rae," Zoe says.

"So you like fantasy, too, then?" I ask.

Zoe taps her lips. "A bit. Why, do you have some suggestions?"

I hold back a smile. "*An Ember in the Ashes* is a fantastic series, or if you like Greek mythology, there's always *Percy Jackson and the Olympians*. You also can't go wrong with *The Hobbit* or the *Inheritance Cycle* series.

Or if you're looking for something a little quirkier, *The Eyre Affair* series is fun, and —"

"Okay, okay," Carrie holds up a hand. "Damn, Rae, sounds like you could get the library started yourself with all of those books."

I give a guilty smile. "Sorry, I didn't mean to overwhelm you," I tell Zoe. "In case it wasn't obvious, I read a lot, too, and you're always welcome to borrow my books."

Zoe grins, then we all eat for a few minutes in happy silence. Mia's food is delicious as usual, and everyone tells her so.

When Nate finishes, he leans forward on the table. "So, guess who came into the clinic today?"

All heads turn toward him, even Luke and Zoe's.

"Big Bird?" Joanie asks dryly. I assume it's her sarcastic commentary on Nate's inability to cut to the chase like she would.

Nate smirks. "Close. Betty McDonald."

"No!" I gasp.

"Yes," Nate confirms. "She said to Maura — that's our receptionist," he adds for Luke and Zoe's benefit, "that she wanted a copy of her medical records for her new doctor in Yakima. Because — get this — she's *moving there*."

Now everyone else gasps. I slam a hand down on the table. "Hallelujah!" I shout, keeping it clean since Zoe is present. "Finally!"

Luke's brows jump. "You're talking about Mrs.

McDonald? The one who used to chase us away from her 'prize winning' flower beds?"

Carrie chuckles and I nod emphatically. "One and the same. She really crossed a line a couple years back, only we just found out recently. I might have given her a piece of my mind and made it less than comfortable for her to stick around."

"Sounds like she had it coming," Luke says drily. "Even when we were teenagers, she would yell at us for 'hanging around looking like we were doing nothing.'"

I roll my eyes. "Do you remember the time she told our parents we were delinquents because we were out after nine p.m.?"

"How old were you?" Zoe asks with a grin.

"Fifteen!" Luke responds. "She was ridiculous."

Luke and I share a smile. The warmth in his eyes hits me right in the chest. And I remember. Those nights we'd wander around, just so we could hold hands a little longer. That's all it was at that age, anyway. Though sometimes, when Pastor McMillan would work late, we'd climb the church's bell tower stairs and clamber onto the roof to stargaze and make out. That part became … more about a year later.

My eyes drop to his lips as I remember. The warmth of his body. His strong hands groping clumsily under my shirt. Gosh, we were so young. So in love. And so naïve, as you always are that first time.

"Well, there's one less thing to worry about," Joanie says dismissively, snapping me out of my trance. "How about we celebrate with dessert?" She rises to help Mia clear the table.

Carrie and Brandon join them, and I make to help, but Mia waves me off, shaking her head and looking pointedly at Luke.

I grimace at her and sit back down. I'll give her a piece of my mind for trying to force us together later.

"So, what *haven't* you seen around town yet?" Greg asks.

"The gym, for starters. And I hear you're just the guy to talk to about that," Luke says.

Greg grins. "You're more than welcome," he says, spreading his hands out. "Though I'm curious if the new fire station will have its own workout equipment."

Luke nods. "Of course. That's a staple. We've got to keep in tip-top shape," he agrees. "But until it's built, you'll be seeing a lot of me."

I swallow hard, trying not to imagine exactly how good of shape he's in under those clothes that more than hint at the already mouthwatering physique he's clearly honed over the years.

"We haven't been to the bakery yet!" Zoe interjects. "Dad keeps putting me off for some reason, but I'm *dying* for pie."

"Did someone say pie?" Mia asks, bringing in a tray of what looks like her mini chiffon pies.

Zoe's eyes go wide. Then Carrie walks in with a tray of mini chocolate cream pies, and Brandon with a tray of mini strawberry rhubarb pies, a newer experiment of Mia's.

"Everyone needs to try the strawberry rhubarb mini pies," Mia announces. "I'm tweaking the recipe for the bakery, so I want to hear what you think."

"Please. They'll be amazing. Stop fishing for compliments," Joanie teases as she pops one in her mouth. She groans. "See? Fucking delicious." Her eyes widen and move to Zoe, then to Luke. "Sorry." She blushes and hides behind her napkin.

Greg bursts out laughing. "We had a conversation about learning to not swear when kids are around, but clearly it didn't stick."

Zoe lifts her chin as she delicately takes a strawberry rhubarb mini pie. "I'm twelve, I'm not a kid. It's not like I've never heard the F-word before. Dad says it plenty."

Luke's cheeks turn pink. "I don't say it *that* much," he protests, popping a chocolate cream mini pie in his mouth.

Zoe turns around to face Mia. "They *are* delicious. If I had anything to offer as a suggestion, maybe the strawberry flavor could use a boost? It's kind of being overpowered by the rhubarb just a teeny bit. Maybe you could add some lemon or nutmeg?"

Mia raises an eyebrow and smirks. "Funny enough, I was thinking the same thing, Zoe. You've got a good palette there."

Zoe beams under Mia's praise, but it's Luke that responds. "She should. Zoe loves baking shows, and she made me take her to every place that sells pie in the Seattle area so she could compare and contrast them —" he holds up his hands "— her words."

Mia is visibly shocked. "Wow. That's … there are a *lot* of bakeries and pie shops in Seattle."

"There are. But there's one pie I miss that can only be found in Alpine Ridge," Luke says, his eyes fixing to mine. "And I hear tell you're still making it."

I smirk. "If you're talking about my Great Grams' huckleberry pie, then you heard right." I turn to Zoe. "You like huckleberry pie, sugar?"

"Love. I *love* huckleberry pie," she replies.

"Well, that settles it. You *need* to come to the bakery. Luke, why haven't you brought this young lady by yet?" I demand. It was meant to be teasing, but the stricken look on his face answers my questions.

He hasn't brought his daughter to the bakery because of me. Or how things are between us right now. Damn.

"You should bring her soon," Mia says softly, taking the sting out of the moment. "She can have a slice on the house for her excellent taste buds." Mia winks at Zoe and she grins, blushing at the praise.

Mia takes a seat and starts in on her own dessert.

Luke looks over at me and asks quietly, "You sure?"

My heart twinges that he'd need to ask. "Of course. You're both welcome anytime," I assure him. "So. Zoe. What are you doing for school now you're here?"

Zoe launches into a lengthy explanation of her plans to "unschool," including classes she's found online, "field trips" around the area for things like hikes and shopping, and so much more.

As we chat, I can't help but marvel at how easy it is to

talk to her. She's bright and curious, with a surprisingly mature outlook for a twelve-year-old. I can't help but wonder if the scars she bears have forced her to grow up faster than she would've otherwise. Kids can be cruel. But I push that thought aside and focus on my new young friend and her undeniable sparkle. I can already tell she's going to bring something special to Alpine Ridge.

I also don't miss that down the table, Mia is grilling Evan about the mysterious celebrity who's apparently building a house in Alpine Ridge.

"Come on, Ev," she wheedles. "Just give me a hint. Is it someone from one of your movies?"

Evan shakes his head, grinning. "My lips are sealed, Mia. They're locked in on a property now, too. You'll find out, eventually."

Carrie laughs. "Oh, you know it's someone good if Evan's going to such lengths to keep it quiet."

Mia groans dramatically. "You're killing me here! Both of you!"

"Wait … is there another famous person moving here?" Zoe asks me in a hushed voice.

"I don't know," I admit, then raising my voice, I add, "I kind of think Evan and Carrie might just be screwing with Mia." I raise an eyebrow in Evan's direction and the table erupts in laughter, and for a moment, everything feels normal. Easy.

Like maybe, just maybe, we can all find a way to coexist in this new normal.

But then my gaze catches Luke's, and the laughter dies

in my throat. Because beneath the surface, there's still so much left unsaid between us. As demonstrated by the fact that he felt like he had to avoid bringing Zoe to the bakery. Or even coming himself, given that I haven't seen or heard from him since he dropped a reality bomb on me. Then again, I did tell him I needed space.

And I did. But I'm realizing … maybe I don't need it anymore. Maybe I'm starting to accept that things aren't what I thought, and that it doesn't have to be a big thing.

After dinner, we're cleaning up and I decide that once we're done, I'll talk to Luke. But before I can, Mia pulls me aside, her expression nervous.

"What's up?" I whisper.

Her eyes dart around, making sure nobody is within hearing distance. "I made an appointment," she says quietly. "With a fertility clinic in Seattle. For early April."

I put my hands over my mouth to stifle a joyful sound. Tears prick at the back of my eyes.

"Oh, Mia. I'm so proud of you. I know it's scary, but you're doing the right thing." I wrap my arms around her, trying to convey how much I feel for her. How much I know what it's like to be where she is.

She nods against my shoulder. "I just … I'm terrified of what they might say. What if they tell me I can never have kids?"

I pull back, looking her in the eye. "Then we'll deal with that together. But don't borrow trouble, okay? Take it one step at a time. And remember, no matter what happens, you have so much love in your life. Nate, me, all of us …

we're here for you." I brush a lock of hair out of her face and cup her cheek. My heart aches, and I wish I could fix this for her.

Mia gives me a shaky smile. "Thanks, Rae. I don't know what I'd do without you." She takes a deep breath, seeming to steel herself. "You know, you should talk to Luke. I think it would be good for you. For both of you."

I bite my lip and nod. "Already decided to, sugar."

She smiles and gives me one last squeeze before slipping away, leaving me with my own demons to face.

So, I reach deep and find my courage. And I go look for Luke. I find him in the dining room, talking to Nate about the architecture of the house, specifically the glass window wall they're standing beside, and how it was designed to make you feel like you're outside even when you're inside. It's one of my favorite things about being in this house, honestly, so I'm not surprised it grabbed Luke's attention. It's hard to grow up in Alpine Ridge and not love the towering pines, snow-capped mountains, and endless blue skies.

"Hey," I say softly. "I'm sorry to interrupt. Luke, can we talk?"

Surprise flickers across Luke's face. "Of course. Would you please excuse us, Nate?"

"Of course," Nate replies graciously, stepping out of the room and pulling the door closed behind him.

For a moment, we just stand there, the silence stretching between us.

"I'm sorry," I blurt out. "For believing people I

should've known better than to trust. It's just ... it always upset me so much because I thought I knew you. I couldn't imagine you doing any of those things."

Luke's expression softens. "Rae —"

"And then my ex-husband," I continue, words I never intended to say tumbling out in a rush. "He cheated on me. With a friend. And I think ... I think I unfairly lumped you two together. Assumed the worst because it was so similar to what I thought you'd done, even though I didn't recognize that's what I was doing at the time."

Luke's eyes widen, a flash of anger sparking in their depths. "Your *husband* cheated on you? God, Rae, I'm so sorry." He runs a hand through his hair angrily and turns to look out the window.

I shrug, suddenly feeling self-conscious about the confession even I didn't expect. "It is what it is. But I'm realizing now that I let it color the way I saw you; like him, a liar and cheater to the core. It's what made it so hard to make the mental shift from what I thought I knew. And that wasn't fair. To you or to me. We both deserve better."

Luke is quiet for a moment. "I understand," he says at last. "And for what it's worth ... knowing that's what you thought of me was hard. Not just because I loved you then, but because as soon as I saw you again, I realized I still did. I don't think you ever stop feeling that for your first love. It becomes a part of you. And thinking you hated me?" He puts a hand over his heart as a pained expression crosses his handsome face. "I couldn't let that go on. I had to set the record straight, even if it didn't change anything else."

"I don't hate you, Luke. I'm not sure I ever did. I was hurt, too," I admit.

He steps forward, looking down at me with an intensity that takes my breath away. "I know the truth can't erase years of hurt. But I hope it can help you heal. Because honestly? I can't imagine being back here and not having you in my life, Rae."

The deep tenor of his voice rumbles through me, straight to my heart. I close my eyes, emotion welling, clogging the back of my throat.

"Don't say things like that," I whisper.

I feel his finger slip under my chin, tilting my head up. "Look at me," he implores. The gentle plea leaves me with no choice but to do as he asks. His warm, liquid brown eyes dart between mine, drinking me in just as surely as mine are him.

"It's just the truth. I'm still drawn to you. I don't think I ever stopped being drawn to you. But I'll take whatever you're willing to give. We can be the kind of friends who only see each other at the weekly dinner party." His thumb strokes under my chin and it makes my knees weak. "We can be friends that spend time together. Lunch at the tavern. Hiking with Zoe." He leans in, his breath fanning over my face as his thumb traces down my neck and across my collarbone, sending pleasant shivers down my spine. "Or we can be more. More than friends. Even more than what we were capable of at sixteen." He steps back, withdrawing his hand. And the absence of him leaves a hole in my heart that I can't deny. "Whatever you want."

I close my eyes, my heart aching. Because part of me wants nothing more than to fall into his arms, to pick up where we left off all those years ago.

But I know I can't. Not yet. Maybe never. I'm too damaged. I swore off serious relationships long ago because of everything I can't be for a man, and never finding one that could be true to me. And while this new reality may change that … we're not there yet.

"I don't think I'm ready for *more*," I reply honestly. "Let's start with friends."

Luke smiles, a sad, understanding smile. "Friends." He looks at me, clearly purposely not asking what kind of friend. "I'd like that."

I nod, afraid that speaking will break the hold I have on all the emotions I feel right now.

But he's as good as his word. Because even as we rejoin the others, I can feel the tentative new beginning taking root between us in the way he talks to me amongst our group. With care and respect for my boundaries.

I feel a glimmer of hope. Because maybe there's still a chance for us to heal. To find our way back to each other, even if it looks different from what it was before.

Only time will tell.

CHAPTER TEN

LUKE

I stand in front of the mirror, adjusting my green bowtie for the third time, wondering if it'll be enough. But strangely, it turns out it's the only green piece of clothing I own, so it'll have to do.

Zoe bounces into the room, wearing a green pajama onesie, a shamrock headband perched jauntily on her head. "Come on, Dad! We're going to be late!" she exclaims, tugging at my arm.

I chuckle, letting her pull me away from my reflection. "Okay, okay. I'm coming, my little leprechaun."

Zoe rolls her eyes at me, and I chuckle. But joking aside, as I grab my keys and head out the door, I can't shake the nerves fluttering in my stomach. All I can think about is seeing Rae again after our conversation last night. The way she opened up to me, the vulnerability in her eyes ... it gave me hope. Even her request that we "start with friends." Because that implies that she's open to ending up somewhere else.

Which is good, since I don't want to be just her friend. I want so much more. But I meant what I said — I'll take whatever she's willing to give. Even if it means tamping down my own feelings, giving her the space she needs, and spending time with her platonically.

The community center is already bustling with activity when we arrive. A shamrock garland hangs around the outside of the entryway, music and laughter pours out the doors, and the smell of frosting hits us hard as we enter. I note the cookie decorating table close to the entrance, piles of colored frosting bags and undecorated cookies beckoning.

But to my surprise, Zoe makes a beeline for the Irish Céilí Dancing lessons, her eyes sparkling with excitement. I follow more reluctantly but soon find myself swept up in the infectious energy of the room. We dance in groups of four, led by an elderly Irishman with a thick brogue and a twinkle in his eye. I don't remember him from when I was a kid.

When Carrie and Evan show up and start dancing with Zoe, she's so over the moon she forgets I'm even there, so at the next break in the routine, I join him. "So, Mr. O'Reilly —"

"Call me Ronan, lad."

I smile. "Ronan. I'm —"

"I know who you are, Luke," he says with a smirk. "I remember you and your gang of begonia-stomping hooligans getting Betty riled every other day." The twinkle in his eye tells me he likely shared my feelings toward Mrs. McDonald.

And it makes me laugh so hard it hurts.

"Wow. All right then, well, that answers my question about whether you lived here when I was growing up."

"The O'Reilly clan has been in Alpine Ridge for sixty years now," he says as the others continue to whirl and stomp. "Brought a bit o' the old country with us, we did." He smiles fondly at the dancers.

"It was kind of you to share it," I reply. "That's my daughter —" I point her out "— Zoe. She needed this kind of joy, I think."

"Well, in that case, tell her she's welcome to come by my home anytime for a spot of fun. I'm just off Main on Mountain View Drive. Mine's the one with an Irish flag. Can't miss it." He pats me on the shoulder. "Good to have you back, son. You'll make a fine fire chief." He gives me a look I've seen before. The pitying kind that tells me he remembers very well why my family left, and why I'm returning as fire chief. It normally chafes, but this time I find myself touched by his empathy and confidence.

Unfortunately, I don't have time to reply, as Zoe whirls to a stop in front of me and pulls me back into the throng, even though it throws off the pairings. But everyone redistributes and we figure it out. As the music winds down, I realize maybe it was the kind of joy I needed, too.

After the lesson, Zoe and I grab some drinks — a non-alcoholic Irish cream liqueur for her, a Guinness for me — and Zoe gets a cupcake and Lucky Charms marshmallow treat to boot. I'm going to have to make her eat broccoli for the next week to account for all the sugar she's eating.

Brandon appears at our side, grinning. He holds up his own beer, clinking it against mine.

"Cheers to the beer that almost wasn't. I had to convince Jerry, the cheap old fart, that it wasn't a St. Patty's Day festival without Guinness," he says by way of greeting.

"Well, thanks," I reply. "You're not wrong."

Brandon nods sagely. "Hey, Zoe, want to come play Shamrock Bingo with me?" he asks.

Zoe nods eagerly, shoving the last of her cupcake in her mouth as the two of them head off, leaving me alone.

I scan the room, my heart skipping a beat when I spot Rae manning the photo booth. She's wearing a vibrant emerald green dress and her shoulder-length blond hair is swept off her neck with a sparkly shamrock clip holding it in place. She's laughing with the group getting their photos taken, and her smile hits me right in the heart.

I make my way over, trying to appear casual. "Having fun?" I ask, leaning against the booth.

Rae looks up, a smile still playing at the corners of her mouth. She taps my bowtie with a finger and grins. "Tons. You?"

"Absolutely. Though I think I might need to practice my jig a bit more."

She laughs, and the sound warms me from the inside out. "Well, lucky for you, there's a photo booth right here. We can document your progress."

Once the folks that were there head off, Rae and I spend the next half hour taking silly photos, first of me attempting an Irish jig, which is hilariously awful. Then we play with the oversized buckled green hats and goofy sparkly gold and green glasses. For a moment, it feels like old times — the two of us, laughing and joking, the rest of the world falling away. Maybe this friends thing isn't so bad, after all.

When Zoe finds us later, her cheeks are flushed with excitement. "I won Bingo! Look at all the chocolate truffles I got!" she exclaims, holding up a small black plastic pot filled to the brim with gold-wrapped candies.

"Great job, sweetheart," I say, congratulating her with a high-five.

"Ah, yes, the truffles. They're my favorites. And the one thing Mia doesn't make at the bakery," Rae comments.

"Want one?" Zoe offers.

Rae laughs. "I've had a good half dozen already today. But you're a doll to offer to share."

"I'd give them *all* to you for a slice of huckleberry pie," she says with a mischievous glint in her eye.

Rae smiles and shakes her head. "Your gold is no good here, sugar. Like Mia said, you come on by whenever you want and get a slice, free of charge."

Zoe turns to me. "Dad, when can I?"

I rub my jaw. At first, I'd avoided taking her so as not

to crowd Rae. But now, well, this week is going to be pretty busy.

"I don't know, Zo. I've got a lot on my plate this week," I hedge.

"Even more reason to bring her by. You can drop her off. I'll feed her and …" Rae winks at Zoe "… I may even teach her how to make my Great Grams's famous huckleberry pie while I'm at it."

Zoe's jaw drops. "No! Really? Would you really teach me?" She bounces on her toes excitedly.

Rae smiles wide at her enthusiasm. "Absolutely." Then to me, "How about tomorrow? Our morning rush is usually over around ten."

"That would be amazing, actually," I admit. "Thank you."

I've been a little reticent to leave Zoe alone so much, but between repairing the old house and gearing up on planning the fire department, I haven't exactly had a lot of time to research activities for her. And this way, I get to see Rae again.

Rae waves me off. "It's nothing. Mia will be thrilled to have her, too. It's a win all around."

"Speaking of winning," Brandon says, sidling up with Joanie, Greg, Mia, and Nate in tow. "Has everyone entered the raffle? Miss Rae here put together some fantastic prizes. And the proceeds will go toward a development project of the townspeople's choice."

"I love that idea," I reply. "Do we vote for one when we enter?"

Brandon shakes his head. "We'll see how much we end up with and match it with town funds, then put together a list of the projects people have asked for that fit the budget it allows."

"How terribly practical," Joanie says drily. She taps her chin. "I have the sudden urge to go buy a few hundred raffle tickets." She winks and heads off toward the raffle table, dragging a laughing Greg along with her.

"Oh, hey, speaking of practical," I say, pulling Nate aside as Rae, Mia, and Zoe start to talk baking. "You mentioned at dinner last night that the clinic is already pretty busy?"

Nate nods. "On the urgent care side, mostly. Which is fine, since a lot of folks already have a primary care physician and don't want to make the switch, so the routine appointments side is slow enough to where that's fine for the time being. But I'm definitely concerned for the future."

"Well, for what it's worth, I'm a trained paramedic, so if you need any help in that regard, don't hesitate to call me," I tell him.

"Really? That'd be amazing. A tremendous weight off my mind, actually. We've had to send a couple of folks to the ER in Ellensburg. But if we had more basic triage in town, it would make a huge difference," he admits.

"I get it. And once the firehouse is up and running, all the guys on my crew will be at least EMT level, if not full paramedics, which most firefighters choose to do. Plus, we'll have a rig that can transport patients," I add.

Nate scrubs a hand down his face. "Damn. Well, that just made my year. I feel a lot better. Thanks, man."

I clap him on the back. "That's what I'm here for. And who knows? If the town grows quickly enough, we may get a full hospital sooner than we think." I laugh, because I know it's possible, but imagining Alpine Ridge being that big is wild.

Nate laughs along with me. "That would be something, but let's not get ahead of ourselves. Eat the elephant one bite at a time, as they say."

"Hey, Dad!" Zoe says, grabbing my arm. "Can we do cookie decorating?" She bats her eyelashes at me. "Pleeeeease?"

I laugh and shake my head. "How can you still want cookies after cupcakes and Lucky Charms treats?"

Zoe shrugs, grinning. "There's always room for cookies."

"She's a girl after my own heart," Rae teases.

"Mine, too," Mia adds, giving Zoe a fond smile.

I shake my head, marveling at her bottomless appetite, but gesture for her to lead the way. Mia takes us over to the cookie decorating table, where we settle in.

She demonstrates how to pipe both the easier shamrock-shaped cookie with thick green buttercream frosting, and the more difficult royal-icing and fondant pot of gold cookies. Zoe tries to go straight for the bigger challenge, but Mia makes her do the shamrock cookie first as a "test" she has to pass to go on. Zoe eats that challenge up faster than the cupcake from earlier.

Naturally, Zoe nails both, though she struggles a little with painting luster dust on the fondant coins and placing them on the pot. Still, the results are impressive, looking extremely similar to Mia's examples.

Despite my best efforts, my cookies come out looking more like blobs than shamrocks. But I sit and watch Zoe, with Mia's patient guidance, create an entire tray of picture-perfect treats. By the time she's done, Mia is gushing over her work, and Zoe is on cloud nine.

As the event winds down, Layla takes the stage to announce the raffle winners. But before she begins, Brandon joins her, holding up a hand for quiet.

"Before we get to the prizes, I have a quick announcement," he says, his voice carrying across the room. "As many of you know, Alpine Ridge is getting a new fire chief. I wanted to take a moment to introduce him to you all. Ladies and gentleman, my brother, Luke McMillan." My jaw drops, but I quickly close it. Damn, I wish he would've told me he was going to do that. Good thing I work well under pressure.

A murmur ripples through the crowd as I stand, feeling a rush of emotion. As I walk toward Brandon, his encouraging smile makes me realize what he's doing. He's trying to reverse the rumor mill and put me on a good footing with the town at the same time. Damn. That's both thoughtful and brilliant.

I clear my throat, nodding at the sea of curious faces. "Thank you, Brandon. I'm honored to be here." I take a subtle, deep breath and decide to lean into it hard. "As many of you know, I grew up here in Alpine Ridge and only left because a fire burned down the town's only church, taking away our father's livelihood as the church's pastor. But that event affected more than my family; it affected the entire town. It's what made me want to be a firefighter. To save families and communities from the fate that befell all of us all those years ago. I'm grateful for the opportunity to return with a wealth of knowledge and experience that I didn't have then that I can use to serve this community."

To my surprise, everyone applauds when I finish. I can feel my ears burning as I step down and Layla takes the mic.

As I head back to my seat, every person I walk by smiles at me. Many whisper greetings and thanks for being here. Each interaction bolsters my confidence in the decision I made to come back and my gratitude for this opportunity.

When I sit back down, Zoe leans over and whispers, "That was really nice of Uncle Brandon."

"Yeah," I agree, my throat tight. "It really was."

The rest of the event passes in a happy blur of raffle prizes, final treats, and hugs goodbye, and before I know it, Zoe and I are heading home, our arms laden with cookies and prizes.

Once the sugar rush has finally worn off at the end of the evening, I tuck Zoe into bed and she yawns, her eyes heavy. "That was the best St. Patrick's Day ever," she mumbles.

I brush a stray curl from her forehead, smiling. "It really was, wasn't it?"

And as I close her door, I realize that for the first time in a long time, I feel like I'm exactly where I'm supposed to be. All the hard work I've done to get to chief. All the risks we took leaving our life in Seattle behind. All the drama I didn't know was waiting for me. It wasn't for nothing. For the first time in a long time, I feel like my life is finally coming together.

CHAPTER ELEVEN

RAE

Monday morning brings the usual wave of caffeine and sugar seekers, but it's who I know is coming after that has nervous energy coursing through my body the whole time.

At ten on the dot, Luke and Zoe walk through the bakery's door. Nerves aside, I can't help but smile at the sight of them, their cheeks flushed from the crisp, almost-spring morning air.

"Happy St. Patty's Day," I greet them, wiping my hands on my apron.

Zoe grins and bounds up to the counter. "Happy St. Patrick's Day!" she returns. "What have you got that's green?" Her eyes start scanning the cases and I laugh.

"Zoe, you're here to make and eat pie. Don't you think that's enough? Especially after yesterday?" Luke admonishes her with a sigh.

"Dad. It's *all* green," she says in a shocked whisper,

seemingly oblivious to what he'd said. She looks up at me. "Food coloring?"

"Matcha," I reply with a wink. Then to Luke, "Off to town hall today, then?"

He nods. "Yep. I shouldn't be too long."

Mia pops out from the kitchen, her face lighting up when she sees Zoe. "Hey, guys!"

"Take all the time you need," I assure Luke. "I think Mia's got big plans for Zoe."

Zoe grins, bouncing on her toes. "Yes! I'm going to learn how to make huckleberry pie today, right?"

"You sure are," Mia agrees. "But that's Rae's specialty, so she'll handle that part. But I definitely have things for you after that."

Zoe's eyes dart back to her father, then to me. She gestures for me to lean close, then when I do, she whispers in my ear, "Can we bake a huckleberry pie for me to take home, too? Dad says it's his favorite."

I chuckle, reaching out to tuck her hair behind her ear. "I think we can manage that," I agree with a wink.

When I look up, Luke's eyes meet mine, and for a moment, the world seems to slow. There's a warmth in his gaze that makes my heart flutter, a tenderness that makes my knees weak.

"I'll leave you lovely ladies to it, then," he says softly. "Thank you. For everything."

I swallow hard, nodding. "Anytime."

As Luke leaves, I turn to Zoe, clapping my hands together. "All right, Miss Zoe. Ready to get baking?"

Zoe nods eagerly, and we head into the kitchen. I walk her through the steps of making my Great Grams' famous huckleberry pie, from rolling out the crust to mixing the filling, to creating the perfect lattice top. She listens intently, her brow furrowed in concentration as she follows my instructions flawlessly.

By the time we put the pie in the oven, Mia has started making lunch. She lets Zoe help her prep the ingredients for panini, though Mia handles pressing the sandwiches because apparently letting non-employees, kids especially, handle heated appliances is a big insurance no-no. Still, Zoe helps to assemble the sandwiches, then plates them afterward, getting a quick lesson in presentation.

As we eat our deliciously gooey cheesy veggie panini, Zoe chatters excitedly about all the things she wants to learn to bake next.

"Slow down there, sugar," I tease her. "We couldn't possibly do all of that today. I think we're going to have to make this a regular thing if you want to learn it all."

"Really? I can come back again?" she asks, her eyes wide and hopeful.

My heart melts, realizing that since her mom died when she was so young, and her dad isn't the baking type — unless something has seriously changed, because he was always hopeless at it when we were kids — that Zoe hasn't had anyone to indulge her passion for baking. To guide and instruct her in it. It's clear she's done some on her own, but there's so much more we can teach her.

I decide that's exactly what we're going to do.

I give Mia a look. She nods. "Of course you can, Zoe," Mia agrees. "In fact, you can come every day this week. We can always use an extra set of hands around here."

Zoe's face lights up like a Christmas tree. "Oh my god, are you serious? That would be amazing!"

"I'm so serious that I think we should clean up our lunch and start making the cookie dough we're going to need for tomorrow," Mia replies.

Zoe quickly grabs all our plates and ferries them to the sink, rolling up her sleeves to begin scrubbing.

I man the front while Mia teaches Zoe. They get through the cookie dough quickly, then Mia shows her how to prepare all the various fruit toppings, compotes, and syrups that we use.

I pop my head in occasionally to join them between customers. As I watch them work, I can't help marveling at how quickly Zoe has learned today … and how she's made her way into our hearts just as quickly. Her intelligence, enthusiasm, and unbelievable natural talent are hard not to love.

When Luke returns to pick her up, Zoe can barely contain her excitement. "Dad, guess what? Mia said I can come help every day this week!"

Luke raises an eyebrow, looking between Mia and me. "Really?" he asks skeptically.

"Really," I assure him. "She's a natural in the kitchen. So helpful and such a joy to have around."

Luke smiles, pride shining in his eyes. "That's my girl."

Zoe slips her hand into her dad's, leading him out as she starts to tell him all about her time with us.

"Zoe?" I call after her, retrieving the pie box we'd stashed under the register. She turns back with wide eyes. "Don't forget this," I mock whisper, sliding the box across the counter.

She leans up and wraps an arm around my neck and squeezes. "Thanks, Rae, you're the best."

I squeeze her back. "Right back atcha, sugar."

I let her go only to find Luke looking at me with an expression on his face that makes my cheeks flush. It's sweetness and gratitude and something ... more. Something I'm not quite ready to acknowledge.

Zoe grabs his hand again, teasing him about her surprise.

"Thanks again, ladies. We'll see you tomorrow?" Luke calls back. But I'm still too stunned by the look he gave me to respond.

"See you tomorrow," Mia agrees when I don't say anything.

After they leave, Mia turns to me, her expression curious. "Are you really okay with seeing your ex and his kid every day? I mean, I know you and Luke are trying to be friends, but you look a little shell-shocked right now."

I shake myself out of it and take a deep breath, considering her question. "Honestly? It's kind of a reminder of all the things I wanted, that's for sure. But in a way, I feel like I get to have them now. Luke and I are friends, and it's good to have him back in my life.

Especially now that I know he didn't cheat on me and father a child with my best friend."

Mia nods, understanding in her eyes. "And Zoe is a pretty exceptional kid."

"She really is," I agree, smiling.

But even as I say the words, I feel a twinge of sadness. Because as much as I'm enjoying having Luke and Zoe in my life, there's a part of me that wishes it were different. That wishes Luke was my husband and Zoe was our child, the way I'd always dreamed it would be.

I push the thought aside, focusing on the present. On the joy of teaching Zoe to bake, on the warmth and gratitude of Luke's smile. It's enough, I tell myself. It has to be.

Thursday afternoon finds me at town hall, fidgeting nervously as I wait for Arthur to see me as he'd requested. When he finally calls me into his office, I take a deep breath, steeling myself for whatever he has to say. Wondering if I did something wrong with the St. Patrick's Day event. If it wasn't what he'd hoped for.

"Rae, thank you for coming," Arthur says, gesturing for me to sit. "I wanted to talk to you about the St. Patrick's Day event. It was a huge success, and everyone loved it."

I feel relief and a flush of pride at his words. "Thank you. I'm glad everyone enjoyed themselves. I sure did, anyway."

Arthur nods, leaning forward on his desk. "As did I. I particularly liked the dancing. Who knew Ronan still had that in him?" He chuckles to himself before continuing. "I also wanted to discuss the future of the community center events. Layla enjoyed helping out, but she's decided to take another opportunity that will occupy her full time. She won't be able to manage future events on her own, though she's still open to assisting when she can."

My heart sinks. "So, who will handle them then? And what happens to the community center?"

"Well, we've talked to Dana — who is currently a masseuse at the wellness center — and since her current position is only part-time, she's interested in running the community center if she can also do that part time. Which we're fine with, for now. But in any case, she wouldn't have enough time to handle the events as well. Which is where you come in."

I blink, surprise washing over me. "Me?"

Arthur smiles. "I'd like to continue hiring you as an independent contractor to run the events. But to do that, we'd need to make things a bit more official. At minimum that would mean you'd need a registered business name, a tax ID number, and liability insurance."

"So basically, you want me to start an event planning business," I say slowly, the pieces clicking into place.

"More or less, yes. I understand it's a big decision, and I want you to take some time to think about it. But Rae, you have a genuine talent for this. You bring something special to the town events that nobody else can provide."

"Wow, Arthur, that's incredibly kind of you to say, thank you," I reply, touched. But then my brow furrows. "You're not just trying to sweet talk me so I agree to do it, are you?"

Arthur chuckles. "A little, but it's still the truth," he admits. "Truly, though, Rae, I'm merely asking you to formalize what you already do. It doesn't have to be more than that."

I nod. "Thank you, Mayor Burton. You've given me a lot to think about. I'll let you know soon."

He rises and extends his hand. I rise in kind and shake it. "It was a pleasure speaking with you, as always," he says, then sees me out the door. With one last smile, I walk away slowly in a daze.

I leave town hall with my head spinning, Arthur's words echoing in my mind. An event planning business. Me. It seems impossible … even if it's something I've secretly always wanted to do. But I already have a job. And left to my own devices, I'm awful at time management and expense tracking and filing all the paperwork that running a business would require. It's crazy … yet, I didn't say no.

That night, we gather at Greg and Joanie's house for game night. It's Luke and Zoe's first time joining us, and I can sense their nervousness. But everyone goes out of their way to make them feel welcome. Mia brings a batch of mini pies specifically for Zoe to try, while Greg and Joanie present her with a new toy to play with Bruiser. I can tell Luke is touched by their efforts to make her feel at home.

We start the evening with a game of Clue. Surprising no one, Joanie's strategic mind and competitive nature lead her to victory. Next up is Apples to Apples, where Evan's wit and creativity shine through, earning him the win.

The room is filled with laughter, jokes, and playful banter, but I find myself going through the motions, unable to fully engage. My mind is elsewhere, replaying the conversation with Arthur, his offer, and the weight of the decision bearing down on me.

Eventually, Brandon notices my distraction and calls me out. "What's going on, Rae? You seem preoccupied."

I sigh, realizing there's no point in hiding it. "Arthur wants me to start an event planning business to handle future town events."

A chorus of excitement and encouragement erupts from the group.

"Rae, that's fantastic! You'd be amazing at it! I mean, you *are* amazing at it," Mia says.

"Totally. I've leaned hard on you over the years, and you always deliver," Greg agrees. "So, what's worrying you?"

I sigh. "It's just … running a business is a big deal, right?"

Joanie shakes her head. "Misconception. It doesn't have to be a big thing, just a shell company if it's only for town events. You could make it a sole proprietorship with a DBA and get an EIN from the IRS. Boom, you're done. Well, except for the insurance, but that's no biggie either. I'd go umbrella if it were me."

I stare at Joanie with confusion. "Are you speaking English?" I ask.

Everyone laughs. "I think what Joanie is trying to say is that it's not as much work — or paperwork — as you think," Carrie explains gently.

I shake my head, finding that hard to believe.

Luke catches my eye and, ever so gently, says, "Rae, you've *always* had a knack for this sort of thing. Even your Grams asked your opinion on everything, and she was the pickiest woman this side of the Cascades. I think you should go for it."

Somehow, of all the voices in this room of encouragement, it's his words that really strike a chord. I'd forgotten how important Grams had made me feel, because she didn't dole out praise easily.

Maybe I do have a knack for event planning. No, I definitely do. I know that. I don't know why I'm questioning that when it's the rest I'm worried about. I bite my lip, uncertainty swirling inside me. Uncertainty that's creeping into other parts of my life. Maybe pushing through this would stop it.

"I wouldn't even know where to start," I admit helplessly.

Brandon leans forward, a supportive smile on his face. "My boyfriend has an MBA and has started multiple businesses. He helped me start up the art gallery, too. I couldn't have done it without him. He was great at walking me through things step by step, so I didn't get overwhelmed. I'll bring him to dinner on Saturday, and maybe we can all brainstorm together?"

I nod, because how could I say no to that? While I'm overwhelmed, I'm also touched by their faith in me. If nothing else, their unwavering support should encourage me.

And yet, even as the games continue, I can't help feeling like I'm still drowning. In information. Doubt. Anxiety.

A second round of Apples to Apples does little to quell the storm brewing inside me, so I excuse myself abruptly and step outside for a breather.

I've taken exactly three deep breaths of the cold, clear air when Luke walks out onto the porch.

"Hey," he says, his eyes filled with concern. "I'm sorry if we overwhelmed you in there earlier. You should know you don't have to do anything you don't want to."

I take a shaky breath. "It's not that I don't want to. I'd love to. But Luke, I can barely keep track of my own life. How could I possibly run a business?"

He takes my hands in his, his touch warm and reassuring. "If you want to, you can do this, Rae. I know you can. And you won't be alone. I'm here for you and so are all our friends." He smiles fondly at the statement, and I realize I'm clearly not the only one grateful for that crazy bunch.

I'm also happy that Luke has quickly found his place here with these people. With my people. With me.

Emotion wells up in my chest, and for a moment, the air between us crackles with a palpable attraction. My eyes drop to his lips, and he takes a hesitant step forward. My breath catches in my throat as my eyes meet his again. They're dark and warm and inviting, and I sway forward.

But before either of us can act on it, Zoe interrupts, popping her head out.

"Dad, come see the new trick I taught Bruiser!"

I inhale sharply, realizing I almost crossed a line I'd sworn not to. "Go on," I encourage him. "I'll be back in soon."

"You sure?" he asks skeptically. And though the years have changed us both, I can tell he still knows me enough to know I'm still reeling. I'm touched that he clearly doesn't want to leave me. To make me feel alone.

"I'm sure," I reply firmly. "Thank you." I swiftly reach out to squeeze his hand, then let go just as quickly.

They go into the house, and I shift my gaze to the stars as I finish my breathing exercises. Once I've calmed down as much as I think I will, I head back inside.

The games have broken up and everyone is chatting and finishing off Mia's mini pies.

As I watch Luke and Zoe interact with my found family, a bittersweet mix of relief and disappointment washes over me. I can no longer deny my growing feelings for Luke, the desire for something more than friendship. Or that I wish we'd had that all along. That life hadn't torn us apart. But that's not how it happened, and no amount of wishing will change that.

Too soon, Luke takes Zoe home, citing preteen bedtime. We can only exchange casual goodbyes, surrounded as we are, but it feels like a part of my heart goes with him, along with all my unsaid words.

I settle back onto the couch and Carrie sinks down next to me.

"Hey, you," she says with a sympathetic smile that tells me she might know exactly where my head is at.

"Hey, sugar," I say, sounding every bit as tired as I am. "How's things?"

"Oh, you know, working my dream job, doing life with my dream man," she says. "So, it's all right."

We both laugh.

"And Evan? How's he adjusting to small-town life after being an international movie star?" I'd ask him, but the man's as much of a people-pleaser as Carrie, so best to get the facts from her.

She chuckles, shaking her head. "Surprisingly, he's really happy. This move has been good for him, for both of us." She pauses. "Am I allowed to ask what's between you and Luke? There's history there, right?"

I take a deep breath and nod, over keeping the truth from everyone except Mia. "He was my first everything. Then, he left. Afterward … someone told me he cheated on me and fathered a child with my best friend, but turns out it was *his* father that did the fathering …" I trail off and grimace. "That made more sense in my head."

Carrie smirks. "I got what you meant. That sounds … messy."

I give her a vague smile. "That's an understatement. Having him back has been an emotional rollercoaster, I'm not going to lie."

"I could tell," she replies honestly. I groan and tip my head back. She pats me on the arm. "Only because I know you so well. I think the only other person who suspects is Mia."

I sit upright and give her a guilty look. "I may have already told Mia."

Carrie feigns indignation. "You mean you told her first? We were *roommates*, Rae. *Roommates.*"

I laugh. "I'm sorry! I couldn't even admit to myself how messed up I've been. I had two more partners after Luke who cheated on me and between that and the fact that my daddy left my momma right after Luke left me?" I shake my head and sigh. "Honestly, I didn't realize how much it shattered me until recently. Or that I've been so afraid of ending up like my mother." It's the first time I've voiced the thought, and it underscores how little I understood why I've been feeling this way.

Carrie's blue eyes are filled with empathy. "I understand how trauma can shape you, but Rae, we're not destined to repeat our parents' mistakes. Look at Mia and me. If we were bound by our family's past, we'd be lost. But we've chosen different paths."

Just as Luke's did earlier, her words strike a chord. I've been living under the assumption that I would inevitably face the same heartbreak as my mother, but that doesn't have to be my fate.

"I can choose a different path," I say out loud. Then I laugh at the simplicity, the absolute freedom of that idea.

"Rae, if I know anything about you, it's that you are capable of so much more than you let yourself believe. I wish you saw yourself the way we do. You're strong, smart, and you have a huge heart. You could rule the freaking world if you wanted to," Carrie teases. But I can tell she believes what she's saying.

"I guess I just need to learn to believe that, too," I say.

"Hey babe, ready to go?" Evan calls to Carrie from the other side of the living room.

Carrie leans in and hugs me. "There's no rush. Stop overwhelming yourself with what you think you can or can't do and focus on what you *want*. Because I love you and I want to see you happy, okay?"

I kiss her on the cheek. "Love you, too, wise woman. Good night." And then I raise my voice toward Evan, "And good night to you, too, hot stuff."

Evan chuckles, but Joanie beats him to the punch.

"Oh good, Rae's feeling sassy again," she comments. "Now I don't have to feel bad about telling you guys to get the hell out so Greg and I can fu—"

Greg clamps his hand over Joanie's mouth in the blink of an eye. "Well, it was great having you all. Rae, I'm glad you're feeling better about things," he says with a nervous laugh.

I can't help laughing myself as I rise while Evan and Carrie hightail it out the door. "Thanks for having me. You two feel free to go at it," I say as I show myself out.

I shake my head, still laughing at Joanie as I climb into the Bronco. She may be brash, but she has an honesty about who she is that I admire.

Maybe Luke is right. Maybe they're all right. I'm surrounded by people who care about me. People with different strengths than me. People I admire, trust, and lean on. Maybe I can lean on them for this, too.

As I drive the short distance home, I feel a glimmer of hope. A sense that I can finally break free from the shadows of my past and embrace a future filled with success, happiness, and even love.

CHAPTER TWELVE

LUKE

On Friday morning, I wake with a sense of nervous excitement. And it's not because I'm meeting the rest of the town council today, though I'm glad that's finally happening.

No, I'm all worked up because of last night. Because of how close Rae was to letting me back in. I could practically taste her yearning on Greg and Joanie's porch. Not just for me to kiss her, but for me to comfort her, despite her fears. Or maybe because of them. Our attraction has always been deeper than physical. She's always gotten me, and I her. It's encouraging how quickly we're making our way back to that, but I realize now how important letting her set that pace is. I almost forgot that while I rediscovered how much she pulls me in.

I close my eyes, a swell of desire rippling through me at the memory of her lips parting with want, the moonlight gilding her hair. She was so beautiful, and I wanted to kiss her so badly. And I know she wanted it just as badly. Whatever magic existed between us all those years ago is still there. And if I thought I'd felt hopeful before …

I take a deep breath and force myself out of bed. There's no time for the kind of wallowing I want to do in those memories. If I don't get up now, I'll be late for the meeting.

I push through my morning routine quickly and encourage Zoe to do the same. On the drive to the bakery, she talks my ear off about how fun game night was, how she thinks we should get a dog just like Bruiser, and all the things she wants to do today.

The dog idea catches my attention. I've always loved dogs. I haven't had one in years, since it didn't feel right living in an apartment and working the schedule I do, but I admit I wouldn't mind it. But I don't say that to Zoe, because we're not there yet. The house isn't there yet. The yard definitely isn't there yet. And maybe I'm not *quite* there yet either. A dog is a big responsibility, and I'd like things to settle down a bit more first.

When we get to the bakery, I don't go in with Zoe like I have been. I know if I do, I'll for sure be late. Though I can't help a longing look past Zoe as she walks in, hoping to catch a glimpse of Rae. But the morning sun is reflecting off the glass front of the bakery, and I can't see much of anything.

With a sigh, I put the truck in gear and drive onward to

town hall. In a couple minutes, I've pulled in, parked, and am heading through reception. I wave hello to Meredith and head down the hall to the meeting room.

As I walk through the door, I breathe deeply to settle myself. While I already know Arthur, Brandon, and Greg, the other five members people seated around the long table don't look familiar.

To my surprise, they greet me with warm smiles and enthusiastic handshakes. I quickly realize they are all long-time residents that, with some reminiscing, I *do* remember from my childhood, because clearly, they sure remember me. And they welcome me with open arms and fond memories, assuring me they always doubted the rumors about Brandon's parentage.

"We knew you were a good kid, Luke," Janet Henderson says, patting my hand. "Never believed a word of that nonsense."

"I always said it was awfully suspicious to blame you, given that your family had just been forced to leave town after the accident," Archie Bennett adds in agreement.

"Now, now, there's no need for any of that. It's all water under the bridge," I reply, though I end up having to repeat myself in various forms as more of them jump to my defense.

I'm touched by their kindness, though I'm fully aware they're probably only saying these things to make me feel more at ease. All that matters to me is that we can all move forward now.

Arthur gives a high level of what the council's role is.

Which is to say, it's not terribly well-defined yet. They're taking things as they come and learning as they go.

Which works for me, because I have ideas of my own, including one I've been mulling over that I share with everyone — I want to offer home and business fire inspections to anyone who'd like them while we work on building the fire station, including offering a limited amount of free equipment from basics like smoke and carbon monoxide detectors, or even just batteries to more extensive tools such as extinguishers, escape ladders, and the like. It'll be a year or two before the fire station is operational, so in the meantime, I want to keep the community engaged and catch any potential issues that could save lives. After all, the town was largely built in the '70s, and fire safety standards have improved by leaps and bounds since then.

To my relief, everyone thinks it's a brilliant plan. Carrie suggests we go talk to her contact at the county next week to discuss moving forward with the fire department build process. I readily agree, feeling a sense of purpose and excitement as things finally start to move from theory and planning to action.

After the meeting, Arthur takes me to lunch, then on a tour of the town, pointing out all the new developments and upcoming projects. The townhouse complex with commercial units housing Joanie's law office, Sera's realty office, and Brandon's art gallery. A new bank and drugstore in the works. Sites that are being cleared for more housing, plots for sale that the council hopes to fill with restaurants, entertainment venues, retailers, and so much more. It's incredible to see how much Alpine Ridge is growing, and I'm thrilled to be a part of shaping its future.

When we get back to town hall, I'm standing next to my truck, ready to offer my thanks before heading over to pick up Zoe when Arthur leans toward me with a somber expression.

"Luke, there's something I need to tell you. Something I should have told you a long time ago," he says in a low voice.

I furrow my brow, concerned by his sudden change in demeanor. "What is it, Arthur?"

He takes a deep breath, as if steeling himself for a tough conversation. "I was part of the church leadership, overseeing the finances, when your father was pastor there. When … the accident happened."

My heart skips a beat at the allusion to the church fire, the memories of that painful time still raw after all these years.

"Before the fire, the church was being audited by the IRS," Arthur continues, his voice heavy. "And when I reviewed my records, I realized someone had altered them. I investigated and discovered it was your father. David had done the tampering."

The revelation punches me in the gut, knocking the wind out of me. How deep does this rabbit hole with my father's transgressions go? On some level, it's hard to believe one man could do so many bad things.

"My dad? Are you sure? I mean … I knew he wasn't … honest, but it's hard to swallow him doing something that bad." And yet, once the words are out of my mouth, it's not that hard to believe. I'm just surprised he did something with such a high risk of being caught. Though, again, that's not really a first for him either. Going so far as to tamper with records isn't that far from stealing from your congregation. Hell, they probably went hand in hand. I guess I'll never get used to learning of the awful things he's done.

Arthur nods grimly. "I confronted him about it. He said he did it for the good of the church, to avoid what little tax we would've had to pay. I pointed out that would be tax fraud, but he didn't seem bothered."

A fresh wave of disappointment washes over me. My father, who was supposed to be a man of God, who I looked up to for most of my young life, truly was a lying bastard. On levels I probably haven't even realized yet and may never even know about.

"He seemed so unbothered, in fact, that it made me realize he wasn't the man we thought we'd hired. Which, in turn, made me wonder if there were other ways he may have taken advantage of the church. So, I dug deeper," Arthur continues, his eyes filled with regret. I have to work not to flinch at whatever is about to come out of his mouth. "I found evidence of theft from the church funds that could only have been your father. I also learned there was a mortgage on the parsonage that shouldn't have existed. The house was owned by the church, funded by a group of Alpine Ridge residents, including myself, who jointly purchased the land and had both built. Your father wasn't part of that group. We hired him after completion to lead the church and we gave him use of the house so long as he held that position."

I shake my head, a sudden realization hitting me. "During the divorce, my father put the house in my name, to keep it from my mother. He said it was because she was trying to 'take him to the cleaners' as revenge for what happened to Hannah. I never knew the house was supposed to belong to the church." I'm spinning, yet again, not just from what he did, but for what this could mean for me and Zoe. How can I keep a house that was never supposed to belong to me?

Arthur sighs heavily. "We didn't know he'd somehow transferred it to his name until it was too late. Until the IRS closed the audit case shortly after your parents' divorce. I noticed their final report omitted the parsonage as part of the church's assets. It didn't take much digging with the county to discover that was because it no longer belonged to the church and hadn't for over a year at that point. And that further, it no longer belonged to your father, either.

"Between the fire, your family moving away, and the fact that your father didn't even legally own the property anymore ... well, the remaining investors and I decided to let it go. There was no hope of rebuilding the church, so what did we need a parsonage for?" Arthur twists his fingers anxiously, belying that this still bothers him as much as it does me. "There were only three of us left at that point, and the other two have since passed away. I'm the only one who knows the truth now, but I felt you deserved to know, too."

I shake my head, my mind reeling at the depth of my father's deceit. The house I grew up in, never truly ours. The life I thought I knew, built on a foundation of dishonesty. But that part's nothing new. My stomach churns with disgust and shame.

"Arthur, I ... I don't know what to say. I'm so sorry for what my father did. The house ... I can give it back to you. I *want* to give it back. If not to you directly, to the town. It's the least I can do."

But Arthur shakes his head, placing a hand on my shoulder. "I didn't tell you this to take the house back, Luke. I told you this because you deserve to know. Because you're a good man, and I know that if anyone can redeem that house, make it serve the town as it was intended, it's you. Your father's sins are not yours to bear. I trust you'll do right by Alpine Ridge. Maybe God saw that the house went to you for that very reason."

Tears prick at the corners of my eyes, the weight of Arthur's words settling over me like a warm blanket. In this moment, I feel a sense of purpose, of belonging, that I haven't felt in years.

"Thank you, Arthur," I manage, my voice thick with emotion. "I promise I'll do everything in my power to make this town proud. To be the man my father should have been but never was."

Arthur offers a small smile, a glimmer of hope in his eyes. "I have no doubt you will, Luke. No doubt at all."

We part ways and I'm so disoriented by what I've learned that have to sit in my truck for a solid fifteen minutes before I'm able to drive the short distance to pick Zoe up. But I compartmentalize it to examine it later. Right now, I have other responsibilities.

I head to the bakery, going inside before I can think about whether it's a good idea to see Rae in my current condition. But turns out she's gone for the day, anyway, so I'm spared having to worry about her seeing right through me and asking what's up. Which is good, because I'm going to need more time to process this before I talk to anyone about it.

In any case, I let Mia know I'll be gone longer on Monday for the county meeting but that I can make other arrangements for Zoe if she's not able to stay at the bakery the whole time. Much to Zoe's delight, Mia assures me it's no problem. I can't help but feel a surge of gratitude for her support and friendship. Especially given the deep hurt and confusion I'm feeling over things my father did. How can near-strangers be kinder than the man who raised me? This whole thing is messing me up badly.

We're almost home when I get over myself long enough to realize Zoe is also uncharacteristically quiet. Besides greeting me when I picked her up and a cursory "it's fine" when I asked how her day's been, she hasn't said anything since we climbed into the truck. I glance over at her, concern etched on my face.

"What's up, kiddo?" I ask gently.

She fidgets with her seatbelt, avoiding my gaze. "Nothing," she mumbles.

I frown, unconvinced. "Zoe, you know you can talk to me about anything, right?"

She nods but stays silent. I decide not to push, giving her space to open up when she's ready.

It's not until we pull up to the house that she finally speaks, her voice thick with emotion.

"Mia let me help in the front today, serving customers," she mumbles.

My heart clenches, a pang of worry shooting through me. My mind goes to the worst-case scenario: someone said something cruel about her scars. The thought brings out my papa bear instincts in a flash, but I focus on not overreacting without the facts. At the very least, I'm going to need to know who I'm going to have to have words with.

"Did something happen?" I ask carefully, trying to keep my tone neutral.

To my surprise, Zoe shakes her head. "No, nothing happened, not like you're thinking, anyway. That's the thing, Dad. Nobody here makes fun of me. Only one person even asked about my scars all day, and they were so nice about it. They told me I'm beautiful, scars and all."

Tears start to stream down her face, and I reach over to take her hand, my own eyes stinging, but my heart lifting with gratitude and relief that it's not what I thought at all.

"Then why the tears, sweetheart?"

She sniffles, wiping her nose with her sleeve. "Because I never thought I'd find a place where people didn't treat me badly because of how I look. Where my scars could make me feel closer to someone, instead of like an outsider. I don't ever want to leave here, Dad."

I swallow hard, a lump forming in my throat. I'm overjoyed that Zoe is finding acceptance and kindness here, but a part of me knows it might not always be this way. That someday, someone might not be so nice. And I wouldn't be a good parent if I didn't caution her of that, but … not right now. For now, I'm just grateful she's getting a respite from the cruelty she's faced for so long. That we're both getting a reprieve from our troubles.

That night, as I'm fixing the leaky faucet in Zoe's bathroom, my mind drifts to the future. Like her, everything that's happened since we moved here has made me appreciate this town more every day. And I can see staying here for a long time. Watching it grow. Being part of a community again. It's already begun.

So maybe it's okay to start putting down roots. Maybe it's okay to want more. Zoe deserves more. She's growing up so fast, and I know the teenage years will bring a whole new set of challenges. She hasn't even had her first period yet, and the thought of navigating that minefield alone terrifies me.

I've always felt like a part of her needed a mother

figure, someone who could guide her through the complexities of womanhood in a way I never could. But as I tighten the last screw, a realization hits me.

Ever since Zoe's mother passed, everyone questioned how I could be a single father. How could I possibly raise a daughter alone? How could I let Zoe go through life without a mother? How will *I* go through life alone? Virginia's parents, Zoe's counselors and teachers. Hell, even my own friends have all expressed these concerns over the years.

While I may not have a partner to help me raise Zoe, maybe … maybe I don't need to feel the pressure to find one anymore. Because here, I'm not alone. We have Mia and Rae, who have already unexpectedly taken Zoe under their wing, forming a special bond with her. And then there's Joanie and Carrie, both strong, kind women.

If things between Rae and I become more, and I hope they will, I'd have everything I ever wanted. But I don't need to put pressure on myself, or her, to make it become more for Zoe's sake. I can't remember the last time I pursued a woman without that thought pushing at the back of my mind. It's … a relief. And it means if it works out, it'll be for all the right reasons.

For the first time in a long time, I feel a sense of peace wash over me. Zoe will have the support and love she needs to grow into a confident, compassionate young woman. She's already well on her way. And I'll have support, too.

And maybe we'll both end up with so much more than we ever thought to hope for.

As I drift off to sleep, I say a silent prayer of thanks for this chance at a better life, for the amazing people who have welcomed us into their hearts.

Alpine Ridge isn't just a fresh start for me and Zoe. It's a chance to heal, to build something beautiful.

And I can't wait to see what tomorrow brings.

CHAPTER THIRTEEN

RAE

It's Saturday night, weekly dinner party night, and I find myself arriving late once again. And once again, with a stomach filled with butterflies. This time it's not because I know Luke will be there — well, not just because of that anyway — but also because Brandon is bringing his boyfriend with the hope that he can help me break down starting my own business into something I feel like I can actually manage.

I dig deep and walk inside, instead of giving in to my fear, running back to the Bronco, and hightailing it the hell out of here at the thought of exposing how clueless and incapable I am.

As soon as I enter, a wall of aromas hits me: tomatoes, garlic, and cheese. It reminds me of my Grams's lasagna, and I'm instantly soothed. I pop my jacket onto a hook and kick off my boots, then head into the living room. Because

I'm a big girl, and I don't have to hide in the kitchen every time my anxiety rears its anti-social head.

I'm rewarded with everyone turning my way with excited faces. "Rae!" the cheer goes up. I laugh and step down into the cozy room, packed with my favorite people.

"I know you're all just excited because that means we can eat now," I tease.

Everyone laughs.

"Damn straight," Joanie agrees from the couch. I smirk at her, and she blows me a kiss.

Then, my eyes land on Brandon, who is sitting on the love seat just beyond the couch. And then on the man next to him. As soon as they do, I can see why Brandon is so smitten. His boyfriend is unobtrusively handsome, with a thick shock of dark brown hair, lively dark brown eyes, and a warm smile topped with a well-manicured moustache that's giving off some serious Pedro Pascal vibes. But it's the fact that he's gazing adoringly at Brandon that tells me everything I need to know about my friend's new love.

"Rae, you're late to the meet-my-boyfriend party! Get your cute butt over here," Brandon calls, gesturing for me to join them. "Alex, this is Rae."

I smile and approach, perching myself on the arm of the loveseat next to Brandon. "Hi, Alex, it's nice to meet you," I say, offering a hand.

Alex reaches out and shakes it. "It's a pleasure. Brandon has told me so much about you. About all of you, really," he replies warmly.

"Well, he hasn't kept you a secret or anything, but he

hasn't exactly told us much either. So, I want to hear all about you," I respond.

Mia's voice interrupts from the arched entrance of the living room, rising over the murmur of multiple conversations. "I feel like I should have a cow bell or something, but dinner's ready."

We all laugh and head in to sit down, starting on the manicotti and salad Mia's prepared. It doesn't take long before everyone starts firing questions at Alex. Where'd you and Brandon meet? Where are you from? What made you want to open an antique shop? The questions go on for a while before Brandon good naturedly ends the barrage, though Alex seems unperturbed. Quite the opposite, actually, especially when Zoe asks him where he and Brandon went on their first date. She's such a cute kid.

And Alex is friendly and easygoing, fitting right in. I can see even more why Brandon likes him so much. And given the groans when asked to stop the impromptu game of twenty questions, I can also see why Brandon waited to introduce him to the gang. Brandon and Alex seem solid enough to handle it, though, exchanging sweet glances and smiles.

"So, is it my turn now?" Alex teases.

"You bet," Mia agrees. "Just don't ask Joanie anything."

Everyone laughs, but Alex looks puzzled. "Why not?"

Joanie smirks and raises an eyebrow, but Greg beats her to it. "Because she has absolutely zero filter, and she's just waiting to give you a raunchy nickname." Zoe's eyes widen and Greg shoots Luke an apologetic smile.

Without missing a beat, Alex turns to me. "So, Rae, Brandon tells me you're an incredible event planner. And that you're considering starting your own business?"

Laughter echoes around the room once more and even I chuckle at his hilarious handling of Greg's comment, though I also feel my cheeks flush at the compliment. "I don't know about incredible, but I do enjoy it. The business side of things is what scares me, to be honest."

Alex nods understandingly. "It can seem daunting at first, but from what I hear, you've got real talent."

I know this is why Brandon suggested he come tonight, but suddenly I'm not so sure. "I know Brandon probably asked you to talk to me about starting a business, but I don't want to dump you into the deep end —"

"Nuh uh. If you won't, we will," Joanie taunts before taking a sip of wine.

Mia shrugs. "I'm with Jo. We all want this for you, Rae."

Brandon gives me an apologetic smile. "What she said. But you've got to want it for yourself, too."

I give Alex an unsure look and he gives me a reassuring smile in return. "I'm happy to use what I know to help. Really. The business aspect isn't as complicated as it might seem. I promise." His calm demeanor and warm smile would melt a stronger woman than me.

Still, I hesitate, my doubts creeping in. "That's so kind of you, but I'm just ... I'm so scattered, always running late, constantly forgetting things. I don't know if I'm cut out for running a business."

"I highly doubt that," Alex says gently.

"Rae, you've seen me learning the ropes of owning a business at the bakery," Mia offers. "He's right. You can totally do it."

"While I appreciate the vote of confidence," I say quietly, "you have a law degree, Mia." I gesture around the table. "And Joanie runs her own business ... and also has a law degree. And Nate, too, with his medical degree. Seems like it takes some serious smarts, if you ask me."

I deflate like a balloon, but Alex just looks at me. "And I've got a bachelor's in art history and a Master's in Business." He shakes his head. "All that means is I paid a lot of money for someone to teach me things I used for the first five minutes of a real job. The rest I had to learn."

"Does that mean I don't have to go to college, Dad?" Zoe whispers to Luke.

Luke face palms and mutters, "We'll talk about it later."

"When?" she whispers back. Carrie snickers at her sass.

"In about five years," Luke hisses, exasperated.

I huff a dry laugh, then turn back to Alex. "That's easy to say when you had a good, solid foundation under you," I say tensely. "School was never my strong suit. Don't get me wrong, I tried a few community college classes after I realized I wasn't going to make it as a singer. I took some French. An accounting course. Then, when neither of those clicked, I went into the nursing assistant program."

"Really? I didn't know you were a nurse's assistant," Nate says.

I scoff. "I wasn't. You think I'm late now? You should've seen me then. I didn't finish the program, what with showing up halfway through class more often than not. So, I dropped out. After that, the only jobs I could ever keep were ones where I worked more than I didn't, and being 'late' wasn't even a thing when the only thing I didn't do was sleep there." I shake my head. "I love you all to death, and I appreciate the point you're trying to make, Alex, but I'm … different. I don't have what it takes. Not like you all." I gesture widely around the table.

Alex tilts his head, studying me for a moment. "Rae, have you ever considered the possibility that you might have ADHD?"

I blink, taken aback. "ADHD? Isn't that for kids who can't sit still in class?"

Alex chuckles. "That's a common misconception. Adult ADHD often looks a lot like what you're describing — difficulties with organization, time management, forgetfulness. There are treatments available that could help you manage it. It might boost your productivity and your confidence."

"I had a classmate with ADHD," Zoe offers. "We all knew when she hadn't taken her medication."

"How?" I ask, curious.

Zoe lifts a shoulder. "She'd show up after the bell and she wouldn't listen to a thing the teacher said. She didn't move around a lot or anything, she just seemed to daydream a lot more than usual."

I sit back, reeling at Zoe's words. Because daydreaming was my main hobby in school. And there goes my stereotype of ADHD kids being fidgety.

Could it really be that simple? Could this explain the struggles I've faced my entire life?

"I ... I never even considered that," I admit.

"I'm ashamed I never thought of it either," Nate admits. I can hear the frustration with himself in his voice. He's certainly known me the longest of those present, save Luke, of course. "If you want to come into the clinic next week, I can get you a referral for a therapist who can evaluate you."

I take a deep breath, my eyes darting around the table uncertainly. But all I see looking back at me is love and encouragement. My eyes well with tears as they settle back on Nate.

"Okay. Yes. Let's do it," I agree. Then, to Alex, "Thank you."

He smiles warmly. "Of course. I'll give you my number before I leave tonight. I'm happy to start helping anytime, in any way I can."

The conversation moves on, but I'm quiet as it does. I feel overwhelmed ... yet encouraged and supported at the same time a newfound sense of possibility taking root in my chest.

Later, as I'm helping Mia clear the dishes, Luke approaches me, his expression soft.

"Hey," he says, leaning against the counter. "That was some heavy out there. Are you okay?"

I smile as I rinse plates. "Yeah, actually. Knowing there might be an explanation for the way I am has me hopeful that I might be able to fix it."

Luke's eyes scan my face. "Understanding yourself is an important part of accepting yourself. I hope it helps you on both counts. Because there's nothing to 'fix'. You're perfect just the way you are, Rae."

I smirk. "I am, aren't I?" I ask airily.

Luke laughs, and tingles erupt over my skin. "Hey, I've been meaning to ask — how's Zoe been doing at the bakery?"

I can't help but smile, darting a glance back toward the living room to make sure she's out of earshot. Not because I have anything bad to say, but because I don't want to embarrass her with praise. "She's an absolute delight, Luke. Such a quick learner, and so eager to help. You've raised a wonderful young woman."

Pride shines in his eyes. "That means a lot, coming from you. I'm just glad it's working out. Zoe adores spending time with you and Mia, and it's been great for me to have a consistent rhythm to get things done without feeling like I'm neglecting her."

I nod, though I can't even begin to fathom the balancing act of single parenthood. I can barely handle my own needs most of the time. "It must be tough, though, getting time for yourself."

Luke shrugs. "It can be, but I manage. Actually, I've been wanting to check out this brewery in Ellensburg that Greg keeps raving about. I don't suppose you'd want to join me sometime?" He looks away, clearly feigning nonchalance. I remember that look. It means he's dying for me to say yes.

I don't know how this gorgeous, successful man could still be interested in me after all these years, but I realize … he is.

My heart skips a beat, but I force myself to play it cool. "Luke, that sounds an awful lot like a date."

He raises his hands in mock surrender, a playful grin on his face. "Hey, I didn't mean it like that. I just … I've missed spending time with you, just the two of us. The more I see you, the more I remember how much fun we used to have together."

I bite my lip, considering. The idea of an afternoon alone with Luke, away from the prying eyes of Alpine Ridge, is undeniably appealing. I miss him, too. And it doesn't have to be anything but two old friends catching up, right?

"Okay," I say at last. "Let's do it. How about the middle of next week? Zoe can hang out with Mia while we're gone."

Luke's face lights up. "Perfect. It's a plan."

As he winks and walks away, my tummy is tied in knots for a whole new reason. First over starting a business, then over a possible explanation for all the things I've struggled with my whole life, and now I've agreed to spend time with Luke. Alone. With alcohol.

I fan myself with the dishtowel, wondering how I got myself into all this. And yet, somehow, it's all a little thrilling. The possibilities. The hope. I breathe deeply, holding onto both hopes gently in my heart, praying they don't slip away like they always do. Praying that this time is different.

The next day, I find myself at my momma's house, the conversation with Alex still fresh in my mind. As we sit at her kitchen table, sipping tea, I decide to broach the subject.

"Momma, did you ever notice any ADHD symptoms in me when I was a kid?"

She frowns and sets down her cup. "Like what?"

I shrug as nonchalantly as I can. "Forgetting stuff. Being easily distracted. Difficulty being on time. That sort of thing."

She waves a dismissive hand. "Oh, Rae, that's how all kids are."

"Yeah, I guess," I agree reluctantly. "But was I … more like that than other kids?"

She shrugs. "How should I know? I only had you."

I roll my eyes. "Surely you saw how other kids behaved at some point."

She lifts her cup back to her lips, taking a slow, deep sip before responding. "It's not the same when they're not yours," she finally says. "You seemed like a normal child." She says it in a final tone. Like she doesn't want to keep talking about it.

So, I refrain from pushing. From pointing out that those traits followed me into adulthood, making everything from schooling to relationships to work more difficult than they seemed for everyone else.

Because I know my momma, I take a deep breath and change the subject.

"There was something else I wanted to talk to you about. I'm thinking about starting an event planning business. Nothing big, just enough to formalize the work I'm already doing for the town."

Momma purses her lips. "A business? You?" She eyes me skeptically with her critical gaze. "What about the bakery?"

My heart drops. "I don't know. I guess I'll have to see how well it does. But I'd keep working there, for now at least."

She huffs out a breath. "Rae, honey, you're good at planning events, thanks to your Grams, but that seems like a lot to take on. Wouldn't you rather focus on carrying on the family legacy at the bakery? Grams would be so pleased to know you brought it back to life."

I press my lips together to stop myself from pointing out it wouldn't have had to be brought back to life if she hadn't run it into the ground. That maybe she's projecting, assuming I can't run a business because she couldn't. But I don't want to be spiteful.

"Mia's doing that just fine," I reply tightly. "I may work there, but she's the one running the show. I'm just trying to find something I'm good at."

Momma pats me on the hand patronizingly as she rises to refill her cup. "Well, you are good at planning your little parties," she says condescendingly. "But, sugar, that's not a business. Don't get me wrong, it's lovely that you help the town out. That's something you can do here and there. But a whole business?" She shakes her head. "No need to get too big for your britches. Stick to what you know."

Her words hit me like a slap, and suddenly, I see the stark contrast between my momma's well-intentioned but limiting beliefs and the endless encouragement of my friends.

All my life, Momma has urged me to play it safe, to think small. But my friends? They push me to dream big, to reach for more. And maybe it's that small thinking that's been holding me back all along.

I've always thought I was just like Momma, destined to follow in her footsteps. But in this moment, I realize that perhaps we're not as alike as I once believed.

Because deep down, I know I want this. I may be forty-six, but it's never too late to go after what you want. And what I want is to build something of my own, to challenge myself and grow. And I want to explore the possibility that there might be a reason behind my struggles, that with the right support, I can learn to manage them.

I'm tired of accepting things as they are. I'm ready for more.

The next morning, I stop into Nate's clinic as soon as they open and make an appointment to get that referral. I'll have to wait two days to see Nate, but it lifts my heart to know that he is doing so well that the clinic is already struggling to accept walk-ins.

With a few minutes left on my break, I call Alex, who agrees to come to next Saturday night's dinner party early so we can start talking business.

While these are small steps, they feel monumental.

As I head back into the bakery, the sun rising behind me, the flicker of hope in my chest that started last night blooms into something more. A desire to do this. To understand myself. To see if starting a business is possible. To see if having Luke back in my life, as something more than a friend is possible. To take one step at a time toward the kind of happiness I never thought I deserved.

And for the first time in God only knows how long, I tell myself I can do this.

CHAPTER FOURTEEN

LUKE

From the moment I wake, anticipation courses through me. I'm taking Rae out today. Maybe we aren't calling it a date, but my hopes are high. The more time I've spent with her, the more I realize that everything I once felt for her is still there … and more. She's kind, and funny, and so damn sexy it literally hurts. I have to push extra hard during my morning workout to tame those particular feelings.

I know even Zoe senses something is off as we drive into town, but she doesn't say anything, jumping out as usual as soon as we park at the bakery. I trail behind, watching with a smile as she embraces Mia and Rae in turn before heading into the kitchen with Mia.

I stop just inside as Rae steps out from behind the counter. In a blue and white gingham dress with a jean jacket, she looks like a sexy, grown-up version of the proverbial girl next door I fell in love with. And never fell out, as it happens. Because the sight of her, the small smile on her face, the nervous energy as she brushes her short, blond hair behind her ear … I just want to take her in my arms and show her how much I hadn't realized I missed her.

Instead, I opt for, "Hey, Rae." I grin at her.

"Hey, Luke," she responds, her cheeks pinkening.

"You look like Spring and my teenage fantasies all at the same time," I tease in a low voice meant only for her.

She wrinkles her nose. "That's not the kind of thing you say on a not-date," she points out.

I laugh. "Did I say it wasn't a date?" She nods slowly, and I shrug. "Ready to go?"

Rae smiles and shakes her head but contradictorily says, "Definitely." She turns and leans over the counter. "Mia, we're headed out."

Mia and Zoe pop out of the kitchen. "Have fun," Mia says with a knowing smile.

"Be good, Zo," I tell my daughter.

Zoe wiggles her eyebrows. "You, too, Dad."

She disappears back into the kitchen too quickly for me to respond, so I'm left standing there with my mouth hanging open.

Rae approaches and places a finger under my chin, snapping my jaw closed. "Come on, before you catch a fly," she teases.

"She's just so sassy. Have you been giving her lessons?"

Rae smirks as we exit the bakery. "Oh, she came to us like that."

I open the truck door for her, and she raises a brow, but hops in without further comment.

With a grin, I round the truck and get in.

I was worried a half-hour-plus drive would be awkward. That it's been so long since we were alone — well, when she didn't think I fathered a child with her best friend — that we'd have nothing to talk about. But I was as wrong as could be.

As we drive, we talk easily, with Rae pointing out all the subtle changes I'd missed while I was focusing on re-orienting myself with the area and keeping Zoe entertained on the drive. New power line runs. Expanded highways and new local roads. Empty fields with "land for sale" signs where farms once existed. Subtle but telling changes of development.

By the time we walk into the tavern, it's like we've somehow both stepped back in time thirty years and brought our previous relationship forward into a new era. It's the best of both worlds. I can't help but feel a mix of nerves and excitement wondering if she feels the same way.

We settle into a booth, making small talk about the food and drinks as we peruse the menu. Once we've ordered, Rae tells me about her appointment with Nate tomorrow, to get a referral to see if she has ADHD.

"I did some reading online yesterday," I admit. "And apparently, ADHD can present differently in girls than in boys. Looking back, I think you definitely showed signs as a kid."

Rae's eyebrows rise in surprise. "Really? Like what?"

I shrug. "Like … you didn't have a lot of friends and shied away from groups. Or how hard it was to get your attention sometimes when you'd zoned out. Which you did a lot. But you never acted out, so I guess I didn't think much of it at the time."

She nods slowly. "I never acted out because I hated disappointing my parents."

The mention of her parents sparks my curiosity. I'm dismayed to realize I hadn't even thought of them since I'd returned, and she hasn't said anything about them. Given that her father was blamed for accidentally starting the fire that burned the church down, surely it affected them.

"Speaking of your parents … is it okay to ask what happened to your dad after I left?" I ask carefully.

Rae's face falls, and I immediately regret bringing it up. But she takes a deep breath and shakes her head.

"No, it's fine. As you can probably guess, the town ostracized him for starting the fire. My parents fought constantly over it, and eventually, he just … left. And my mom … well, she was a mess, especially once the divorce was finalized. Honestly, between their split and finding out that you had cheated on me and gotten Beth pregnant, I was a mess, too."

I flinch at the mention of my supposed infidelity, the old accusation still stinging even though we both know the truth now.

"I was so angry," Rae continues. "At the townspeople for how they treated my dad, at my dad for leaving us, at

Beth for what I thought she'd done, at you for … well, you know. I got into fights, vandalized property. I earned a well-deserved reputation as a troublemaker that's followed me to this day."

She shakes her head, lost in the memories. "Anyway. Without my dad's help, the bakery struggled, too. Momma had to shut it down the next year. She took a job at the grocery store, and I started working at the tavern. We barely made ends meet."

My heart aches for her, for the hardships she endured in my absence. And I can't help it. I reach out and wrap my hand over hers. She looks up, blinking rapidly against the sheen of tears in her eyes. "Rae, I'm so sorry. I had no idea it would be that bad."

She gives me a sad smile. "It's in the past."

"I'm still sorry." I pause. "Wait, the bakery closed?"

She nods. "Mia only reopened it recently. Her grandmother had bought it from my momma."

I blow out a breath, still stroking my thumb over the back of her hand. "That bakery was everything to your family. Your Great Grams must've been so disappointed."

Rae huffs a breath out of her nose. "She was devastated. But not for long. She started to lose her faculties shortly after." She sniffs deeply, clearly troubled by the memory. And I understand why. Once the bakery was gone, her Great Grams had no reason to keep going. "She passed when I was twenty. That's when I left Alpine Ridge."

I take a deep breath and nod slowly, recalling

something she'd said previously about moving to Seattle to try to make it as a singer.

"To pursue your singing career?" I prompt.

Rae nods. "I got some small gigs at clubs, but I never hit it big. And then I met my ex-husband. We wanted a family, so I had to give up on being a struggling artist. I worked full-time, and there was no room for singing anymore. And ... well, you know the rest."

"He cheated on you," I say softly, shaking my head. "Why would *anyone* cheat, much less on you?"

Rae sighs. "Turns out I couldn't have children ... but she could." She looks away.

I start to respond, my heart breaking for the dreams she lost after I left. My gut twists knowing I was probably one of them. But our food arrives before I can, and she changes the subject to Alpine Ridge's development, a topic we thoroughly discuss over our meal.

After, we decide to take a walk around downtown Ellensburg, the quaint, colorful shops and the warming spring day too inviting to deny.

We walk in silence, our hands brushing together. The tension has me so amped up I have to say *something*. "Isn't Alex's shop around here somewhere? Maybe we should drop in and say hello."

"It's closed Mondays and Tuesdays," she responds. "But he's coming to Mia and Nate's weekly dinner party again this Saturday."

"Oh yeah? That's great. He seems like a good guy.

Brandon seems happy, anyway, and that's what matters most," I reply.

Rae pauses in front of a boutique and looks at me thoughtfully. "Is it weird to have a brother? After …" She trails off, her cheeks turning red.

"After Hannah died?" I offer. She nods. "It's okay to talk about her, Rae. And no. It's not weird. I miss Hannah every day. I'd like to think she'd be excited to have another brother. I am, anyway, despite the circumstances. Brandon and I just … click." I smile down at her. "Kind of like you and me."

Rae's blush deepens, but she doesn't look away. "We always did. Even when you were just the scrawny pastor's kid." She smiles fondly at the memory. "And then you grew up."

I nod, remembering the day I came into the bakery after being away for a summer at my grandparent's house. I'd grown a good three inches, and my voice had dropped. And I remember the look on her face that day. The day she saw me as *more*.

"I've grown up even more since the last time I saw you," I point out.

Rae tips her head back and laughs. "You sure have, Luke McMillan." Her eyes trail over me and my skin hums under her gaze.

"I have to admit, part of why I came back to Alpine Ridge was the hope of spending time with you. To see if there was more than just a click."

Rae bites her lip, a playful gleam in her eye. "And? What do you think? Is there?"

I look at her. Really look at her, gazing deep into her eyes, noting her hesitation but willing her to see everything I'm feeling and can't quite put into words. Because Rae and me? We fit in a way I'd never found before her.

Back then, I was in love with her before she ever even noticed me. And I was an idiot to think I could leave a love like that behind and never look back. Because Rae's still a part of me. And she still draws me in. Possibly even more now for having been away from her so long. Too long.

Her lips part as her eyes soften. And it's the permission I didn't know I needed. I raise a hand to her cheek, stroking my thumb over the delicate skin. Her breath catches and I smile.

"So much more," I murmur, leaning in. I close my eyes and run my nose along hers, waiting for her to give me full permission. Full access to her luscious mouth.

She hesitates for a moment, and I start to think I've misread her. But then she mumbles, "Fuck it."

We both stop holding back, our lips crashing together in a kiss so heated it's almost frantic, with lips quickly giving way to tongues, hands wrapping around each other until there's not an inch of space between us. Her body molds to mine, and I groan into her mouth at the familiar feel of her in my arms.

God, I missed this. I missed her. I missed *us*.

When we finally pull apart, foreheads still touching, we're both breathless.

"So much for this not being a date," she breathes.

I chuckle. "I'm not mad about it." And then I kiss her again, slower this time, relishing the feel of her soft lips against mine.

But when we break apart this time, she pulls back, and I see uncertainty again in her expression.

"Is this a good idea?" she asks.

I run a thumb down her jawline. "Why wouldn't it be?"

She breathes in, slow and deep. "It's … I'm not good at relationships. And this one? There are bigger stakes here."

I draw my head back and furrow my brow. "Such as?"

She gives me an incredulous look. "Zoe, for starters. Don't get me wrong, I already love her to death. But I don't want her to think I'm trying to take her mother's place. And then there's you."

I huff a laugh. "What about me?"

Rae shifts uncomfortably, pushing away gently. "You seem so certain I'm what you want, but you've only been back a few weeks. You don't even know who I am now. I'm afraid you're interested in the idea of me more than who I actually am."

I reach out, taking her hand in mine. "Rae, slow down. We're just starting again. At least, I hope we are. We can take this as slowly as you need. And Zoe adores you. She'll be thrilled that we're spending more time together. And if it wasn't obvious, I'm pretty into you, too. You. The you who, yes, is still a lot like the girl I knew. But you've grown up, too," I point out. "And I see that. It's not like we haven't spent time together. Everything I've learned about who you are now has brought us to this moment. And I hope I get to keep learning about where you've been, what you want, and what we might be together at this stage of our lives. Because I'm still drawn to you, Rae. And I don't want to pretend that I don't think about you all the time anymore."

Rae takes a shaky breath. "Honestly? I think about you all the time, too." She looks up at me, stepping back in and allowing me to take her hand. "You're right. I'm sorry for being silly. I just ... I don't know how to navigate this."

I give her hand a squeeze. "For a woman with so much heart and so much talent, you're awfully unsure of yourself. Maybe you need someone to remind you every day how amazing you are."

Rae's eyes shine with unshed tears, and I realize with a pang that she probably hasn't had enough of that kind of support and encouragement.

"I do limit myself," Rae admits softly. "But no more." She lifts a hand to my face. "Do you want to go steady with me?" She bites into her bottom lip, fighting a smile.

I laugh. "I'd love nothing more than to pick up where we left off," I murmur, drawing her toward me with a finger under her chin and kissing her softly.

She pulls back with a happy sigh. "Let's look at it as starting fresh," she suggests. "I feel like there are so many things I believed to be true that weren't. About you. About myself. About life. I want to start something new. Something better."

My heart swells with ... yes, with love. Damn. I bite

back the words, determined to make sure I'm not getting caught up in the moment. But I'm filled with love for her right now. Amazed by her bravery, her honesty, and her heart.

"And I'll be right here beside you, every step of the way," I promise.

As we continue walking hand in hand, I feel a sense of rightness settle over me. I know with every fiber of my being that I'm exactly where I'm meant to be.

I can't wait to see where this journey, this new start, takes us.

CHAPTER FIFTEEN

RAE

After Luke drops me off at the bakery and leaves with Zoe, Mia corners me, her blue eyes sparkling with curiosity. "So, how was the date?" she asks, a knowing smile playing at her lips.

I feel my cheeks flush. "It wasn't supposed to be a date," I protest weakly. But then I sigh, a grin tugging at my mouth. "But yeah, it kind of turned into one. A *really* good one."

Mia squeals, clapping her hands. "I knew it! Congratulations on finally giving in to your feelings."

"My feelings. For Luke."

Mia smirks. "Did you not know? Because it was obvious, to me at least."

I raise an eyebrow. "Obvious? I've spent the last few weeks going from being angry with him to dealing with the confusing fallout of what really happened." I shake my head, trying not to dwell too much on the whirlwind that has been Luke's return to town. Because I can't deny my feelings anymore, and right now I'm tired of looking at them too closely.

Mia huffs impatiently. "Rae, even when you were furious, you still looked at him with love in your eyes. And only someone you truly love can hurt you that badly."

Her words hit me like a ton of bricks. She's right. I can't deny the truth of it. I probably do still love Luke, even though there's an enormous chunk of his life I've missed. Yet he seems like the same guy I fell for all those years ago. Despite thinking he'd done something awful, I think deep down I always knew who he was. Still, there are a lot of blanks to fill in.

"Maybe. But I don't know him anymore, not really. Though I guess I'll get the chance to learn about all of that while dating him," I muse aloud.

Mia grins. "Exactly. It's like having your cake and eating it, too."

We both burst out laughing, the sound echoing through the empty bakery, and my empty heart. Well, not so empty anymore.

The next day, I find myself sitting across from Nate in his office, nerves fluttering in my stomach as I await the referral to see a therapist about possibly having ADHD.

Nate gives me a reassuring smile. "You know, this appointment is mostly a formality for the insurance company," he says gently. Then his expression turns contrite. "But honestly, it's also a chance for me to apologize. As your friend, I feel like I should have noticed the signs sooner. I'm sorry, Rae."

"I didn't realize, how could you?" I reply dismissively.

He shrugs. "I'm a doctor. It may not be my specialty, but I should've picked up on it."

"Don't beat yourself up," I say. And then I add nervously, "Do you think I really have ADHD?"

Nate leans forward, clasping his hands. "You have all the hallmarks — difficulty being on time, getting easily distracted, feeling overwhelmed and anxious, among other things. But most adults with ADHD are so used to masking their symptoms to appear 'normal' that they don't even think about it."

I lean back in the surprisingly comfortable office chair opposite Nate's old oak desk and absorb that. "Masking," I repeat. "That's … yes, that fits." I nod, mostly to myself. The pretending to be paying attention. Setting a slew of alarms to be on time so nobody would realize how hopeless I was at keeping to a schedule. Forcing myself into social situations that sent my anxiety spiraling, all while pretending to have fun. "So, what will the therapist … do?"

Nate smiles patiently. "If seeing a therapist is too daunting, that's okay, Rae. These days, lots of people self-diagnose," he assures me. "But all a therapist will do is ask questions to confirm the diagnosis and maybe make you fill out some questionnaires. The real benefit to going the official diagnosis route is access to treatment. Though it can take time to dial in what works for you. But even just having an official diagnosis and the treatment options that go with that can give you a mental health boost."

Nate looks down at a form, checking a few boxes and then signing the bottom before handing the top copy to me. "Here's your official referral. We'll fax a copy to the therapist's office this afternoon and they should be contacting you within a few business days. That'll give you some time to think about whether you want to proceed."

I let out a breath, grateful that he understands my reticence. But anxiety aside, I've already made my decision. "Thanks, Nate."

"Anytime," he assures me, rising and walking me out to the waiting room. He leans in and drops his voice. "I'd give you a hug, but then everyone else would want one, too." He winks at me and straightens up.

I chuckle. "No worries, I'll just go get one from your wife," I tease with a wink back.

Nate laughs and waves goodbye, heading back toward his office.

I leave, referral in hand, feeling supported and relieved. I'm finally walking the path to understanding myself better.

Am I anxious about convincing a complete stranger how badly I struggle sometimes? Honestly, yes, I am. But you can't be courageous without fear. And I seem to have somehow finally found my courage.

At the end of the day, Luke stops by the bakery a bit earlier than expected. Zoe and Mia are still in the kitchen formulating some new cupcake concoction.

"You're early," I say after sending Janet on her way with her daily chocolate chip muffin.

He grins, leaning over the counter. And since Janet was the only customer left, I lean in and meet his mouth with mine. Warmth floods me as his lips work against mine, his tongue lightly teasing me.

When he pulls away, I have to take a moment to compose myself. It's been a damn long time since I've been kissed period, much less in a way that makes me dizzy. I remember long make-out sessions with Luke when we were teenagers but even kisses while on the giddy high of first love don't compare to how his kisses make me feel now. If it's any indicator, Luke has developed some incredible skills and I'm trying very hard not to think about what kind. I'm determined to take this slowly.

But then, I was determined not to date him at all. I give what I'm sure must be a dazed smile as I fill a cup full of decaf for Luke and hand it over.

"So, how was your day?" I ask, knowing he'd started interviewing architects.

Luke runs a hand through his gray-streaked dark blond hair. "Boring as hell. And not nearly as important as your meeting with Nate. How'd it go?" He takes a sip of coffee and gives an appreciative rumble that makes me shiver.

I blink a couple of times while I try to remember his question. Oh. Yeah.

"It was good. I've got the referral. They're supposed to call me in a few days."

"Is there a reason you're waiting for *them* to call *you*?"

I chew on my lip. "I … no. There's no reason. I'll call them once I'm off." I nod resolutely.

"Good. You deserve answers."

I lift my chin. "I do, don't I."

Luke laughs, and the sound warms me from the inside out. "Look at you, already more confident. And I haven't even told you how gorgeous you look today," he murmurs, his eyes scanning down my powdered-sugar-covered apron.

I snort. "Got a thing for hot messes?" I tease.

Luke smirks. "Got a thing for you, Rachel Donovan."

I blush hard at the suggestive look on his face.

"I don't remember you blushing so much," he says slyly.

And I blush harder. "I'm just flushed. Hormones." I shrug even though I know I'm not convincing anyone.

"Hormones," he repeats skeptically.

"You've never heard of perimenopause? Hot flashes? Sweating?" I know I sound nervous because I am. And I also know he sees right through me.

Luke chuckles and sets his coffee down on the counter, pulling me forward by the hand and running his nose down the column of my neck. Shivers erupt across the sensitive skin and my whole body flushes with heat.

"Then why does it happen when I do this?" he murmurs huskily against my skin, kissing just under my ear.

"Definitely hormones," I mumble, craning my neck to

give him better access. He chuckles against my skin and the warm puff of air has me tingling all over.

We hear feet shuffling and voices coming toward the kitchen door and we spring apart.

"To be continued," he promises.

I bite into my bottom lip to hold back a grin as Zoe emerges and gives Luke an earful about her day. He manages a quick thanks to Mia and a brief goodbye before she's tugging him toward the truck, still chattering nonstop.

He's such a wonderful dad. And she's such an amazing kid. I can't screw this up.

As the week goes on, Luke makes a habit of coming early to pick up Zoe so we can talk. It's hard to get in much besides how our days are going, so we end up texting between things late into the night until it's time for bed. Apparently, texting is easier, since talking on the phone with Zoe around is nearly impossible. Like most twelve-year-old girls, she's — in Luke's words — nosy as hell. I correct him that she's got an inquisitive mind, which is a good thing.

Still, texting it is. Which I've never been big on, but it's a surprisingly good way to ask random questions about his life, and vice versa. I learn about his time in the military after high school. How he hasn't talked to his mom since his sister's death. That one gets me, and I can't help asking how she could walk away from her other child. He says he doesn't know, but he suspects it has to do with his dad, and the fact that Luke himself made sure it wasn't easy to find him so that once he cut contact with his dad, he couldn't be sucked back in.

Still, his family situation pulls at my heart. Then again, it's not like mine's any better. Even though our fathers had very different roles in the fire and what came after, it seems the results for their families were equally disastrous. It's strange bonding over shared pain like that, but … cathartic. It's not something I even share with folks who don't know, much less feel like they could ever understand. But Luke does.

It's not all heavy, either. I learn his favorite food is takeout Chinese. When he can find the time, he loves rock climbing — in nature, not at a gym. And his goal has long been to become a fire chief, to look after a town, city, or even county to ensure the safety of as many families as he could.

Apparently, after training in first response, rescue, and firefighting in the military, he used the GI bill to go to school for occupational safety and leadership, then started working his way up the ranks of the Seattle Fire Department. But chief always eluded him. While the guys are used to working as a team, according to Luke, they can be savage in competing for promotions. And Luke is many things, but cutthroat is not one of them.

We must send hundreds of messages over the week. He asks to see me on Friday night, but Saturday is an early day at the bakery, so I have to decline.

> I have to be at work at 4 am. But I'll see
> you tomorrow night at Mia and Nate's,
> right?

His reply is swift.

LUKE

You bet your sweet ass.

I chuckle.

> If anyone around here has a sweet ass,
> it's you. I can't wait to see it in uniform.

I watch the dots bounce on the screen, biting my thumb nail as I sink under the covers and switch off the light.

LUKE

I'd much rather you see it out of uniform.

I nearly swoon at the response and my whole body flushes with heat once more. It's been happening more and more these days, but Luke has a next-level ability to trigger it.

> That image isn't going to help me sleep.

LUKE

Mmm. I can think of a few things that
could, but you won't come over.

I fan myself with one hand as I respond with the other.

What's gotten into you?

LUKE
You don't like it?

My insides tighten at the response I can almost hear him whispering in my ear. God, this man is going to be the death of me tonight.

You know I do.

Or maybe he doesn't remember how much I liked it when he'd whisper those sorts of things to me as we made love. If he even remembers. Because I sure do. Clumsy and unskilled as our trysts may have been, he always had a knack for getting me so worked up I could barely think straight. Clearly, he hasn't lost it.

LUKE
Do I? It's been a while. I think I need you to remind me what you like and how you like it.

God. Damn.

This is taking it slow?

But as soon as I send the message, I know what he's going to say. Because clearly, he's in that kind of mood.

LUKE

Oh, I'd be happy to take it very slow with
you. I've got all night, Rae.

Forget fanning myself. I throw off the covers and get out of bed, cracking the window open to let the chilly night air in. I'm tempted to strip, too, but I don't want any reminders of being naked, and what can happen in that state.

You're playing dirty. And don't make that
sexual!

I chuckle as I lay back down, my feverish skin finally cooling under the icy breeze from outside. My phone buzzes, so I lift it back up.

LUKE

Fine. I'll be good. For now. Sleep well,
beautiful.

I grin, putting my phone on the charger and closing my eyes. I'll bask in this part while it lasts. Because we'll either keep getting to know each other, and we'll get there eventually, or ... well, I don't want to think about the alternative. I don't want this to end in disaster like every other relationship I've ever had. Because it's been a long time since I've even let myself take this chance. All I can do is hope it's worth it.

The next evening, I arrive at Mia and Nate's house even earlier than I told Mia I'd be meeting Brandon and Alex there. More than a little proud of myself for managing it, I knock but get no response, so I let myself in, as we're always told to do.

When I step inside, Mia's voice floats down the hall. "But what if the tests say —"

"Don't what if this," Nate interrupts. "Whatever the results are, we're in this together. And no matter what, I love you. Understand?"

I pause, holding my breath as I realize they must be discussing their visit to the fertility specialist. I knew they'd headed there after the bakery closed early yesterday, but I'd forgotten until just now.

Not wanting to intrude, I quietly reopen the front door, then loudly slam it closed, calling out a greeting. "Hey guys, I'm here!"

Mia's head pops out of the kitchen. "Rae! You're early!"

I leave my coat and shoes at the door, trekking down the hall to join her. One look at her puffy eyes tells me she has, indeed, been what-iffing herself to death. I haul her into my arms and squeeze her tight. "Hey, sugar. You okay?"

Mia squeezes me back. "I'm … no, not really."

I let go, holding her at arm's length. "Let's cook and you can tell me all about it."

Mia smiles at me gratefully and, with some prompting, tells me about their visit. Which is to say, not much. They were informed of the full barrage of testing that is their routine, but Mia clearly took that to mean they'd already concluded something was horribly wrong with her. I gently insert that I went through this, too, and that it's all standard. That this doesn't mean anything is wrong with her, and to do what they say and hope that it'll show an easy fix. Because it very well may. And that I'd happily cover for her that day at the bakery, and she shouldn't worry about a thing.

By the time the roast is in the oven, Mia is clearly doing better. We're getting started on side dishes when I hear voices at the door heralding Brandon and Alex's arrival.

I step out of the kitchen to go meet them only to run into Nate, who I quickly realize had probably never stopped listening after he left the kitchen.

"Thank you," he mouths, his eyes darting toward Mia.

I shake my head to say that there's nothing to thank me for, then I pull the big, muscly lug into a hug of his own. And damn if he doesn't hug me back just as hard. I pat him on the shoulder reassuringly before heading toward Brandon and Alex.

"Hi, guys," I greet them enthusiastically, suddenly excited for what's coming.

"Rae, darling, you look fabulous as always," Brandon says, kissing me on my cheek.

I pinch his cheek in return. "You're my favorite."

"And I'm here to give him a run for his money," Alex teases, pulling me in for a hug.

"Oh good, you're a hugger," I reply, squeezing him back. "Why don't we go into the living room?"

We troop down the hall and settle around the coffee table. As usual, there's a fire roaring in the fireplace, making the room warm and cozy. I sit on the floor at the corner of the table, flexing my bare toes in the long, cushy pile of the plush beige rug.

Alex settles down and pulls a laptop out of his bag, opening it up on the coffee table so we can all see.

"So, before we get into it, I just want to say that you should think of the business plan as mostly for you at this point. Your first plan doesn't have to be long or detailed. It's more a way for you to organize your thoughts and get an idea of what it would take to do what you're thinking about doing and then decide if you want to keep going. Make sense?"

I tip my head to the side. "Yes, actually, and that sounds way less scary than I thought."

Brandon chuckles. "Alex can make anything approachable."

Alex gives Brandon a loving smile. "I wish. You're just smitten with me."

Brandon grins. "Damn straight." He leans over and gives Alex a sweet, chaste kiss.

"Aww, you two are just too damn cute. Can we focus now?"

They both look at me in shock. "Are you already on meds?" Brandon jokes. "Because *you* just told *me* to focus."

I laugh. "I'm not, though maybe soon. And to be fair, if my boyfriend were here, I'd probably have trouble focusing, too."

Brandon raises a brow. "Boyfriend?"

Shit.

I smile innocently and turn back to Alex. "So, you were saying about the business plan?"

Alex looks between us for a moment as if trying to decide which one of us to side with.

"Yes, the business plan," Alex finally agrees, turning the computer toward me. "I'm going to cut to the chase so as not to overwhelm you. Before you can start, there are five questions you should answer."

I arch a brow. "You're giving me homework?"

He shrugs. "I mean, yes? Even if you know the answers now, it would still be good to think about them and actually write out your reasoning, since they'll be the core of the rest of the plan."

I shrug. "Okay, Yoda, show me the ways of the force."

Brandon snorts and Alex turns the screen to me, reading the questions aloud. They really are simple, but I see how they'll be key to making a plan.

"What is your service and why is it unique?" he reads. "The former is a straightforward answer, but I'd encourage you to really think about the latter part. Maybe even look around at what other event planners do, that sort of thing."

I nod, pulling out my phone and taking notes. I glance up at the next question. "Who will be my customers? At least that one's easy."

Alex nods. "And the one after, too — how will you reach your customers? You're lucky in that your business is serving an existing customer. Though if you decide to expand, you'll want to revisit that question."

My eyebrows fly up. "Whoa there. One thing at a time."

"Sorry," Alex says sheepishly. "I don't want to overwhelm you, but honestly, if you're going to have a business, it's better to plan for growth from the start than pretend like it could never happen."

"Straight facts," Brandon says in agreement.

I blow out a slow breath. "Okay. Noted." I can do this. I. Can. Do. This.

"Next question: how will you make money?" Alex reads, then turns to me with a thoughtful expression. "Have you made money on the events you've run so far?"

I shake my head. "We don't charge attendees, so no. But honestly … since my friends often end up pitching in, I've thought about what I would have to charge to have the events pay for themselves, at least, so they didn't have to keep dumping their own money in. So even though it'll be the town paying, I have some idea of what I'd need to charge."

Alex nods. "That's a great start. Have they talked to you about payment for your services?" he asks.

I lift a shoulder, fighting against the discomfort of a lifetime of authority figures and employers telling me never to discuss compensation. "Arthur paid for everything for the St. Patrick's Day event and I received a non-employee compensation check that was way more than I thought I deserved," I admit.

Alex's eyes narrow. "We're going to talk industry rates at some point. But I'm glad they're clearly willing to pony up the necessary cash."

I huff a laugh. "Now I just have to get used to talking about money," I mumble.

"You're going to have to get comfortable talking about a lot of things," Brandon adds. "But not all right this second, so tell that anxiety I can see on your face to shut the fuck up."

This time I full-belly laugh. "Damn, B, you just said a mouthful." I shake my head, wiping away tears of laughter. "I'll work on it. All of it."

Alex smirks. "Which brings me to the last question: what does your team look like?" He pauses. "I know your friends have pitched in, but if you're going to run a business, you need employees, not just friends."

My heart sinks. This. This is the part of running a business that really freaks me out. I'm so used to doing everything myself, only allowing others to pitch in under very carefully controlled circumstances. But hiring and managing people I don't already know and trust? I can already feel my anxiety levels jumping back up.

"I take it by your silence that this is the hardest one," Alex says delicately. I nod, unable to respond with words, to explain. "Allow me to offer a solution?"

My brows bunch together. "What do you mean?"

Alex's eyes dart to Brandon, who has an equally

confused look on his face. Alex clears his throat. "If you're open to a business partner, I would be interested."

My jaw drops. "You're joking," I gasp.

"I'm not," Alex says plainly. "The antique shop is practically running itself these days. I'd been thinking about opening another here, but it doesn't feel like Alpine Ridge is quite ready for that. So, in the meantime, I'd love to have a heavier hand in your event planning business. You bring the event planning experience, I bring the business experience. And we can learn from each other as we go." He darts another nervous look at Brandon. "And that means I can be here more. So, you'd really be doing me a favor."

Brandon stares at Alex, and by the heave of his chest I can tell he's close to hyperventilating. I lean back, unsure if he's upset or … Brandon launches himself at Alex and gives him a full-on, open-mouthed kiss.

Okay, he's happy.

I chuckle with relief.

They break apart and Brandon caresses Alex's face. "You'd do that for me?"

Alex swallows hard. "For us," he breathes. Then, to me, "And for you, Rae. I feel strongly that I could be there to help you get off the ground … and slowly fade out when you're ready for me to. Does that sound like it would work for you?"

Now it's my turn to be speechless. So, I take a cue from Brandon, knocking Alex over with a hug. Brandon and Alex both laugh.

"I'll take that as a yes," Alex murmurs in my ear as Brandon joins in on the hug.

I nod, tears brimming over. "Yes," I choke out. "Thank you."

"Are we having a hug party?"

I barely have time to look up before a smaller body crashes into us and Zoe joins our pile.

I pull back, laughing as I wipe the tears away to find Luke standing in the entryway to the living room, looking unsure.

I grin and gesture for him to join us. "Alex and I are going into business together," I explain.

Luke's brows jump in surprise. "Really? That's … wow, that's great. Congratulations to you both," he says, reaching over and shaking Alex's hand.

There's not much time for talk as the rest of the gang arrives and the house fills with laughter and lively conversation. Followed by even more over another amazing meal from Mia, followed by the cupcakes that Mia and Zoe perfected this week.

Everyone praises Zoe's creativity at the flavor combination — lavender, lemon, and blueberry. She beams under the praise, and I'm so damn proud of her. She's already a better baker than I ever was, which I tell her. Her surprised look and wobbly lip tell me that my approval means something to her. The realization is simultaneously flattering and heavy. Because I'm seeing her father now. I brush off thinking about the implications of it, which is good, because everyone has already moved on to discussing what they want to do after dinner.

I help Mia clean up and miss most of that conversation. That is, until I vaguely hear Carrie make a comment to Evan, the only part of which I pick up is my name, causing Evan to turn to me with a mischievous grin.

Oh, no. I'm not sure I like whatever's going to happen next. I look at him warily.

"Rae, darling," Evan says winningly, sidling up to me and slinging an arm over my shoulders. "We're thinking a little after-dinner music would hit the spot. And it's been brought to my attention that it's been way too long since we sang together."

I blanch, totally surprised. We did one duet forever ago, that I hadn't even remembered until now.

I look at him skeptically. "Now? Really?"

But then Zoe pipes up, her eyes wide and pleading. "Please, Rae? I want to hear you sing!"

Well, damn. How can I say no to that face? "Okay, okay," I relent. "One song."

Evan rubs his hands together gleefully. "How about 'Don't Know Much'?"

I snort. "Too serious. Let's do 'Don't Go Breaking My Heart' instead."

He laughs. "Okay," he agrees, then leans in and stage whispers, "But your age is showing."

I swat at him playfully. "Shush. That song came out the year I was born. It's a classic."

We launch into the duet, our voices blending together

like they were made to harmonize, just as before. And I'm once again blown away that Evan is a handsome, talented actor and an amazing singer. It seems like too much for one person to be good at.

As we sing, I lose myself in the music, memories of belting out tunes with my hairbrush as a microphone while imagining my bright future as a famous singer flooding back.

When we finish, the room erupts into cheers and applause. Zoe bounces up and down, grinning from ear to ear.

"Wow, Rae! You should have been a superstar!"

Her words simultaneously thrill and sting, a bittersweet reminder of the dreams I once chased. Still, I smile and take a little bow, basking in the warmth of my friends' praise.

Joanie suggests we do full karaoke in the living room, and Evan can't get there fast enough, taking most of the gang with them, including Zoe who, if she wasn't smitten before she knew he could sing, too, may now never leave his side.

While I stay to help finish clearing out plates, Luke appears, his hand grazing the small of my back. He tilts his head towards the dining room, and I follow him in, curiosity blooming in my chest.

Once we're alone, he turns to me, his brown eyes soft and filled with wonder. "Zoe's right, you know," he says quietly. "Your voice is even more beautiful than I remember." He reaches up, tucking a strand of hair behind my ear.

"You don't have to say that," I admonish him.

"Even if it's true?" He smiles down at me, his eyes full of emotion. "Do you remember when you used to sing to me, Rae? Because I do."

I swallow hard, nodding. It was his favorite kind of foreplay. We'd find an empty field and lay a blanket on the grass. I'd sing while we watched the stars. Then we would make love. A fact I hadn't remembered until just now. And suddenly I'm feeling very weak in the knees.

"I still dream about those nights under the stars," he admits. "And somehow you're even more beautiful now than you were then."

"Luke." I can't tell if his name on my lips is a protest or a plea.

"Rae," he whispers as his lips capture mine in a slow, sensual kiss. I melt into him, my hands coming up to rest on his broad chest. The rest of the world falls away, narrowing down to just the two of us, lost in a moment of pure, perfect bliss.

"Ahem."

We spring apart at the sound of a throat clearing. Zoe stands in the doorway, a huge, triumphant grin on her face.

"I knew it!" she crows. "I knew you two liked each other!"

Heat rushes to my cheeks, and I bury my face in Luke's shoulder, mortified at being caught making out like teenagers.

"We do," Luke admits. "Is that okay?"

"Okay?" Zoe asks incredulously. "That's *awesome!*"

Luke chuckles and I manage to beat back my mortification enough to lift my head and offer Zoe a feeble smile. "Did you need something, Zoe?"

Zoe gives me her most winning smile. "Will you come sing some more, please?"

My smile broadens as my anxiety relaxes. "Sure thing, sugar. I'll be right there."

"Yes!" Zoe cries triumphantly, turning tail and heading back to the living room.

Luke kisses the side of my head as I stare at the spot where Zoe was standing. "See?" he says. "She's thrilled."

I turn and look at him. And the happiness on his face hits me right in the heart. I realize in this moment that despite his reassurance, I was still afraid she might object to me and Luke being together. But the sheer joy that was radiating from her tells a different story. She's happy for us.

And just like that, one more piece of the puzzle clicks into place. With Luke by my side, Zoe's approval, and the unwavering support of my friends, I feel like all of the hurts of the past are being healed by the joy of the present.

Luke and I can do this slowly, and I don't have to fear a relationship with him. Zoe isn't worried about me taking her dad's attention away or seeming like I'm trying to be a mother figure. And Alex, in what should qualify him for sainthood, has offered to start a business with me, meaning I won't have to do this alone. I feel like in this new world, there's nothing holding me back. Nothing I can't do. And everything to look forward to.

CHAPTER SIXTEEN

LUKE

Spending time with Rae every day when I pick up Zoe from the bakery has quickly become the highlight of my days. On Wednesday, we don't get to spend as much time together as usual since Rae is covering for Mia. But on Thursday, Mia makes it up to us by giving us some extra time alone.

We decide to go on a walk, our hands intertwined as we stroll down Main Street. Spring is in full bloom, and the evergreen hills are dotted with budding maples, cottonwoods, and willows; shades of bright greens splayed over deep emeralds, contrasted against the clear blue sky. Rae looks beautiful in a flowy green polka dot dress that shows off her toned calves.

The conversation flows easily between us, ranging from who is the better cook — we agree it's her, since my attempts to cook for Zoe and me have been feeble at best — to how we hope all the changes to the town shape its character — with both of us hoping that more families with kids move in and bring new life and energy with them.

At one point, Rae turns to me, her hazel eyes sparkling with curiosity. "What's it really like being a firefighter?" she asks. "I mean, beyond the hero stereotype."

I take a deep breath, considering my response. "It has its ups and downs," I admit. "Obviously, there's a lot of good — saving people, their homes, their livelihoods. But it's not all about saving people and rescuing kittens from trees."

I go on to explain how, everywhere I go, I can't help but notice potential fire hazards. Lit candles left unattended, missing or non-functional smoke detectors, blocked fire exits I feel compelled to clear. It's a constant state of vigilance that I can never quite turn off.

"And sometimes," I continue, my voice growing quieter, "in my dreams, I can't unsee some of the horrors I've witnessed on the job."

Rae squeezes my hand, her expression sympathetic. "But you bear that burden so that others don't have to," she points out softly. "Luke, I'm so proud of you for turning a tragedy into a lifelong career of helping people."

Her words wrap around my heart like a warm blanket. She understands, perhaps better than anyone, the impact of the fire that changed the course of my life.

I clear my throat, needing to be fully honest with her. "The reality is, being a firefighter can be hard on relationships, too," I confess. "The crazy shifts, the danger, the emotional toll ... it's a lot for someone to handle."

Rae stops walking and turns to face me fully, her hand coming up to cup my cheek. "We can deal with that when we get there," she says firmly. "Together."

"You said *when*," I point out, my heart expanding at her obvious message: she's in this for the long haul. I already knew I was but hearing her talk that way does things to me.

She grins. "Yeah. I did."

In this moment, gazing into her eyes, I know with absolute certainty that I love her. That she's the one that got away all those years ago, and I'm sure as hell not letting that happen again.

But I hold back the words, not wanting to overwhelm her when we're supposed to be taking things slow. Instead, I lean down and capture her lips in a tender kiss, pouring all my unspoken feelings into showing her. As she kisses me back passionately, I can't help but feel like this can't be real. It's just too good to be true.

On Friday, as I'm going over the architect's notes for the new fire station schematics, my phone rings with an unfamiliar number. I mentally note that's a firefighter tic I didn't mention — I never let calls go to voicemail in case it's an emergency. So, I pick up.

"Hello?"

"Luke? It's ... it's your mother."

I nearly drop the phone in shock. "Mom?" I manage, my voice strangled.

She takes a shaky breath. "I got your letter. I wrestled with whether to respond, but... I decided you deserved to know the whole story. The truth about why I left your father."

My chest tightens with anticipation and old hurt as I listen to her explain what really happened the night the church burned down. How Rae's father caught her mother having sex with my father in the church. How the two men fought, knocking over a candle, which started the fire. How my father threatened Rae's dad into silence, forcing him to go along with the story that Chet accidentally started the fire by flicking his cigarette butt into the bushes in front of the church.

She also confirms what Brandon and I discovered — that my father was the one who got Beth pregnant, not me. Apparently, he paid her off and got her to blame it on me during their divorce proceedings, which is how my mother found out. Her lawyer also uncovered evidence of my father skimming from the church's tithe for years.

I'm not surprised by my father's actions, having known him for the fraud and liar he is. I share with my mother how Arthur had already figured out the financial misdeeds.

"Thank you for telling me all this," I say sincerely. "But Mom … why did you never reach out before? After the divorce, after I joined the military … I thought …" I trail off, unable to voice the abandonment I'd felt.

"Oh, Luke," she sighs, her voice thick with tears. "I tried. The divorce gave me visitation, but your father blocked me at every turn. And then you were off serving, and I couldn't find you. I assumed … I thought maybe you didn't want to be found. That you were angry with me for leaving. I'm sure your father spun it that way."

"He did," I confirm. "But I never believed him. And I'm not angry, Mom. Not anymore. I understand now, and … I'd really like to have a relationship with you, if you're open to it."

"I want that more than anything," she whispers.

We end the call with tentative plans to meet up soon, and I lean back in my chair, absorbing everything she revealed. On one hand, I feel a sense of relief, a few more missing pieces of the puzzle clicking into place. But on the other …

My father was responsible for the fire that ended up killing my sister. And he used God only knows what against Chet to get him to take responsibility. Probably convincing him that nobody would believe him over their pastor. Chet had a reputation for cheating. On his wife. People out of their money. Even at simple card games. He was an easy target for my piece of shit father.

Sadly, none of that is what's really upsetting.

What I'm really worried about is Rae.

God, how am I going to tell her about her mother's role in the fire? The implications are staggering, the potential fallout for our burgeoning relationship terrifying.

But she deserves the truth, no matter how painful.

With shaking hands, I text her, asking if I can come over tonight. She agrees readily, and I call Brandon to see if he can watch Zoe for the night. He agrees, asking that I drop her off at his place. She'll be thrilled. Rae? She'll be devastated. I scrub my hands over my face, steeling myself for my world to potentially come crashing down around my ears in a few hours.

When I get out of my truck at Rae's place, I stand staring at the small, quaint house. All I can think is that I never wanted to see her home for the first time under these circumstances. I'd pictured coveted time alone. Dinner. Conversation. And, honestly, taking her to bed.

As soon as Rae opens the door, her face falls at what I'm sure is my somber expression. The first words out of her mouth are, "Luke? What's wrong?"

"Can I come in?" I ask.

She frowns, but steps back. "Of course."

I step inside into the living room. It's cozy and eclectic, with bright colors and interesting art, and it smells like sugar and vanilla. Or maybe that's just Rae.

I guide us to the couch and take a deep breath, steeling myself. "I'm not sure if I mentioned, but after I spoke to my father about Brandon, I … well, I tracked my mother down and sent her a letter."

Rae puts a hand on my knee, which I cover with my own. "You didn't. Did she respond?"

I nod. "She called me today." I give her a wary look. "You're not going to like what she had to say."

Rae lifts her chin. "Don't handle me with kid gloves, Luke. Give it to me straight."

I huff out a humorless laugh. "Okay." And I do. I tell her exactly what my mother told me about the night of the fire. About her parents.

Rae listens in stunned silence, her face growing paler with each revelation. When I finish, she stands abruptly, pacing the small living room.

"I can't … I don't …" She shakes her head, pressing her hands to her temples.

"I know," I agree. "It's a lot."

"It's … I can't believe it," she mutters.

I grab her hand as she paces by me. "I understand that. And maybe …" I quickly go back over my mother's claims. "Maybe my mother only knew what my father told her. I don't know when she got there that night and what she did or didn't see, or if it was just her lawyer that told her. Maybe you should talk to your mother about it. Ask her what the truth is."

Rae continues her pacing, shaking her head. I don't feel ignored. I can tell she's completely overwhelmed by this. After a few minutes, I rise, and she stops abruptly before she runs into my chest.

"What do you need from me?" I ask gently, aching to touch her but not wanting to add to her turmoil.

She shakes her head again. "I don't know. I … I think I just need some space. To process all of this."

My heart sinks, but I nod in understanding. "Of course. Take all the time you need." I press a kiss to her forehead. "I'm here when you're ready to talk, okay?"

She gives me a brittle smile, and I let myself out, my mind whirling with worry and what-ifs.

As I drive home, I can't shake the feeling that just when things were finally falling into place, the secrets of the past have once again thrown us into chaos. I can only hope that, once she's had some time to process this, Rae and I will weather the storm together.

Because I'm not giving up on us. Not now, not ever.

CHAPTER SEVENTEEN

RAE

I'm overwhelmed. My mind is spinning with the implications of what Luke just told me about my mother's role in the church fire. I feel like an asshole for shutting him out, but I just need some space to think this through. Though my head is already full of thoughts and starting to ache. But I can't stop now that I'm spiraling.

Hearing that my mother cheated on my father with Luke's dad, causing the fire and everything after … that would change everything. I've looked up to her my whole life. I knew my dad was no saint, and that they'd had problems, but they always seemed to make it work. Until they didn't.

Unfortunately, if this is true … well, it would make my father's actions after the fire make so much more sense. The anger, the fighting with Mom. And thinking more on it, I can see my mom cheating, knowing that my father was unfaithful, too. She may want to put on a proper front to save face, but I've seen glimpses of her selfishness before. I just thought everyone had a bit of that. But could it really run this deep?

I don't even know if Mrs. McMillan was there or if this is all just hearsay, even if it fits. I'm so upset that I know I need to talk this out with someone before I confront my mother and say all the wrong things.

I consider talking to Mia or Carrie, but that doesn't seem quite right. Maybe Nate, since he's known me so long? But that doesn't feel right either. None of my friends really understand everything I've been through, and I don't want to relive it all on top of this.

Then it hits me. It's Luke who has known me the longest, who understands what this all means to me. Who was there when it happened and has also suffered the fallout. Though after all but kicking him out, it would be selfish to bring him back just to dump my feelings on him. Especially since he's going through it, too. But mostly? I'm worried it'll strain what we've rebuilt. A relationship that is already resting on the unsteady foundation of the ashes of our shared past.

Caught in my own anxieties, I do nothing but pace and worry and cycle through the same negative thoughts, spiraling until I'm too exhausted to continue. Then, feeling overwhelmed and alone, I lie down and cry myself to sleep.

I wake to my six a.m. alarm with swollen eyes and a scratchy throat. I know I'm not really sick, it's just from crying, but either way I'm in no state to deal with my perky best friend-slash-boss and demanding customers. So, I decide to do something I've never done while working for Mia and call in sick.

"Hey, Rae, what's up?" Mia answers, sounding distracted. I hear shuffling that sounds like pans going into the oven.

"I'm so sorry to do this to you, sugar, but I'm not feeling up to coming in today," I say, sounding every bit as awful as I feel. Emotionally, anyway.

"Oh, Rae, you sound horrible," Mia replies. "Of course, don't worry about it."

"I'm sorry to leave you in a lurch," I apologize sincerely.

"Gosh, no, I'll be fine. I'm sure Carrie or Joanie can come pitch in. You just focus on feeling better. I can drop off some food for you on my way home if you want, since you obviously won't be making it over for dinner?" she offers.

And now I feel even more like an ass. She's too good to me. But I know even if she had all the facts, she'd probably still say the same. I'm lucky to have a friend like her.

"I'm good here, don't you bother about me," I assure her. "But thank you. I'll see you on Monday, hopefully."

"I hope so, too, but like I said, just focus on getting better, and let me know if you need anything, okay?"

Tears well in my eyes, my emotions still so near the

surface. "Thanks, Mia," I reply thickly. I hang up more abruptly than usual. But it was necessary, as I start bawling, Mia's kindness a stark demonstration of a level of support I never realized I wasn't getting from my own mother all these years. Making me realize maybe I haven't seen her for who she truly is, idolizing her simply because she's my mom. And that maybe she really is capable of worse.

That evening, I'm still deep in my pity party, wrapped in a blanket on the couch, enjoying a threesome with Ben and Jerry, when there's a knock at my door.

A glance through the peephole tells me it's Luke, and my heart drops. I swing the door open, stricken.

"Luke, is everything all right?" Surely, he must be here because something so bad happened that he didn't want to tell me over the phone. Oh god. Or maybe he's come to end things with me, thinking maybe I'm just like my mother.

Luke's brown eyes scan me from head to toe, and I'm suddenly very self-conscious that I haven't showered today and probably look a mess from sleeping like crap and wallowing all day.

"Thank God, you're okay." He shakes his head. "Everything's fine. I came because I showed up at Mia's for dinner and she said you were sick. I thought … I don't know what I thought," he admits. He takes a tentative step toward me, running a hand through his hair. "I was just worried about you."

I let out a breath. Fucking anxiety. I'm over here

catastrophizing and he's making sure the latest drama in our saga didn't make me ill, or worse.

"I'm … fine," I say lamely, stepping back and gesturing for him to come in. He crosses the threshold and grabs me as I swing the door closed, pulling me into a crushing hug.

"You went into self-protection mode, didn't you," he murmurs into my neck.

I blink back tears. "Yeah, I guess I did."

He pulls away, cupping the back of my neck with his hand. "I get it. I've been tempted to do the same. The one upside of being a single parent — wallowing is not an option."

I huff a dry laugh. "That's an upside?" I bunch my brows. "Where is Zoe, anyway?"

The corner of his mouth tips up. "When Mia realized I was leaving to take care of you, she offered to have Zoe sleep over. And naturally, Carrie and Joanie jumped in saying they had to make it a full girls' night. After that, Zoe couldn't get rid of me fast enough," he says, rolling his eyes.

My heart nearly bursts with gratitude. That my friends jumped in to care for her. That they knew it was so Luke could care for me. That Luke is here. Though I'm a little sad that I'm missing out on that party. I blink against fresh tears and Luke sees where I'm at in an instant, pulling me back into his arms.

"Whatever you're feeling right now, it's okay," he murmurs soothingly. "You're allowed to feel all of it. I sure am."

I tip my head back to look at his face. The creases in his forehead are more pronounced and the corners of his lips are pulled down. "Are you mad at my mother for her part in Hannah's death?" I ask bluntly.

Luke closes his eyes. "Honestly? Yes," he breathes. "But I'm angrier with my father."

I pull him toward the couch, sitting down and drawing him next to me. He hauls me into his lap so he can keep me wrapped in his arms, like he needs it as much as I do. But then again, I imagine he does.

"I'm sorry," I whisper.

He shakes his head slowly. "It's all shades of disappointment. It was a new addition to an already awful situation. I already knew my dad was a cheat and a liar. I'm mostly upset for *you* having to learn that both of your parents were, too, though in different way. In any case, you most definitely do not have a damn thing to apologize for."

"I'm not apologizing, I'm empathizing," I clarify.

Luke gives me a vague smile that affects me no less than usual for its sadness. He's beautiful, even in our shared grief for the continued loss of faith in the people who were supposed to be protecting us and setting the example of what being a good human looks like. I can't imagine failing my own children as badly as they failed me. Not that I'm going to have any of those, but still.

"What are you going to do?" he asks softly, breaking me out of my thoughts.

I sigh. "I guess I have to talk to her, don't I? Even though I've realized it's probably all true ... she's my mother. I should at least give her a chance to tell me her side of the story."

Luke nods. "That's how I felt about my father, and you know what his response was. I wouldn't expect much more from your mother."

I lift a shoulder, deciding against explaining that I've been trained to expect the bare minimum. Instead, I say, "Expect the worst, hope for the best."

Luke kisses my collarbone. "I guess in this instance I can understand that philosophy." He looks up into my eyes. "But I'm here to get you used to expecting the best and getting it. Because you deserve it."

I melt at his words. I was so, so stupid not to call him back sooner. Because he's saying exactly what I needed to hear. Reminding me that I do deserve good things.

I put my hands on his face. "I don't know what I did to deserve *you*, but I'm so damn happy you're here."

He nuzzles into me and pulls me in tight, holding his ear against my heart. I stroke his thick hair, running my fingers through the almost indistinguishable intertwined strands of blond and gray.

"Me, too," he murmurs. "Just tell me what you need, Rae. I want to be here for you through this."

I crack my first smile since before I knew. "A proper dinner would probably be a good start. Because a pint of ice cream sure isn't it."

Luke looks at the empty carton on the coffee table and chuckles. "Probably a good idea since I left before I could eat at Mia's. Tell me what you want, beautiful, and I'll do my best to make it happen." His voice is so husky and sincere, it does things to me.

I bite into my bottom lip and the sudden dirty thoughts that run through my head. How can I possibly be thinking about sex right now? Then again, my emotions are all over the place, and I am tightly pressed up against the taut muscles of Luke's chest and thighs, wrapped in his strong arms.

I push off his lap and put some space between us to cool down my dusty libido, heading toward the kitchen.

"I'm sure I've got something I could whip up."

He follows, wrapping his arms around me from behind as I stare into the open fridge. "I'll help."

The feeling of him pressed against me … that definitely won't help us focus on food. So, I decide what we'll make and put him to work, so he's at least not touching me while I'm trying to think clearly.

We work together seamlessly to throw together a simple meal and, as if by unspoken agreement, we don't mention my mother, the fire, or anything else related for the rest of the night.

We talk late into the night about anything and everything else, though. I don't realize how late until I crack a deep yawn.

"I should go," Luke murmurs, rubbing my knee like he wants me to move it so he can get up.

"Stay," I find myself saying. Then I blush hard at the look he gives me.

"Are you sure?" he asks.

I take a slow, deep breath, trying to decide how to put this. But it's Luke. So, I let him see the tears I was tempted to hold back.

"I don't want to fall asleep alone and crying again tonight," I admit.

Luke's expression falls. "Oh, Rae —" I put a finger to his lips to silence him, unable to handle the heartbreak in his voice.

"Don't. Just … stay," I plead.

He nods and lets me lead him to the bedroom. Since I never got out of the joggers and tank top I sleep in, I climb into bed. Luke kicks his shoes off and slides in on the other side, pulling me against him. He wraps his arm around my waist, threading his fingers through mine.

"I'm here," he assures me in a whisper against my ear. "You're not alone."

My eyes drift shut like they were waiting for his words. His embrace. And the safety I feel being with him.

My eyes open to full daylight, and it takes me a moment to realize I'm not late for work. It's one of the rare Sundays I've had off, and it's a good thing I do. Because I also remember my new reality. And that I'll need to talk to my mother today, since I'm supposed to go over for my weekly visit.

A sleepy groan behind me reminds me I'm also not alone like I usually am. I roll over to a sleep-rumpled

Luke checking the time on his phone, then putting it back on the nightstand. He rolls back toward me with a lazy smile.

"Well, aren't you just the most beautiful sight first thing in the morning," he says.

My breath catches as he kisses me, soft at first, then with increasing urgency, the lengths of our bodies pressing together. I feel his arousal against my hip and pull back, breathless.

"I'm sorry," he says quickly. "I didn't mean to get carried away. I just wanted to distract you from … everything."

A smile curls my lips. "You succeeded. But don't you have to pick up Zoe?" I ask.

"Not for a couple of hours." He pauses. "But I'm happy with this." He kisses me gently once more. "I don't expect anything more."

I close my eyes against a wave of desire that washes over me. He may not expect it, but I'm ready for *more*. It's been so long since I've wanted a man, much less been with one. And Luke has been here for me in a way I haven't had … well, since he left. He's everything I thought he was before I believed the lie that tainted what we'd had all those years ago.

But there are no more lies between us. No secrets. And the love we shared then hasn't gone. It's just changed. Matured. Grown into something … more. Luke has always owned a piece of my heart, and now he has it all once again.

I reopen my eyes and stare into his. "But you want it?" I ask, slipping my hand over the bulge between us.

He sucks in a sharp breath, his eyes darkening. "I do. But you'd better be sure you do before you do that again," he says huskily.

I bite into my bottom lip and stroke him once more.

And just like that, his tether snaps, and his mouth is on mine, his tongue pushing into my mouth, his hand hauling my leg over his hip as he grinds into me. The hot, hard length grazing my core has me molten in seconds and I gasp into his mouth.

He pulls away, nipping a blazing trail down my neck, his hand now covering my breast, teasing the tip with his thumb.

Well, that went from zero to a hundred in no time at all. And as he pulls my tank top down to expose my breasts, I know it's exactly what I need right now. What *we* need. To feel something *good*. Oblivion. Passion. Connection.

I grind against him, chasing it all.

"Fuck, Rae," he curses. And since he so rarely does, I know he's losing control just as much as I am, and it makes me feral for him.

"I need you, Luke."

He pulls away and makes short work of ripping my tank top over my head and my panties and joggers off after in two quick, powerful moves. He tosses them away before doing the same with his own clothes.

As he crawls back onto the bed, I admire his toned,

hard body, shivering in anticipation. He pauses, hovering over me, his eyes full of desire.

"You are so beautiful, Rae," he says in a soft tone that is filled with need.

I reach between us and spread my legs, guiding him home.

"I'm yours," I say simply. "Take me, Luke."

His head tips back for a moment before he sinks in slowly. We both groan at the tight fit, the mind-spinning pleasure, and the feel of skin on skin.

Once fully seated, he pauses. I don't know if it's to give me time to adjust or so he can keep it together. But based on his sharp, panting breaths, he's just as turned on as I am right now. I put my hands on his face until his eyes meet mine.

And then he moves. Slow and deep, he watches me while he brings me more pleasure than I can ever remember having.

I have to break eye contact to tip my head back, my entire body clenching with tightly coiled anticipation as he drives me quickly toward my peak. Everything is heightened by the emotions that have been swirling inside of me, and it seems that's affected me physically, too.

And when he shifts us, his chest now touching mine, his face buried in my neck while he pistons his hips, I can barely stand the intimacy of it.

"This is nothing like it was," he says.

"It's better," I agree.

"It's everything," he whispers against my skin.

I arch against him, my breasts scraping against his chest. "I'm yours," I repeat, tears filling my eyes.

"And I'm yours," he breathes, pumping faster. Harder. His breaths coming more quickly.

Knowing he's close, I start to lose it, grinding into him, chasing my own orgasm. His gasps turn to frantic puffs, a desperate noise escaping him with each. I whimper at the depth of pleasure swirling inside me, as I feel myself approach the edge.

"I need more," I beg.

He sits up, looking down at me with an expression I can't quite place, then takes me harder. Faster. I nod encouragingly, watching his face as he moves inside me.

And it undoes me completely. My orgasm washes over me, unlike any other I've had. Because it's so much more than that. I'm shattered. Broken. Exposed. His.

Luke comes on a cry and fills me, giving a few last shuddering thrusts as he finds his release. Then he leans back down, our sweat-soaked bodies slick against each other. I wrap my legs and arms around him as he sinks down, and everything I was is forever changed. Because this wasn't just sex. I've had just sex. This was so much more than that. I'm wrecked, in the best way possible. Because this was an act of love. I've believed enough pretty lies and had enough meaningless sex to know the difference now.

Luke pulls his head back just enough to look in my eyes. "You okay?"

I give him a lazy, sex-soaked smile. "Perfect. You?"

He brushes a sweaty lock of hair from my face. "Incredible. Words can't even do it justice."

I nod, understanding.

We lay like that a few minutes more before taking the most sensual joint shower of my life. Slippery skin touches and sexy, sated looks that fill a hole in my chest I'd long pretended wasn't there.

When we're done and dressed once more, we stand at the door, preparing to part ways.

"You ready?" he asks softly, running a hand over my shoulder, down my arm, then twining his fingers with mine.

I breathe deeply. "As I'll ever be."

I smile up at him, unable to put to words the deep sense of gratitude I have for him. He's grounded me. His touch makes me feel invincible. And with his encouragement, I know I can handle this conversation with my mother, and so much more.

I go up on my toes and kiss him gently. "Thank you."

Luke laughs, lifting my spirits even higher, somehow. He pulls me against him and the smile drops off my face, my eyes going wide. "I should be thanking you," he murmurs. "That was the best sex of my life."

I huff a laugh. "I wasn't thanking you for the sex, Luke," I say drily. Then, with a smile, "But it was for me, too." I shake my head. "Thank you for being here for me. I needed this to find the courage to face my mother today."

"I'll always be here for you. But you don't need me for that. You've always had courage, Rae."

My brows bunch together. Because I don't feel like I have. "Really?" I ask skeptically.

"Really. Nobody can give you courage. All they can do is help you find what you already have."

I pull him down and kiss him firmly on the lips. "I'll call you later?"

He nods, kissing me one last time. "You'd better." He winks as he opens the door, and we step back into reality.

The whole drive over, I reflect on the things Luke said. I deserve to be treated well. I have the courage to have this conversation with my mother. I have people who love me. I'm not alone. I can do this.

Even though it's earlier than I usually stop by, I don't call ahead to warn my mother I'm coming. I just show up, my heart pounding as I let myself in.

"Rae? That you?" Mom calls from the living room.

I tuck my keys into my pocket instead of putting them on the table like I usually do and leave my shoes on.

I walk into the living room to find her in her armchair, another bodice ripper resting pages down on her lap.

"It's me," I confirm unnecessarily, leaning against the wood-framed entrance to the room and crossing my arms.

"You're early," she replies, picking her book back up.

"Yes, well, I didn't have work today," I say.

She looks up. "Why are you still standing there? Sit down."

I ignore her suggestion, and say instead, "You remember I told you Luke McMillan is back in town?"

Mom sets her book down again. And now that I'm

paying attention, I notice her tells. Her pinky taps the cover nervously.

"I do. And I heard tell he didn't actually father the Thompson boy."

I make a noncommittal noise. "No. Pastor McMillan did."

My mother's nostrils flare. "That's a big accusation, young lady."

And now she's deploying the "I'm the boss of you" tactic. God, I never connected that to her deflecting until now.

"It's not an accusation. They got a blood test that proves it." I tilt my head to the side before delivering my first blow in what may be our last fight. "Luke recently reconnected with his mother, too, and she confirmed it. It's part of the reason they divorced after they left town."

Mom huffs. "Guess the fire devastated their marriage, too," she replies, her eyes not meeting mine.

"Oh, she certainly had a lot to say about the fire." I tap my finger on my arm and stare her down. I don't know where this confidence is coming from — or maybe I do, thanks to Luke — but it's clearly keeping her from pushing back. For now.

After a few solid moments, she waves a hand dismissively. "That was years ago. I don't know why she'd dredge that whole mess back up."

I huff an annoyed laugh. Clearly, she has no intention of fessing up, but I'll give her one last chance.

"Is there anything you want to tell me about that night?" I ask plainly.

Now she looks at me. And it's with vitriol I've never seen her direct my way.

"No," she says firmly.

I narrow my eyes. "Really? So, you're saying Dad didn't catch you having an affair with Pastor McMillan that caused him and dad to fight until they knocked over a candle and burned the church down?"

My mother's face pales. "Your dad admitted he started the fire with a cigarette. What would she know? She wasn't there."

My brows raise. "And to know that *she* wasn't, *you* would have to have been," I point out.

Mom's mouth pops open in surprise at being caught.

An inappropriate sense of glee courses through me. And I make a mental note to thank Luke again for helping me be calm so I could give my mother enough rope to hang herself with.

"Now, don't go jumping to conclusions like you always do," she chastises. "Your father was there, wasn't he? You don't really think *I'd* cheat on *him*, do you? Honestly, Rae, I thought you had more sense than that." She shakes her head.

She's good, I'll give her that. If we'd had this conversation a few months ago, I'd feel embarrassed for assuming the worst. But now I see it for the gaslighting it is.

"I'm onto your tricks now," I warn her. "And I notice in that little speech you didn't actually deny anything."

She clenches her jaw and glowers at me. The silent tension is thick between us.

"So, are you going to spread that gossip around like you do all the rest?" she finally asks, lifting her chin.

I scoff and shake my head. "Wow. Really? That's your response?"

Her lips tighten into a frown, and I can see her trembling. "Your father left, and I had to raise you all on my own. You'll forgive me if I don't want the judgmental busy bodies making my life hell over things they only think they know about. If you love me at all, you wouldn't subject me to that."

And now I'm mad again. She's all but admitting it, though she can't even manage that properly. And all she cares about is what other people think of her? Though obviously, I'm not on that list.

I take a deep breath, but it does nothing to quell the anger surging through me. "With all due respect, go to hell, Mom. You cheated on Dad and went along with a lie that destroyed this family. A lie that also cost me thirty years of love with the only person who has ever put my needs first. And the worst part? You were part of the reason Luke's sister died!" Now I'm yelling.

"Hannah's ... dead?" she asks, placing a hand to her throat.

I flinch. Is that ... remorse?

But in a flash, whatever it was is gone and she lifts her chin defiantly once more.

"Whatever happened to her wasn't my fault. I didn't even know she was asleep in the Sunday school room," she protests. "And it wasn't me that knocked over the candle."

"I thought it was a cigarette? Now you're admitting it was a candle?" I shake my head, disgusted by her lack of actually admitting what she did and taking responsibility. "You aren't the woman I thought you were," I tell her, my voice shaking. "You're an awful person. And while Dad wasn't perfect, letting him take the fall was unforgivable. Pretending like you had nothing to do with what happened to Hannah … to *all* of us is unforgivable."

Her eyes narrow. "Well, you're not the woman I thought you were either. I thought you were a good, loyal daughter."

I laugh bitterly. "You're right, I'm not the woman either of us thought I was. I'm stronger and more capable than I realized. Than you ever let me believe." I push off the frame and march forward, looking down at her. "You always kept me small, and now I know why. Because Pamela Donovan only cares about Pamela Donovan. We can't have Rae getting 'too big for her britches' and having a full life that might take her away from her daughterly duties." I take a deep breath and walk backward. "But I'm done with that now. I'm only going to surround myself with good people who lift me up and encourage me. You are neither of those things."

I stop at the entrance to the living room, waiting for her

response. Any response. But it doesn't come. I shake my head, my rage gone, replaced only with disappointment.

"I hope you have the life you deserve, mother."

She blanches at my usual lack of endearment — Momma; the name I called her from the time I could talk. But she's no longer the mother figure she was to me. Despite her obvious distress, she doesn't respond.

So, I leave.

I don't let the tears stream down my face until I get in the Bronco and start driving away. They don't stop until I get home, and only because I pull myself together enough to call Luke.

"Hey. How'd it go?" His warm, concerned voice soothes me.

"About as we expected. She admitted nothing directly and took responsibility for nothing. It's done. I'm done."

"I'm so proud of you, Rae," he says softly. "You did the right thing."

"Thank you," I whisper. "For everything."

There's a noticeable pause before he finally says, "I love you, Rae. I didn't want to say it for the first time again over the phone, but I needed you to know."

My heart swells, tears flowing afresh. For a good reason now. "I love you, too, Luke," I admit with my whole, healed heart. Because he was what it had been missing. "I'm guessing you can't come tell me that in person?"

He pauses, and I know the answer is no. He's a dad. He has responsibilities. "Zoe and I had already planned to take off for the day, and we aren't supposed to be back until late," he hedges. "But I can come home if you need me. Just say the word."

"No, please, don't worry about it, I get it," I assure him. "Go on, have fun."

"Are you sure?"

"I'm sure," I confirm.

"I'll tell you tomorrow, I promise," he says.

"Tomorrow," I agree.

"Get some rest, beautiful."

"Bye, handsome."

As I hang up, my emotions are bittersweet. I'm just starting to mourn the loss of the mother I thought I had … while regaining the love I thought I'd lost.

I'm realizing that sometimes you don't get to pick what shape your life takes. And sometimes it shapes you.

CHAPTER EIGHTEEN

LUKE

Monday morning comes and goes in a blur of meetings and phone calls as we're still deep in the architectural draft phase for Alpine Ridge's fire station. It's not until I'm on my way to pick up Zoe from the bakery that I realize I haven't seen or texted with Rae all day.

When I arrive, Mia tells me Zoe's just finishing up a task in the back. I take the opportunity to steal a few moments alone with Rae.

"Hey," I say softly, pulling her into a hug. "How are you feeling about the confrontation with your mom after sleeping on it?"

Rae sighs, leaning into me, and I notice a dab of frosting on her neck. I resist distracting her by licking it off.

"The anger is fading. It's all in the past, really, and I don't want it to affect my future." She looks up at me with a small smile. "Our future."

My heart swells at her words, at the promise they hold.

I was so terrified that "going slow" meant she had too many doubts. That she'd eventually decide it wasn't worth the risk. I've never been happier to be wrong.

"Though I'm disappointed in her and have no plans to speak to her, given that she's clearly not sorry about any of it," she adds, her expression clouding.

I'm about to offer some words of comfort when suddenly, the shrill wail of smoke alarms fills the air. Rae and I exchange a panicked glance before sprinting to the kitchen.

We burst through the door to find a small fire in a pan on the stove, which Mia is already putting out. My gaze immediately seeks Zoe, and relief crashes over me when I see she's okay, standing back from the stove with wide eyes, her face so pale the ridges of her scars stand out.

"What happened?" I ask, my voice tight with concern as I rush over and check Zoe over from head to toe, needing to reassure myself she's unharmed.

Mia gives me an apologetic look. "Zoe just set the oven too hot by accident and the oil in the pan burned. It's my fault, I should have been watching more closely."

Zoe's bottom lip trembles. "I'm sorry, Dad. Are you ... are you not going to let me keep baking now?" Her voice is small, afraid.

I lean in, taking her hands in mine. "Did it scare you, Zo?"

To my surprise, Zoe shakes her head. "No. I know I'm safe here."

Mia nods, offering me a reassuring smile. "Zoe was

calm and knew exactly what to do to put out the fire. You've taught her well, Luke."

Pride swells in my chest, temporarily overshadowing the residual fear. A year ago, an incident like this would have triggered Zoe's PTSD, sending her into a panic attack. Hell, it probably would have triggered mine, too.

But as I look at my brave, resilient daughter, I'm struck by how far we've both come. How much stronger we are here, in this place that's starting to feel like home in a way nowhere else ever has.

"No, sweetheart. I would never stop you from doing something you obviously love so much," I assure her.

Zoe wraps her arms around me, squeezing hard. "Thanks, Dad. Let's go home."

I rub her back, my eyes meeting Rae's. She looks relieved as she watches us lovingly. And I realize in a sudden rush I want Rae to go home with us, too. Today, particularly. But … maybe every day. One thing at a time, though.

"Rae, would you like to come over for dinner tonight?"

Her face lights up. "I'd love to."

When we get back to the house, I can't help noting once again how badly it needs a coat of paint. And I still hate that damn yellow.

At least the yard has been beaten back some, but it still needs the full treatment. Several dead bushes line one side of the house, and the huge maple behind the house needs trimming for sure. But then, I've been focusing on the inside. I'll get there, and though I want the place to look presentable, I know Rae won't really care.

Once inside, I busy myself with getting everything ready, nerves fluttering in my stomach. It's still a work in progress, but I'm proud of how much I've accomplished so far. All the appliances have been replaced. All the plumbing and electrical is now in tip-top shape. The bathroom and kitchen fixtures still need updating, and the décor is … horrid, honestly. But everything is in working order, finally.

When the doorbell rings, I take a deep breath and go to let Rae in. Her presence immediately fills the space, warm and radiant.

"Hey, beautiful," I say, pulling her in for a hug. But I can't resist sneaking a kiss, too, seeing as Zoe is upstairs in her room.

"Hey, you," she replies, giggling as I kiss down her neck. God, I love her neck. Long and graceful and it's where her vanilla sugar scent is the strongest.

"Let me give you the grand tour," I say, taking her hand.

As I lead her through each room, pointing out the repairs and updates I've made, Rae listens attentively, offering compliments. But when we reach the living room, she pauses, a playful glint in her eye.

"I have to say, Luke, the repairs look great. But …" She gestures around at the mismatched, dated furniture and decor. The living room is by far the worst, aesthetically speaking. "You really need help with everything else."

I laugh, rubbing the back of my neck. "It could use a woman's touch, huh?"

Rae smirks. "Stop hinting and just ask."

"Okay, okay." I hold up my hands in mock surrender. "Rae Donovan, would you do me the honor of helping me redecorate this disaster zone?"

"God, yes, please. You have to let me get rid of that awful wallpaper," she replies with a sheepish grin.

I flick my eyes up to the faded peach and pale green stripes. She's not wrong. What were my parents — and everyone in the 80s — thinking?

From the top of the stairs, Zoe lets out a whoop of excitement. "Yes! Rae, we can make this place look so good!"

"Zo, have you been eavesdropping this whole time?" I call up.

She charges down the stairs. "Nooo," she replies unconvincingly. "I was just coming down because I'm hungry. When's dinner?"

The oven timer dings and Rae laughs. "Good timing, kiddo."

I roll my eyes. "Why am I not surprised?" Zoe has always had a sixth sense as to when food is going to be ready. I guess it's part of what makes her such a great baker.

Over dinner, Zoe chatters animatedly about all the things she wants to do with Rae now that she's officially my girlfriend. Rae indulges her enthusiasm, suggesting shopping trips, craft projects, and more that have Zoe practically bouncing in her seat.

It warms my heart to see the two of them bonding, to know that Zoe is okay with having Rae in our lives like this.

Later, once Zoe's upstairs reading before bed, Rae and I settle on the couch, her head resting on my shoulder.

"Is it hard being back in this house sometimes?" she asks quietly. "With all the memories it must hold?"

I sigh, considering my answer. "Sometimes I'm reminded of the bad times," I admit. "But there were good memories here, too. And more than anything, I want to make new ones. With Zoe." I press a kiss to the top of Rae's head. "And with you."

She tilts her face up to mine, her eyes shining with emotion. "I can't wait."

As I hold Rae close, the warmth of her body seeping into mine, I'm filled with a sense of contentment, of rightness. Yes, the past held its share of darkness. But the future stretching out before us is filled with light. Rae is my light. My love. And while it's not surprising, I'm relieved to see how well she fits in here. In this house. And with Zoe and me.

Rae is literally everything I ever wanted. Even after we left when I was sixteen, she was the one I compared all of my girlfriends to. And I'm just now realizing that's probably why I never got married. Never stayed with anyone that long. Sure, the job made it tough, but … none of them were her.

Now I finally realize, I've been waiting for the last thirty years to come back to this place, by her side. We've already worked through some heavy, emotional issues, and her relationship with Zoe absolutely melts me. She fits perfectly into my life. If I have my way, I'll never leave again.

CHAPTER NINETEEN

RAE

As I sit across from the psychologist in her cozy Ellensburg office, my nerves are buzzing with a mix of anxiety and anticipation. I've been waiting for this moment, for answers, for so long.

The therapist, a kind-faced woman named Patricia, who appears to be in her fifties, looks up from her notes and smiles. "Rae, based on everything we've discussed, it's clear to me that the issues you've been struggling with align with an ADHD diagnosis. Specifically, the Inattentive type."

I let out a breath. Hearing it out loud, having it confirmed by a professional, is equal parts validating and overwhelming.

"Okay. And Inattentive type — that means I don't have the fidgety stuff?"

Patricia smiles patiently. "Yes, basically. Nor are you

impulsive. Your issues are all around difficulty focusing. And there are plenty of ways to help manage that."

The anxiety in my chest unravels at her reassuring words. We spend the rest of the session discussing strategies for managing my symptoms. Some of it I'm already doing — creating routines, setting alarms, breaking down tasks into manageable chunks. Some of it I'm not — meditation, regular physical activity, and continued therapy with Patricia. All sound perfectly reasonable and manageable. Though I have been doing other therapy, with the woman Mia recommended. I've done a couple of sessions with her to process the issues with my mother, which has definitely helped with the anxiety I've felt since our confrontation. To help continue my progress, Patricia also recommends starting me on a low dose of methylphenidate, better known as Ritalin.

"How long will it take to help?" I ask, trying to tamp down my eagerness.

She chuckles softly. "Oh, about an hour."

My eyes widen in surprise. For some reason I thought you had to take that kind of medication for weeks or even months before seeing results. But knowing that relief could be just around the corner? It's incredibly encouraging. For the first time, I feel like I can get a handle on this, on myself, sooner than I ever thought possible.

Leaving the therapist's office, I'm filled with a renewed sense of hope and determination. And I know exactly where I need to channel that energy.

The bell above the door jingles as I step into Alex's antique shop. He looks up from the counter, a warm smile spreading across his face when he sees me.

"Rae! I wasn't expecting to see you today," Alex greets me from behind a long, oak counter with beautiful scrollwork on its front.

I grin, pulling a folder out of my bag and holding it up triumphantly. "I was in the area. And I come bearing gifts."

Alex raises an eyebrow as I hand him the folder. Inside is the answers to the questions he gave me as homework. But there's also a draft business plan. The result of hours of research and brainstorming since our last conversation. Once I started thinking about it, it was kind of hard to stop. And I'm pretty damn proud of what I put together.

"Is this what I think it is?" he asks, his eyes going wide as he opens it. He gasps. "It is! It's … a business plan?" He looks back up at me in shock.

"It's just a draft," I hedge.

"That's … wow. Mind if I skim it really quick?" he asks.

I wave a hand, gesturing for him to go ahead. And instead of letting my anxiety build watching him, I glance around the shop. It's tidier than I'd expect of an antique shop, with well-marked sections for various types of items. There's a full bookcase of old typewriters to the left of the counter, and the entire corner on the other side is full of clocks. But there's too much to take in, and he clears his throat sooner than I'd expected.

"Rae, I'm impressed. This is ... incredibly thorough for a draft. I can tell you've put a lot of thought into this."

I nod, shifting my weight from one foot to the other nervously. "I have. And I know it still needs work, but Alex ... I'm ready to do this. Like, really do this. I even have some money set aside. As you probably noticed in the plan, I include leasing a space for the business, since my house is too small for what I'm thinking."

Alex nods. "I agree. Especially since you included Ellensburg in your target market. Even once I knew what kind of business you wanted to start, I didn't realize until looking at this that Ellensburg doesn't have *any* event planning services. But ... there's something you should know ..." His lips press together and my pulse races.

"Did I mess something up? Or is leasing a space too much too fast?" I ask self-consciously, bunching my suddenly sweaty palms in my skirt.

"No. It's only ... the last open shop space in Alpine Ridge was just leased."

My heart sinks. "Oh. Well, I guess we'll have to look elsewhere then."

But then Alex's face breaks into a grin. "It was just leased ... because I leased it. For us! I'm ready, too, Rae."

My shock gives way to mild indignation and total elation. I reach over and slap him playfully on the arm. "Don't do that to me, Alex!" I laugh. "Are you serious?"

"As the heart attack I apparently almost gave you," he replies with a chagrined smile.

"Well, damn, sugar. I think I need to give you a hug." I

reach over and pull him into my arms, squeezing tight. "Thank you."

"No, thank *you*," he says, squeezing me back. Then he pulls away. "Truly. I was feeling … blasé. Like I needed a new challenge. Between that, and Brandon and I getting more serious and commuting back and forth, I knew it was time to make a change. And then Brandon told me his sweet friend Rae was looking to start a business and needed help."

"I didn't expect to get quite this much of it," I admit. "But I'm so grateful, Alex."

"Oh, honey, we're just getting started," he says slyly. "I've been going through my inventory to see what event-related pieces we could use in the new space. Want to see?"

I clap my hands gleefully. "Is that even a question?"

Alex laughs and goes to the entrance to flip the open signed to "be back soon," then he takes me into the storeroom behind the counter. It's not huge but is still crammed with many beautiful objects. He leads me to the ones he's picked out, and I'm speechless. Vintage garden arches perfect for floral arrangements, sets of delicate, ornate china, an array of gorgeous vases … it's like a dream come true.

"Oh, Alex, it's all beautiful. But are you sure?" I ask, fingering the gold edge of one of the beautiful sets of plates.

Alex reaches out and squeezes my shoulder. "Absolutely. These are almost all duplicates anyway. We can keep some here for Ellensburg-based events, and take these to Alpine Ridge for events there," he replies.

I feel tears prick at my eyes. I put a hand to my chest, speechless from all of the emotions I'm feeling right now. I take a few deep breaths and collect myself.

"That's … this is all just *perfect*," I breathe.

Alex smiles warmly. "Can you meet me early again this Saturday? At our new office?"

Happiness so strong and acute thickens my throat and I swallow hard. *Our new office.*

"Absolutely," I agree.

We finalize the details, and I leave, practically floating. All I can think on the drive home is that I can't wait to share the good news with Luke. But I want to wait to tell him in person. This is too big to share over the phone, and I don't want to get emotional while driving. Especially since I have one more stop to make. One more difficult conversation to have today.

When I pull up to the bakery, I sit in the Bronco for a minute, taking in the storefront. Mia kept the original style but had the "Alpine Ridge Bakery" repainted to look fresh. I usually don't pay attention, because it reminds me of too many memories. But now I've made new ones here. Better ones. Though my path is about to take me down a different road, this place will always hold a special place in my heart.

I head inside to find Mia transferring the few remaining

pastries for overnight storage in the back. She looks up, surprised and her face lights up.

"There you are! How did it go with the therapist?" she asks eagerly.

"It went great, actually. Better than I expected," I reply, setting my coat and purse down on one of the tables and sitting down.

"I want to hear all about it," she replies. "Need a pick me up?"

I go to decline before deciding … what the heck. "Sure, why not. You choose."

She grins and shuffles around for a minute before emerging from behind the counter with two plated brownies. She plunks one in front of me, then sits across the table with the other.

"So?" she prompts, taking a bite of the oversized chunk of gooey chocolatey goodness.

"Alex was right. I have ADHD." I leave it there, doubting she cares about the details. "She had some helpful tips, and we're going to try some meds. I'll keep seeing her, and hopefully things will get … easier." I shrug, then take a bite of my brownie. It was a good choice, as the combination of nostalgia and chocolate calm my heightened emotional state. It's the perfect reward for everything I've accomplished today.

"That's fantastic, Rae. I actually expected to see you sooner, and I was starting to get worried."

I chuckle. That's Mia. Even though she's like a little

sister to me, she still has the tendency to mother me. And everyone around her, really.

"I stopped at Alex's antique shop to talk about moving forward on the event planning business." Mia perks up, clearly curious. "He leased that last retail space next to Sera's realty office. We're doing it, Mia."

"Oh my god," she says, wiping her mouth with her napkin before half-standing to lean over and hug me. Good thing I wasn't taking a bite. I chuckle as she sits back down. "Sorry, I'm just so happy for you!"

"Thanks. And don't worry, I'll stick around until you find someone to replace me here," I assure her.

But Mia waves off my concern. "Oh, don't you worry about that. I'm just thrilled to see you chasing your dreams." She pauses, her expression turning slightly shy. "Actually, I have some good news of my own. The fertility doctor found a hormone imbalance and put me on medication to correct it. We should be able to get pregnant now. Well, at the normal odds, anyway." She smiles softly, her eyes shining with cautious optimism.

I let out a gasp of delight and now it's my turn to leap forward and hug her. "Mia, that's wonderful! I'm so, so happy for you and Nate."

"Thank you," she responds when I pull away. "For being there for me. For encouraging me to get checked out. I don't think I would've done it without that push."

"What are friends for? You did some pushing of your own, too. And I'm grateful for that," I admit, referring to her encouraging me to be honest with myself about my feelings for a certain fire chief.

"How *are* things going with Luke?" she asks, leaning forward.

I close my eyes and smile, my heart swelling with all the joy I feel today. "Amazing," I admit on a sigh. I open my eyes to her sparkling smile. "It's hard to believe he's only been back a couple of months. There's been so much that's come to light, and we've faced it all together." I shake my head. "You were right. I never stopped loving him, same as he never stopped loving me. And now that we're getting to know each other with all the facts on the table?" I bite into my lip to stop the tears. Mia puts her hand over mine.

"He's The One, isn't he?" she asks softly.

I nod, a tear spilling over my cheek.

"Always has been. Always will be."

Now Mia's eyes are glistening. "Have you told him that?"

I sniff deeply, wiping the tears from my eyes. "Not in so many words," I admit.

Mia squeezes my hand and pulls back. "You finish that brownie and go tell that man how you feel, Rae. Life's too short not to."

I laugh. "You've got that right," I agree. I raise my fork, and she meets it with hers, the small clink a toast to our friendship. Started from a mutual love of pie. But now it's so much more.

As we eat and talk a bit more, I'm struck by how much

joy there is in seeing the people you love get exactly what they've been hoping for. It's a feeling I could definitely get used to.

That evening, I'm bustling about getting ready for Luke and Zoe to come over for dinner at my place. For some reason I'm nervous to have them both in my personal space. Even though Luke has been here before, Zoe hasn't. And they definitely haven't together. It feels almost like being interviewed to be part of their family. I shake it off, stirring the pasta sauce. I'm being silly.

Still, I'm nervous when the knock on the door comes. I wipe my hands on a towel and go to answer it. Zoe bursts in as soon as I open the door.

"Rae! We're here, and we brought dessert!" she exclaims, holding out a box.

"Why, that was so thoughtful of you, thank you," I tell her, secretly starting to regret the giant brownie I had this afternoon. Still, always room for more sugar, I suppose, especially if Zoe made it.

Luke comes in tentatively, as if compensating for Zoe's enthusiasm. "Hey, beautiful," he murmurs, giving me a chaste kiss on the cheek. He smells amazing, like soap and pine. "How was the appointment?"

I start to answer, but Zoe has clearly been cataloging sights and smells. "Gosh, your house is so cute! And something smells amazing," she gushes.

I chuckle, ruffling her hair affectionately. "Well, thanks.

I hope you're easily impressed, because it's just Spaghetti Bolognese."

"I'm not, but I'm sure it will be delicious because you made it," she replies. "I consider myself a foodie, you know. I might even go to culinary school someday."

That catches me by surprise. I look at Luke, who just shrugs. "Culinary school? I would have thought you'd want to go to pastry school, given your love of baking," I tell her.

Zoe's eyes go comically wide. "There's a separate pastry school?"

"There sure is."

"I thought it was just part of culinary school!" She clutches at Luke's arm, practically vibrating with excitement. "Dad, forget culinary school. I want to go to pastry school!"

Luke laughs, pulling her into a one-armed hug. "Zo, you can do whatever you set your mind to. You're a smart, capable young woman, and I will support you no matter what."

The look of pure joy and pride on Zoe's face is enough to melt even the coldest of hearts. She beams up at her dad before turning to me.

"Oooh, I just remembered you told me you like to read! Where are all your books? Can I pick one?" Zoe asks, switching subjects on a dime like only children can.

I laugh. "Sure thing, sugar. The ones that are okay for you to read are on the white bookshelf," I point to the second bedroom, "in that room. Why don't you check them out while I finish getting dinner ready?"

"Awesome!" she cries, bounding off.

Once she's gone, Luke laces his fingers through mine. "Want to tell me about your day while we work?"

I smirk at his use of "we." He has a lot to learn about how I operate in my own kitchen.

"Sure, I'll tell you about my day while you *watch* me finish dinner and stay out of my way," I tease, leading him toward the kitchen.

He holds up his free hand. "Whatever you say, boss." I laugh. "You look happy, so I'm guessing things went well today?"

I grin. "They did." I stop at the counter and go up on my tiptoes to give him a kiss on the lips. I keep it brief, in case Zoe decides to pop out. "The therapist was great. She confirmed the ADHD diagnosis and put me on some meds. There's more, but that's the gist. In slightly bigger news …" I chew on my bottom lip and Luke's eyebrows jump. "Alex and I are officially going into business together. I gave him my draft plan … and he's already leased a space."

Luke's jaw drops and I grin at his shock. "For real?" I nod. He picks me up, spinning me around before placing me gently back on my feet. Then he kisses me much less gently. His mouth consumes mine greedily, his excitement palpable in the rough stroke of his tongue against mine. It lights me up from head to toe, and I'm dizzy and breathless when he pulls back. "Rae, I'm so fucking proud of you," he murmurs huskily.

"Damn, you must be if you just cursed," I tease him.

He smirks down at me. "You have no idea." His gaze is so intense it sends shivers over my skin. "We need to celebrate. A real date, just you and me. What do you say?"

"I say, it's about damn time, Fire Chief McMillan," I tease, giddy with happiness. "Now go sit over there so I can finish dinner. Chef Zoe needs to pass judgment, after all."

Luke chuckles and sits at the stool on the other side of the counter.

As I work, I can't resist starting a conversation I've been meaning to have with him. "You're an incredible father, you know that?" I say, stacking plates to bring to the table.

"I'm just trying my best to be what she needs. It's not always easy, but I got lucky. She's an amazing kid."

I hesitate for a moment, biting my lip. There's a question I need to ask him, but I'm almost afraid to hear the answer. "Luke ... do you think you'll want to have more children someday?"

I can't help darting a glance his way as I head toward the dining room table next to the kitchen. So, I see the understanding that dawns in his eyes. I look away to put the plates on the table and turn back just in time to find him putting himself between me and the kitchen.

He looks deep into my eyes, trailing his fingers down my arms. "Rae, even if you and I hadn't found our way back to each other, I can honestly say that more kids were never part of my plan. I love Zoe with all my heart, and she's more than enough for me."

Relief washes over me, followed by a swell of emotion so intense it nearly takes my breath away. "Good. Because I love you, Luke. I realized I always have. And I want a future with you, more than anything."

His answering smile is blinding. "Rae, before I even came back, you were the love I could never forget. The one I compared every love after to, and they all fell short. Now that I have you back … well, I've never been happier than I am right now. We've already wasted too much of our lives apart. While I don't want to scare you off … well, I already know I want to live the rest of my life with you."

He watches me as if waiting for me to run. But why would I, when we clearly found our way back to each other, through lies and secrets and heartache, only to fall right back in love? We're clearly meant to be.

I slide into his arms, tilting my head back to look at him. "Didn't you hear me? I love you, Luke McMillan, and I wish we hadn't wasted time either, so I'll take that offer."

"Are you sure? You haven't lived with a firefighter before," he says, his eyes twinkling. "The smoke smell, the gear everywhere, the schedule —"

I go up on my toes and silence him with a kiss. He smiles against my lips, wrapping his arms around me and pulling me in deeper. His mouth is demanding and giving all at once, loving and sensual, anchoring me to the moment while promising forever. It's a kiss that fills me with a bone-deep certainty that this — Luke, Zoe, the life we're building together — is exactly where I'm meant to be.

And for the first time in my life, I'm not afraid to reach out and grab hold of the happiness that's being offered to me, with both hands and an open heart.

EPILOGUE

RAE

EIGHTEEN MONTHS LATER

I stand at the edge of the crowd, watching Luke interact with the new firefighter trainees and townsfolk at the fire station opening gala. I may have planned this event, but I still can't believe it's happening. Though that, perhaps, has more to do with the rocky journey it took to get here. And I can't help but reflect on how much has changed.

I've moved in with Luke, and waking up next to him every morning fills me with a joy I never knew was possible. Zoe has accepted me into their lives with open arms, treating me like a parent, though I always try to defer to Luke when it comes to the big decisions. We even got a husky that Zoe promptly named Cinnamon. She says we need a white cat now that she plans to name Sugar.

Zoe herself is thriving, having fully embraced the

unschooling life, mastering whatever subject catches her fancy and still far outstripping what's expected at her age. She's still firmly set on pastry school, and now that's she just turned fourteen, she can officially work for Mia at the bakery.

My mother, in a perhaps not terribly surprising turn of events, moved out of Alpine Ridge to a senior living community in Ellensburg. Janet Henderson caught the movers in action, who spilled the tea. I can't decide if I'm relieved or disappointed, but either way, it's nice not to have that worry hanging over my head.

On the flip side, Luke's mother moved back to town in a bid to re-establish their relationship. I'm sure having a grandchild she'd never met helped, too. She's here tonight, beaming with pride as she watches her son fulfilling his dreams. Their relationship is still fragile, given the hurts they've both suffered, but seeing them work to mend it warms my heart. Between Luke's ever-strengthening bond with Brandon, and now his mother being here … well, it feels like our family, and our love, just keeps growing.

Speaking of growing … across the room, Mia is positively glowing at Nate's side as she sips sparkling cider, one hand resting on the swell of her fast-expanding belly. They just found out they're having a girl, and the joy radiating off them is palpable. Mia's hired several new helpers for the bakery, besides Zoe and Penny, who returned from college, and plans to be more hands off once the baby comes. I'm happy she's taking that time. It's all precious, as I'm learning with Zoe.

Joanie and Greg are here tonight, too, but have been jet-setting more often than not these days, determined to see the world. But as Greg confided in me when they picked up Bruiser after their last trip — Zoe has been happily pet sitting when they're gone — it's only to get the travel bug out of their systems before they settle down and have kids. He says he wants four, but Joanie insists they should start with one and see how it goes. I can't help but chuckle at the thought of their future negotiations.

And then there's Carrie and Evan, who shocked us all by eloping at town hall a few months back. Everyone was furious at first, until they explained their desire for privacy, given Evan's celebrity status. We couldn't fault them for that.

Speaking of celebrities, Evan's famous friend who built a vacation home here? Well, we're not supposed to say who it is, and somehow the secret still hasn't gotten out. But Evan let it slip at one of our weekly dinner parties last month when Joanie acknowledged that he couldn't *say* it, but maybe he could do an impression of whoever it is. And as soon as he bellowed "Adriaaaaan!" — besides sending us all into a fit of laughter — it was immediately obvious who it was. And now there's buzz about one of the Amazon execs building a house here, too.

Our little town is certainly growing, and not just in residents. New businesses are cropping up left and right; a drugstore, a bank, a hardware store, a beauty salon … well, you get the idea. Plus, the police department is being built, having started about six months after the fire department's construction began. And Zoe got the library she'd been after from the moment she moved here. Hell, we may even get that mall Carrie keeps asking for soon.

Though first, Alex and I are going to need a new office. Our event planning and antiques shop has grown to where we're looking to hire. It helps that through therapy and tweaking my meds, I'm more focused and productive than I can ever remember being, and I feel like I can hold my own amongst my much more educated business-owning friends now. I'm *proud*. I'm doing things I only thought of as wild dreams not so long ago. And it's all because of the man of the hour.

Speaking of whom, my attention snaps back to the present as Luke steps up to the podium, his brand spanking new firefighter dress uniform crisp and his eyes shining with emotion. There aren't words for how good he looks up there, and it's not just the uniform. I've got love goggles on big time for this man. He's become my everything, and I've never been happier. The crowd hushes as he takes the microphone.

"Thank you everyone for coming tonight. I'd like to dedicate this fire station to my late sister, Hannah Jane McMillan," he begins, his voice thick with emotion. "Nearly thirty-two years ago, Hannah died as the result of a fire here in Alpine Ridge. It was a tragedy that shaped the course of my life, sparking a passion for firefighting that has brought me to this moment."

He pauses, taking a deep breath. "Becoming Fire Chief, being able to make decisions about fire safety that could truly make a difference … it's the culmination of a dream I worked decades to achieve. And to have it happen in my hometown, surrounded by the people I love? It means more than I can say."

Luke's gaze finds mine in the crowd, and I feel tears prick at the corners of my eyes.

"I want to thank everyone for their support, but especially Rachel Donovan. Rae, your love and encouragement have been my guiding light. I couldn't have done this without you."

As the room erupts in applause, Luke cuts the ceremonial ribbon, officially opening the Hannah Jane McMillan Fire Station.

The party resumes, music swelling and laughter filling the air as Luke makes his way through the well-wishers, shaking hands and accepting congratulations. I smooth my black velvet sweetheart neckline cocktail dress nervously as I feel assessing glances from the people he leaves behind.

When he finally reaches me, there's a mischievous glint in his eye. He grabs a bottle of champagne from a passing waiter and tilts his head toward the back of the building invitingly.

Curious, I follow him outside, the cool evening air a welcome respite from the crowded room.

"What's this about?" I ask, gesturing to the champagne.

Luke grins, handing me the bottle, which I clutch uncertainly against my chest. "A private celebration."

He leads me behind the firehouse, where twinkling

lights have been strung up, creating a magical atmosphere. Suddenly, he pulls me into his arms, his lips finding mine in a kiss that steals my breath.

When we part, he reaches into his pocket and drops to one knee. My heart stutters in my chest as he opens a small velvet box, revealing a sparkling diamond ring.

"Rae, I let you go once, long ago, and it was the worst decision of my life. I should've fought for you, for us, and the future we could've had. And while I can't go back and undo the past, I can do better this time around. I know we'll be together no matter what, but I want us to be everything to each other. You were my first love, and I want you to be my last. Will you marry me?"

Tears blur my vision as I nod, a shaky laugh escaping my lips. I try to speak, but my "yes" can't get past the tears choking me up.

Luke raises a brow, his grin widening. "Take a deep breath, love, then let me hear it."

I laugh, breathing in deeply. "Yes!" I yell.

He laughs with me, rising to slide the ring onto my finger. I don't even look at it. I can do that later. Right now, I only have eyes for him. He stares back into mine, and the look is filled with promise and desire. As we lose ourselves in each other, the sounds of the party fade into the background, and I'm overwhelmed by the sense of rightness, of belonging.

And when Luke's lips meet mine, I lose myself in him completely. The heat of his mouth warms me soul deep. The slide of his hands over my back makes me press closer to his strong chest. I feel safe, and loved, and whole in this moment, and I never want it to end.

I always believed this kind of love was an elusive concept that could never be real. And Luke was my most elusive love … until he wasn't. Until he showed me that true love does exist. Though it happens in its own time, and you have to be ready for it.

I never believed I was worthy of love, so it was hard to accept. But Luke helped me realize it's what I deserve. And now I know that this is where I'm meant to be. With Luke, in this town that has seen us through so much.

And as I look to the future, to the life we're already building together, surrounded by family and friends, I know that whatever challenges may come our way, we'll face them hand in hand, heart to heart.

Always.

Thank you so much for reading! Please take a minute to leave a review on any retailer, goodreads, and/or BookBub. Even if it's just a couple of sentences, your opinion is important to potential readers and to me.

Want more Alpine Ridge? Get ready for the series collection with exclusive bonus content, coming soon! In the meantime, go back to where it all started with Mia and Nate's story, *Tough Love*

http://melanieasmithauthor.com/books-tough-love.html

Sign up for Melanie A. Smith's newsletter to get a FREE book plus all the latest news and more

https://melanieasmithauthor.com/newsletter.html

ACKNOWLEDGMENTS

Thank you to my ever-supportive husband and son for putting up with my agonizing over writing. And not writing. And back stories of every character that barely show up in the book. And for just generally putting up with living with an author.

To Erin, my book bestie, for encouraging me, checking in on me, and commiserating with me. Wouldn't want to do any of this without you, you amazing human.

To Anne, who checks on me under the guise of teaching me the most amazing Scottish-isms. I'm grateful beyond words for both. And for giving me the inside scoop on what it's really like to live with a firefighter. As you can see, your insights went straight from your fingertips into Luke's mouth because they were too perfect not to include. I continue to be amazed by how our experiences and lives are intertwined, and I'm thankful for our cosmic connection.

And thanks always to my readers, who with every single purchase, review, share, or message give my author journey meaning and immeasurable happiness. I hope you've enjoyed Rae's story and the Alpine Ridge world.

ABOUT THE AUTHOR

Melanie A. Smith is an award-winning, international best-selling author of steamy romance with smart, self-sufficient heroines and strong, swoony book boyfriends with hearts of gold. A former engineer turned stay-at-home mom and author, when Melanie is not lost in the world of books you'll find her spending time with her husband and son, crafting, or cross-stitching.

Connect with Melanie on:

MelanieASmithAuthor.com

facebook.com/MelanieASmithAuthor

x.com/MelASmithAuthor

instagram.com/melanieasmithauthor

BOOKS BY MELANIE A. SMITH

The Safeguarded Heart Series

The Safeguarded Heart

All of Me

Never Forget

Her Dirty Secret

Recipes from the Heart: A Companion to the Safeguarded Heart Series

The Safeguarded Heart Complete Series: All Five Books and Exclusive Bonus Material

Life Lessons

Never Date a Doctor

Bad Boys Don't Make Good Boyfriends

You Can't Buy Love

The Heart of Rutherford: Life Lessons Novels 1 – 3

Alpine Ridge Series

Tough Love

Recklessly in Love

Unscripted Love

Elusive Love